Ju Lawn

Debby Fowler

A Felicity Paradise crime novel

ISBN 978 185022 247 7

First published in 2014 by Truran
www.truranbooks.co.uk

Truran is an imprint of Tor Mark, United Downs Industrial
Estate, St Day, Redruth Cornwall TR16 5HY

Printed in Cornwall by Booths Print, The Praze,
Penryn TR10 8AA

*This novel is a work of fiction. Names and characters are the
product of the author's imagination and any resemblance to actual
persons, living or dead, is entirely coincidental.*

ACKNOWLEDGEMENTS:
Where to start? – with my husband and children, of course,
for putting up with my 'scribbling' as they call it and for the
subsequent erratic catering, thank you.

I would also like to thank Diana Palmer for the use of her flat
in St Ives and the resultant peace and quiet to write. Thank you too
to Sally Gilbert for her vital courier service and to Geoff in the
Wharf Post Office for nagging me endlessly to keep writing. Thank
you to my daughter, Dr Lucy Mackillop, for her advice on all things
medical and to Heather and Ivan Corbett and Kate Richards.

And as always, the biggest thank you goes to Jo Pearce – how
you put up with me, I do not know.

For my mother

'The darkest hour is just before dawn'
Anon, mid 17th century.

PROLOGUE

Berlin, December 1938

Her father's telegram was an order, not a suggestion.

Headstrong and with an independent streak which both astounded and disturbed her parents, Sophia Charlesworth was used to getting her own way. She was stubborn, determined, self-assured and very, very beautiful. Although only nineteen, she already recognised her beauty, understood its power and could be quite ruthless in the use of her charms to get her own way. Today though, she was pleased to be told what to do. She was deeply frightened, out of her depth, a child again. Instead of resentment, she felt a profound sense of relief.

She was suddenly alone in Berlin. It was just over a month since Kristallnacht, the Night of Broken Glass, when Jewish businesses and homes had been destroyed in an orgy of violence and terror. Since that day, many Jews had been rounded up; there were beatings in the streets and rumours of rape and torture. It was unreal, terrifying and for once in her young life, she needed to be told what to do.

'Go at once to the British Embassy,' the telegram read. 'Ticket waiting for train/boat to England. 16 December. Vital you come home immediately. Father.'

It was a bitterly cold afternoon. There was snow in the air. Sophia hurried through the streets to the British Embassy. It was only a ten minute walk from her digs but she was frozen by the time she arrived.

Edward Rashleigh, assistant to the Vice-Consul, could not have been more helpful and efficient. Within fifteen minutes she was on the way back to her lodgings with her ticket in her bag and the promise that the British Embassy would send a car to pick her up and take her to the station on the day of her departure. The relief was enormous. Just two days ago, Mary Cummings, the girl who had travelled with her to Berlin for the Olympic Games and to study German, had been summoned home, leaving Sophia alone in a city thick with menace. Then terrifyingly, the previous day her landlady and husband had completely disappeared. Sophia knew nothing of their whereabouts; she was now entirely alone in the house.

She was almost there. The sky was heavy with unshed snow causing a premature dusk. She nearly missed him, but a slight movement made her stop and peer into the gathering gloom. A tiny figure was huddled against an unlit lamppost. She hurried over and bent down. The child was whimpering and shivering with cold. She spoke to him in German. 'Are you lost?'

The child shook his head.

'Then why are you here? You must be lost, you're freezing.'

'My mummy,' he wailed, 'the nasty soldiers took my mummy and daddy.'

Gently Sophia lifted him to his feet; he could barely stand. Then she saw it, the tell-tale Star of David on his coat sleeve and immediately she understood everything.

'Come with me,' she said. 'Come to my house, I'll make you warm.'

He hesitated for a fraction of a second, then stumbled forward, almost falling. She bent forward, scooped him up into her arms and hurried down the street, looking left and right for any signs of military patrols. Mercifully the street was deserted.

Once home she placed the boy in a chair by the range and piled some coal into it, rattling it around with the poker to warm it quickly. She heated up some milk and gave him a cup. He drank

3

it greedily. She followed this with a little bread, cheese and sausage. Everything disappeared in seconds. She established that his name was Otto, that he was four years old and had been wandering the streets since very early that morning when it appeared that the Nazis had raided his house and taken away his parents. His mother had pushed him into a cupboard as their front door was being broken down. Once his parents had gone, he had been too frightened to stay at home and to a four-year-old, it had probably seemed logical to go out looking for them. She asked him no more questions, his eyelids were drooping. She left him in the chair, rushed upstairs for a blanket and wrapped it around him, then stoked the range again. There was no question of going to bed herself. She could not leave this poor little boy alone after what he had been through so she sat opposite him, sleeping fitfully until a grey dawn broke over the city. During the long night, Sophia remembered her landlady kept some clothes in the house for a visiting grandson. The boy, she judged, was only a little larger than Otto.

The following morning, after a meagre breakfast and with some protesting, she put Otto in a bath and then dressed him in clean clothes and a jacket with no star. She then walked with him through the streets to the British Embassy. Her heart in her mouth, she was terrified that they would be stopped and asked for their papers.

Edward Rashleigh was surprised to see her again but listened sympathetically to Otto's story.

'You're running an enormous risk with the authorities by looking after him,' he said, with a look of mild rebuke.

'I know, I know,' said Sophia, 'but I was thinking about the Kindertransport. A train with Jewish children left for England earlier this month, didn't it, and there are going to be more, aren't there?'

Edward Rashleigh nodded.

'I wondered if we could get him on one of those and then when he arrives in England I can help him – that's if he can't travel with me?'

'He definitely cannot travel with you,' Edward Rashleigh said swiftly. 'That way you could find yourself in all sorts of trouble. Hang on a moment, I will talk to my boss, Frank, and see what he can suggest.'

While they talked, Otto sat solemnly and silently on his chair. He seemed to understand the importance of behaving himself if these people were to help him. Rashleigh returned a few minutes later.

'There is a train, a Kindertransport train,

leaving shortly after six in the morning the day after tomorrow. If you take him to the station you should be able to put him on it, but you can't go with him. It is for children only.'

'But who will look after him?' Sophia said, her voice full of anxiety.

'The children are having to look after one another, that is the only way the Nazis will allow this to happen. It's children only, absolutely no adults: nobody over seventeen. With a bit of luck you'll find an older girl who will be prepared to take care of him.'

Sophia said nothing; already the act of handing over Otto to strangers seemed unthinkable.

'Frank is very worried about the next couple of days,' Rashleigh continued. 'We will drive you both home now and get some shopping for you on the way. What you must not do is go outside with Otto again. You took a terrible risk coming here with him today.'

'I couldn't see what else to do,' said Sophia.

Rashleigh smiled for the first time. 'I do understand, but you must be very careful. We will send a car for you at five in the morning the day after tomorrow to take you to the Kindertransport train, but we can't help you once you're there in case the authorities believe we're involved or think the child is someone important and try to stop him boarding. We can't send an Embassy car either. I will borrow one from a member of the Embassy staff, a private car that won't draw attention to you or the boy. I am afraid that is the most we can do, it's up to you to get him on that train.'

'I'll get him on,' said Sophia, quietly.

The two days Sophia and Otto spent together wereilluminating for both of them. Sophia was an only child with no experience of younger siblings or even cousins. Otto, too, had no brothers or sisters and certainly no experience of exotic if volatile teenagers. Still, they muddled through between them. Otto insisted on calling her 'beautiful lady' and she called him 'Otto baby'.

'I'm not a baby, I'm a boy,' he said repeatedly, enjoying the joke.

At five o'clock, on Otto's day of departure, as good as his word, a car arrived to collect them for the station driven by Rashleigh himself. Sophia had re-dressed Otto in the clothes in which she had found him, washed and sponged to the best of her ability. Together they climbed into the back of the car and sat holding hands during the short journey to the station.

When they arrived Rashleigh said, 'Jump out quickly. Good luck! I'll wait for you and drive you home. I'll be down that side street opposite. I don't want you wandering around at this time of the morning on your own.'

Sophia nodded and helped Otto out of the car. The station was in chaos; there seemed to be hundreds of children and parents milling around. Nazi guards were shouting to put the children on board and Sophia rushed to the train dragging Otto behind her, looking desperately for a friendly face. The train was building up a head of steam, whistles were blowing, guards shouting. Then she saw a girl leaning out of the train window waving at an elderly man, tears streaming down her face. She looked about fourteen.

'Excuse me,' said Sophia, 'would you take care of this little boy, his name is Otto?'

'I don't know,' the girl began.

'Please, please,' said Sophia. 'He has no one, his parents have been taken.'

The girl looked at Otto and Otto at her.

'All right,' she said, 'you'd better pass him through the window.'

Sophia lifted him up and the girl grasped him under the arms, dragging him unceremoniously through the window. She heard a thump the other side and then Otto's face appeared, the height of the window obscuring all but his eyes which were filled with tears. The train was shuddering, the guards were whistling.

'Beautiful lady,' he wailed. 'My beautiful lady.'

'Otto baby, don't worry, I'll find you again, I'll find you again, I promise.'

The train began to move. On the platform, parents who had desperately held back their grief in front of their children, began to sob. Sophia didn't notice them. As she walked from the station towards the waiting car, the only grief she registered was her own.

1

St Ives Cornwall, March 2011

Keith Penrose strode down the coastal path from Man's Head towards Porthmeor beach. It was a mad March day, the sun bright with the promise of spring, the wind blowing small cotton wool clouds across an otherwise brilliant blue sky. Harvey, Felicity's Jack Russell, had a distinct case of wind under the tail and was prancing ahead of Keith. As they neared the steps down to the beach he stopped and looked hopefully in Keith's direction.

'Aren't you hungry, it's way past your breakfast time?' Keith said to the dog. Harvey wagged his tail. 'OK, so you want to go the long way around, go on then.'

With a bark of delight Harvey ran down the steps and onto the beach heading for the nearest flock of seagulls. 'What am I doing?' Keith thought, as he followed the dog down the steps. 'Talking to a dog! Is this what retirement does for one?'

While on the beach watching Harvey tear around, he stopped at a favourite rock and sat on it for a moment gazing out to sea. The tide was way out. Was he happy? Yes, of course he was, he was living with a marvellous women who he adored, in a town of which he was becoming increasingly fond. He was healthy and mercifully most of his faculties appeared to be still functioning. He let out a small sigh – was it of contentment? He wasn't sure.

He had been retired for nine months and Felicity had done her best to keep him busy. Now living with an artist, he had started to take an interest in art. Under her careful tutelage, he regularly visited the Tate and had accompanied her on several trips to London to see not only the more obscure ones, visiting new struggling artists in places like Brick Lane. It was all fascinating stuff, but it was difficult to fill the enormous hole in his life created by his retirement. In many ways he was living the life he had always imagined retirement would bring. He swam in the sea most days in the summer, twice a week in the Sports Centre in the winter. He walked Harvey twice a day and read a great deal. History was his particular passion. He and Felicity went to plays and concerts at the Minack, at the Hall for Cornwall in Truro and to the cinema. They regularly had friends to dinner and their big adventure in early January had been a trip to Australia.

He had been longing to see his children, now both settled there, but had been more than a little anxious about Felicity meeting his wife Barbara – wife in name only now but it was still nerve-wracking. As it happened, he need not have worried. It had been an extraordinary success. Each woman had told him confidentially and in no uncertain terms that he was a very lucky man to be loved by the other – not that he needed telling.

The trouble was that none of these things entirely compensated for a lifetime's work in the police force. His career had been all-consuming and had equipped him for no other sort of life. That's the problem, Keith thought, sitting on his rock, I'm a retired policeman but in my heart a policeman is what I still am, I don't seem to be able to move on from it.

Felicity had suggested a job, but what sort of job could he do? Who would have him at sixty-five? She had also suggested travelling. Her daughter, Mel would look after Harvey and perhaps they should go off with a couple of backpacks and have a gap year like students. Somehow the idea, although appealing, didn't feel quite right. Felicity's view was he couldn't bear to be away from

Cornwall that long, and maybe in a way she was right. But what he really felt was that first he needed to sort out his day-to-day life before running away from it.

He stood up, whistled to Harvey and made his way along Porthmeor beach towards the Island. Harvey gave him a defiant look and ran in the opposite direction. Still if the worst came to the worst the dog knew his way home. From experience Keith knew that ignoring him usually brought him back so he continued to walk along the sand, head down against the wind. Of course, he was aware of what was depressing him. Felicity had caught the sleeper to London the night before. She was seeing a publisher today about a commission for some drawings. He was pleased for her but also a little jealous. Her life had purpose, his seemed to have none. The day stretched ahead of him. He had promised he would cook supper tonight and pick her up at St Erth shortly after sieven. He glanced at his watch, it was only half past eight – nearly ten hours stretched ahead of him and apart from the supper, there was absolutely nothing he had to do, nor even particularly wanted to do.

Felicity was having a lovely day in London. An early morning visit to her publisher had resulted in the commissioning of eight paintings to illustrate a gardening book, one of which would adorn the front cover. The money was fabulous and she was very excited. Following her meeting, she met her god-daughter, Ellie, for lunch in Covent Garden. Ellie was bubbly and enthusiastic about her life and there were frequent references to a boy named Jake. When questioned about him, Ellie vehemently denied there was anything going on between her and Jake, but Felicity could tell she was protesting too much. I hope he is kind to her – Ellie is too vulnerable for a broken heart, Felicity thought as she climbed into a taxi and waved goodbye.

She arrived at Paddington just after two. She scanned the departure board and saw that her train was already at the platform. She began threading her way through the busy crowds and then stopped. She was feeling thirsty after the glass of wine she had drunk at lunch-time. She turned on her heel and headed off towards the newsagents; she would buy a bottle of water and a newspaper. She glanced at her watch, she had plenty of time. The thought that Keith would be waiting for her at the end of the line made her smile as she walked. She wondered what he had cooked for supper: cooking was not a great skill so far as Keith was concerned, but he was learning. She would have a proper talk with him tonight. There was a persistent niggle in the back of her mind. Ever since their return from

Australia, while he had been his usual cheerful self, she felt he was drifting, there was no sense of purpose to his day. He denied it of course, said after all his years of work it was wonderful and relaxing but she didn't believe him, not for a moment. Something would have to be done.

She reached the newsagents and began to go inside when suddenly a name sprang out at her from the news stand – 'Otto Juniper'. She stopped so abruptly that a man behind her bumped into her.

'Sorry,' she murmured, her eyes fixed on the name – 'Otto Juniper' and the single word, 'Tragedy'. She forced herself to go first to the drinks cabinet and remove a bottle of water. She then made herself buy a newspaper without stopping there and then to read it. She must have looked slightly peculiar because the girl who served her stared at her a little oddly. On legs that threatened to buckle, she made her way out across the station concourse, put her ticket through the machine and then walked the length of the platform until she found an almost-empty carriage. She climbed aboard the train, put her bag on the luggage rack, sat in a mercifully single seat and with trembling fingers at last opened the newspaper.

'Otto Juniper,' the headline ran, 'still the Wworld's finest violinist but will he ever play again? The Maestro is said to be devastated by the sudden death of his partner and muse'.

A little cry escaped Felicity's lips, she closed her eyes and laid the paper on her lap. She heard other passengers boarding and finally the whistle, followed by the gradual movement of the train as it pulled out of the station, but she could not open her eyes, she could not read any more.

Keith decided to walk over the bridge at St Erth to meet Felicity on the platform. He parked the car, climbed the wooden steps and crossed the bridge towards Platform One. As he did so, he saw the London train come snaking around the corner towards him. He felt his heart lift, she would be with him in a moment. He had lit the fire in the sitting room and a fish pie was ready to be warmed in the oven, a bottle of Sauvignon Blanc waited in the fridge, a salad just needed a dressing. The train ground to a halt and passengers began disembarking. He looked up and down the length of the train but couldn't see her. Then suddenly there she was, but he had to look twice to make sure it was her. She was walking like an old woman, as if the cares of the world were on her shoulders. He hurried forward taking her bag and kissing her on the cheek.

'Darling,' he said, anxiously, 'what's wrong? What on earth's the matter?'

She looked up at him, her face forlorn. 'Nothing, why do you ask?'

'Something is wrong, you look awful.'

'Thanks very much,' she said with a trace of smile.

'You know what I mean,' he said. 'Maybe you're just tired? Come on. Let's get you back to the car.'

On the short journey to St Ives he questioned her about her day. She answered his questions politely but her voice was expressionless, her thoughts clearly somewhere else.

'I'm so proud of you for getting that commission,' he said, in an effort to engage her.

'Yes, it is good,' she answered, but without enthusiasm.

He parked the car in Barnoon car park and getting out of the car collected her bag from the boot and then took her by the hand.

'Come on,' he said, 'I've got the fire lit at home.'

'That's a bit indulgent in March.'

'No, it's not. It is a beastly evening. You look cold, perished in fact.'

They said nothing on the short walk down to Jericho Cottage.

'I'll just freshen up,' Felicity said as soon as they arrived and disappeared into their bedroom.

Keith stared after her, as she closed the bedroom door. She was behaving very oddly. Harvey came bounding down the stairs and stopped in amazement; his mistress had come home and yet he had not been her first priority.

Keith looked at him sympathetically. 'Come on, old boy, let's open some wine.' Keith took a bowl of olives out of the fridge, opened the wine and poured two glasses. Then he put the fish pie on the bottom shelf of the Aga and stood around anxiously wondering what to say or do. In all the ups and downs of their relationship, Keith had always felt at ease in Felicity's company. There had been rows and misunderstandings of course, and the heartbreak of forcing themselves to stay away from each other for a time, but never this. At last he heard the bedroom door open and she came up the stairs. Even her walk sounded different, she was dragging one foot after the other. In her hand she carried a newspaper.

'A glass of wine, my love?' he said. 'Come on, come and sit by the fire.'

'Thank you,' she said, taking the glass and following him through to the sitting room.

They sat down together on the sofa in front of the fire. Harvey came and lay at her feet but cautiously: he too was picking up on the atmosphere. They clinked glasses and drank in silence for a moment. A sudden fear gripped Keith. Was she ill? Had she really visited her publisher or had she gone to see a doctor? He couldn't bear it any more.

'Felicity, darling, you know how much I love you?'

Felicity cast solemn eyes in his direction and nodded.

'Something is terribly wrong and I am thinking the most dreadful thoughts about what it might be. Please, please tell me what it is, share it with me.'

She hesitated. 'I was in the station, at Paddington,' she added unnecessarily, 'and…' she hesitated, 'and I saw a banner headline on a news stand, it was about Otto Juniper.' She placed the newspaper on his lap.

'Otto Juniper,' Keith said, 'he's marvellous. Barbara took me to a concert of his once, his playing made me cry.' He stopped short seeing, the expression on Felicity's face. 'What is it, what is it darling?'

'The thing is, the thing is … my mother has just died.'

2

Keith took Felicity's hand in his. 'Your mother has just died?' he repeated, incredulously, 'but your parents are both dead, you told me that years ago, soon after we met.'

Felicity stared down at her feet, gripping Keith's hand like she was drowning. 'My father died about five years before Charlie, so mercifully he never knew I was widowed so young but my mother has been dead to me since I was six years old.'

'What does "dead to me" mean?' Keith asked, 'and what has it to do with Otto Juniper?'

'It means she walked out of my life when I was six years old and I haven't seen her since,' Felicity said. She took a gulp of wine. 'I'm sorry,' she said placing the glass on the table nearby, 'I should have explained. She left to live with Otto Juniper but I don't tell anyone, even the children don't know. Nobody knows.'

'Not even Charlie?'

'No,' Felicity said, 'Gilla knew, but then she

was my best friend from when we were babies. She knew because she was there when it happened.'

'I don't understand,' Keith said, 'help me here.'

'My mother was in Germany, in Berlin, in 1938, just before war was declared. You know they started persecuting the Jews, they broke all the shop windows and destroyed their businesses and homes.'

'Kristallnacht,' Keith said.

Felicity looked up at him, surprised. 'Yes.'

'We learnt all about it at school,' Keith said.

'While she was there, waiting to be brought back to England, she found a little boy, a little Jewish boy.'

'When you say found?' Keith asked.

Felicity shook her head. 'I don't know any details. I know very little of the circumstances. I just know that she took care of him and managed to get him on the Kindertransport that was saving Jewish children.'

'I know about the Kindertransport,' Keith said. 'It was marvellous; they saved ten thousand children.'

Felicity nodded. 'She saved him anyway and got him on a train and she herself came home from Germany a few days later.'

'What has this got to do with why she left you?'

'The little boy she saved was Otto Juniper.'

'Oh!' Keith was silent for a moment. 'Now I

understand a little more. I know he has a muse, the love of his life, the woman who inspired him to play. Is her name Sophie?'

'Sophia,' Felicity corrected.

'This was your mother? Wasn't she a lot older than Otto?'

Felicity nodded. 'My father took her to a concert at the Sheldonian Theatre in Oxford. Otto Juniper was playing and as soon as she saw him, even after all those years, she recognised him as the little boy she had rescued. She had tried to find him apparently, searched for years.'

'What sort of ages would they have been then?'

'I don't know exactly how old Otto was at the time – in his late twenties I think, but my mother was forty-two and I was six. I was six,' she repeated.

'And what happened?' Keith asked.

'She left. She went to live with Otto. She left me and my father and she never came back. The paper says she was ninety-two when she died yesterday. Otto is seventy-eight. The age gap still sounds ridiculous, even at her great age.'

'Why haven't you seen each other in all these years?' Keith asked.

A curious look came over Felicity's face. 'I didn't want to see her. My father was a good man but he was not very imaginative and a very poor communicator. He had no idea how to deal with a child, nor any wish to, I suspect.'

'She must have known all that,' Keith said quietly.

'Of course she knew that but she still left me for Otto. After a few years she tried to make contact but I wouldn't see her and neither did my father encourage it. We were both still so … so damaged by it. It was so sudden, you see, no warning. She just left us and she was such a strong person, the glue that held our little family together. Without her, we just existed. Years later, when my engagement to Charlie was announced in *The Times*, she must have seen it and asked to meet me. But I still refused. The last time she made any attempt at contact was after the birth of Jamie. Again she must have picked it up from an announcement in the paper.'

'Didn't you really want to see her again?' Keith asked.

'No,' said Felicity, in a small voice.

'But she is your mother, *was* your mother,' he corrected.

'She didn't behave like a mother, she left me. I cried myself to sleep night after night. I couldn't believe she would never come back. My father wouldn't talk about her. He couldn't see that I needed to know things. It hurt so much; I thought the pain would never go.'

'Poor little girl,' Keith said, putting down his own glass and taking Felicity in his arms. 'While I've got breath in my body, I promise you will never be alone again, my darling,' he said, holding her close. She was still cold and trembling. He withdrew slightly and studied her face. 'Are you wishing now she has died that you had made contact with her?'

'No, never,' Felicity shocked him with her vehemence. 'Never, ever,' she said. 'It was just a shock, that's all. Ridiculous really, bearing in mind how old she was, I should have been prepared.'

'Would you like to go to the funeral?' Keith suggested.

'No,' Felicity stood up abruptly and walked over to the mantelpiece; the hand resting on it, he noticed, was clutching the edge of the granite so tightly that her knuckles were white.

'It might …' he hesitated. 'What is that appalling American expression, it might provide closure?'

'No,' Felicity said, 'I am not going and I'm certainly going nowhere near that man.'

'He can't be all bad. Think of the pleasure he has brought to the world.'

'He took a mother away from her child,' Felicity said. 'He was a lost child himself, he must have known how it felt. He of all people should have realised the enormity of what he had done.'

Keith frowned. 'I remember reading about their relationship somewhere. Whether it was in the programme at the concert I went to or whether it was in a newspaper, I can't remember, but they say that he didn't or couldn't reach the height of his brilliance until your mother was with him; that she was the catalyst that made him such a great violinist.'

'That makes it all right then?' Felicity asked, bitterly.

'No, no of course not. I'm simply trying to understand what happened. There must have been a very strong bond between them.'

'What happened,' said Felicity, 'is that my mother aged forty-two went off with a much younger man without even considering what she was leaving behind.'

'You're very bitter,' Keith said.

'Yes, I am,' Felicity said.

'And yet you've hidden it, from Charlie, from your children, from me; you've hidden it from everyone all these years!'

'It was the only way I could cope with it. All through school, can you imagine, Mother's Day cards, that sort of thing?'

'I can't imagine,' said Keith. 'I do realise how lucky I was, being brought up in a close family. My parents loved one another and me and my sister. I can't imagine what it must have been like but I know bitterness isn't the answer. She has died now, darling, this is a boil that needs to be lanced.'

'How?' Felicity asked.

'I think we should go to the funeral and take your children and your grandchildren. I think you should meet Otto, hear his side of the story and make your peace with him. He is an old man.'

'Never!' said Felicity. 'I am not going to the funeral and I will never speak to that man.'

'Then the wound will never heal.'

'Keith, I am well over halfway through my life, I have had years and years to learn to live with this. I have the children, my grandchildren, your children and above everything else, darling, I have you. The wound healed years ago. It was a shock, that's all.'

'Would you ever have told me about her if I hadn't asked why you were upset?' Keith asked.

Felicity stared at him, struggling hard to be honest but at the same time not wanting to hurt him. 'Probably not,' she admitted.

'That makes me very sad,' Keith said, 'that you didn't trust me.'

'It's not a question of trust,' Felicity replied, 'if I had told you about it, it would have made it real again, brought back the hurt.'

'And isn't the hurt back now?'

'Yes, yes,' said Felicity, 'of course it is. She was my mother and she died yesterday. She was a person in her own right yet so far as the newspapers are concerned, her death is all about Otto. Will he ever play again without his muse and all that stuff. I was sacrificed at the altar of Otto Juniper's talent, it seems my mother was too.'

Keith made one last effort. 'Burying stuff – feelings – it doesn't work, in my experience. They fester, they reappear, they influence.'

'It's worked for me into my fifties. I don't see why it shouldn't go on working.' She smiled suddenly, her face relaxing a little. 'Is that fish pie I smell?'

Keith nodded.

'You clever man, did you do it all yourself or did you get Annie to help you?'

'Damn!' said Keith, with a smile.

'Annie made it for you?'

Keith nodded. 'I went round to ask her for her recipe and she took pity on me. She said I was useless, she wouldn't even try to teach me what to do – in fact she said there was no point. I should have been offended but I knew she was right.'

Felicity laughed. 'Well, it is going to be a very good fish pie if Annie made it. Come on, let's lay the table and enjoy the evening.'

'OK, I'll just put a log or two on the fire,' Keith said. He watched her with worried eyes as she hurried through to the kitchen. 'Let's enjoy the evening' – the evening you had just learnt your mother has died. He shook his head, it wasn't right, it wasn't right at all.

3

The following morning found Keith Penrose out on the beach once more with Harvey, who was in particularly high spirits whirling around in pointless circles yapping at seagulls. The yapping was particularly unwelcome. Keith was aware that he and Felicity had drunk too much wine the night before, which in the circumstances was hardly surprising. This morning he was glad of the fresh air to clear his head but he could have done without Harvey's enthusiasm.

The question was, what should he do now? Nothing, which was Felicity's wish, or something, which was his inclination. The bitterness she felt towards her mother, he was certain, would remain with her for the rest of her life unless she dealt with it in some way and now there was an opportunity to heal the wound. He had made the point to Felicity during the evening that Sophia had been a grandmother and a great-grandmother, that Mel and James and their children had the right to say goodbye if they so wished, even if they had never said hello.

'There is no point in saying goodbye to somebody they never knew existed,' Felicity said.

'But what if they decided in the future to explore their ancestry? They would learn that their grandmother had been alive throughout their childhood and what would they think of you for lying to them?'

'They're not likely to do that,' Felicity had said.

'On the contrary, it's all the rage now,' Keith had argued. 'You are essentially an extremely honest person, it would come as the most appalling shock to them to realise you had lied to them about your own mother.'

'She was dead to me from when I was six, so she was dead to them too,' Felicity said, angrily. 'Now can we please change the subject.'

And so they had tried but there was an atmosphere between them and all night long they had tossed and turned. Felicity had at last been asleep by the time Keith crept from their bed and headed out into the early morning with Harvey.

He was on his way back, having just circled the Island, when his mobile rang. He looked at it and frowned; George Staple, his former boss.

'Hello, sir,' he said.

'Oh, Keith, I think we can drop the "sir" now, don't you? Particularly after all these years. My name is George.'

Keith thought of his austere and sometimes inscrutable boss. The idea of calling him George seemed quite impossible. 'I'll do my best,' he said, without much conviction.

'I'll cut straight to the point of the call,' George Staple said, never one to waste time. 'I was hoping you could meet me for lunch today, I have a job for you, not a paying job … well, not really, but something that I think might interest you.'

Keith was intrigued. 'What sort of job?' he asked.

'Your last case,' George Staple said, 'the McAllister' one, it impressed the powers that be. It was good work Keith, no doubt about it.'

'Thank you,' Keith said.

'The thing is, another cold case has come to light and we would quite like you to have a look at it.'

'But I'm no longer a policeman,' Keith said.

'I'm aware of that,' said George, patiently, 'but I can explain to you how it works, hence the lunch. Should we say Bustopher's Bistro in Lemon Street, twelve-thirty today?'

Keith hesitated; not only was the thought of a job intriguing, it felt almost like being thrown a lifeline, something to do, something to seize his interest. Immediately, though, he thought about Felicity. Was it sensible to leave her alone today? He hesitated.

'It is urgent, Keith, if you are interested in helping us out with this one, we do need to get on with it.'

He made a decision. 'That'll be fine,' he said. 'I'll be there at twelve-thirty. Thank you for thinking of me.'

Felicity was up and dressed when he returned and looking perfectly normal if perhaps a little pale.

'We drank too much wine last night,' she said, smiling at him ruefully and giving him a hug. 'Ooh, you smell nice, all salty.'

'I've just had a call from George Staple,' Keith said.

'Really, what did he want?'

Keith explained as much as he knew. 'He wants us to meet for lunch today in Truro, is that all right with you?'

'Yes, of course,' said Felicity, 'why wouldn't it be?'

Keith busied himself filling the kettle. 'Well, you know in the circumstances ...'

'Keith, listen to me.'

He put the kettle on the Aga and turned to

face her. 'Yes,' he said.

'We had this all out last night. As far as I am concerned the subject of my mother and her death is now closed. I don't want to talk about it to anyone, even you, ever. Is that understood?'

Keith studied her in silence for a moment. This was a side of Felicity he had never seen before. She was so kind, compassionate, interested in other people, fun, humorous… this hardness, this bitterness was so totally out of character. 'My darling, I don't want to do anything that is going to upset you and if you want to ignore the fact that your mother has just died then I must respect that but understand, no, I'm afraid I don't.'

Felicity's face softened a little. 'I'm sorry you don't understand. I can see why you don't but I must ask you to just accept it. We all have different coping mechanisms for the difficult things that have happened to us in our lives. In my case, the only way I coped with losing my mother … no, not losing her, when my mother abandoned me … the only way I coped when my mother abandoned me was to close the door on my feelings for her. If I had allowed myself to continue as that lost, lonely, grieving little girl, I would never have recovered, I know I wouldn't. I just had to slam the door on what she had meant to me and get on with the rest of my life. After all, it is what she did, I was only following her example. And it has worked, it's worked very well but as a result, the fact she has just died means nothing to me, nothing to me at all.'

'I understand what you are saying but it's just this apparent lack of feeling is in such contrast to the normal you.' He looked bewildered.

'Darling,' Felicity came forward and took Keith's hands in hers. 'I'm glad you feel like that, that I am normally a caring person, I hope. Maybe my mother leaving even gave me more of an understanding about life's frailties. I don't know, and I don't want to know. I don't want to explore my feelings for her. There no doubt will be a bit of a fuss in the papers for a day or two until her funeral takes place and then again one day when Otto dies but nobody else in the world but you will link me to them.'

'I suppose I should be flattered that you told me at all,' Keith said.

'It's because I love you so much, I don't want secrets between us,' said Felicity, 'but you are the only person I have ever told or will ever tell.'

'Then promise me one thing,' said Keith.

Felicity nodded. 'If I can.'

'If you ever want to talk about it, about what it felt like to be abandoned or about growing up without a mother but knowing she was alive, will you at least try to talk to me about it?'

'I don't want to talk about it,' said Felicity, 'as I've explained, I've slammed the door on all that.'

'I know,' said Keith, 'and I do understand, or at least I am trying to, but now you have at last confided in someone, in me, all I am saying is that I am here if you feel the need at any time, now or in the future, to talk about it, that's all.'

'Thank you,' said Felicity, 'but I won't. I won't want to talk about it, Keith, now or ever, but thank you for the thought.'

Keith drew her into his arms and held her close. Heaven knows, he was no psychiatrist, but forty years in the police force had taught him a little about human nature and he felt sure that burying all this grief and sadness could not be good.

Punctuality was important to Keith Penrose so he arrived at Bustopher Jones Bistro ten minutes early and was surprised to see George Staple already seated at a table, a bottle of red wine already started. He stood up and shook Keith's hand.

'Well, something is agreeing with you,' said George, 'you look ten years younger than when I saw you last.'

Keith smiled. 'Something to do with not having to deal on a daily basis with man's inhumanity to man, I expect.'

'Possibly,' George agreed.

George Staple had just missed looking avuncular, Keith always thought. He was a huge man, broad-shouldered with a large head accentuated by a big mop of white hair but there was also a toughness about him that made him anything but cosy. Keith didn't mind the slight air of menace, he liked George Staple because he was straight, an honest, decent copper who had made his way up through the ranks in an honest, decent way.

George lifted the bottle. 'It's a half-decent Merlot, I thought you'd appreciate it.'

'Thank you, sir,' said Keith, 'Just the one glass, I'm driving.'

'We're dropping "sir", I thought we agreed,' said George, smiling.

'I'm trying,' said Keith, 'but it is a difficult adjustment after all this time.'

'Let's order,' said George, 'and then we'll talk.'

They ordered their food, clinked glasses and George sat back in his chair. 'What I have to offer you, Keith, is not much. We have a cold case with which you are familiar and the powers that be were so impressed by your last case before you retired that they want you to have a crack at this one.'

'I'm familiar with it?' Keith asked.

'Do you remember the woman who was pulled out of the sea on Porthminster beach in St Ives, six years ago? It was a presumed suicide.'

'She had stones sewn into her pockets,' Keith continued, 'yes, of course I remember her. Morwenna Nicholls, she had two boys named ...' Keith searched his mind.

'Graham and Christopher,' George said. 'Yes, they were six and thirteen at the time. The father, Colin, maintained there was no way that his wife would have committed suicide and having thoroughly investigated the family, we agreed with him but there was no apparent alternative reason for her death. There were no obvious signs of foul play, no abrasions other than being tossed about in the waves. The coroner recorded an open verdict; there was nothing else he could do, nothing any of us could have done.'

Keith nodded. 'It was awful,' he said. 'Those poor boys, suddenly made motherless, terrible.'

'What was your view at the time?' George asked.

Keith leant back in his chair and sighed. 'Well, it was a very difficult one. Someone had definitely sewn stones into the pocket of Morwenna's coat, which would suggest the action of someone intending to commit suicide. However, her husband, her mother, her father, her brother, her sister and her best friend – everyone who knew her well said she was as happy as could be. She had everything to live for – a happy marriage, two great kids. They lived over at Marazion, with a view of St Michael's Mount – a marvellous spot. What happened to the boys?'

'I don't know any details,' said George. 'They are twelve and nineteen now. I know the elder boy is at university. The twelve-year-old is obviously at school. They've moved up country since the tragedy. They live in Exeter now.'

'So why are you suddenly interested in this case?'

George took a sip of his wine. 'The same thing has happened again, Keith. This time at Church Cove, Gunwalloe on the Lizard. The woman was about the same age and again stones were sewn into the pockets of her coat. They have compared the two garments – the coats are different, the thread is different but the stitching is very much the same.'

'What? Are you saying that somebody murdered these two women six years apart?' said Keith.

'I don't know what I'm saying at the moment,' said George, 'which is why you are here. This time it involves a professional family. They are Truro-based. There is one son aged sixteen, the husband is a solicitor and his wife, the one who was found dead, was a doctor working in A & E at Treliske Hospital. The boy is doing well, he is at Truro

School and likely to go to Oxbridge, a clever chap. The husband seems to be stable and loving and absolutely destroyed with grief at what has happened. We've interviewed all her colleagues at the hospital and her friends – there appears to be absolutely no reason why she would take her own life.'

'Was she visiting Gunwalloe when the incident happened?'

George shook his head. 'No, she left the hospital as usual and her car needed a service so her friend dropped her in town, the idea being that she should walk home. Their house is near your old home. She told the friend that she was going to do a bit of shopping, but she never came home and it is impossible to get to Gunwalloe without a car.'

'That's very different from Morwenna Nicholls,' said Keith. 'Morwenna was on Porthminster beach; people saw her walking down there.'

'Yes, I agree but in all other respects, the two so-called suicides are identical.'

'OK,' said Keith, 'so there's this homicidal maniac who is rather good at sewing. He sews stones into two random women's coats while presumably, what, they are tied up, drugged, bashed over the head?'

'No they certainly weren't drugged, drugs

weren't found in either body,' said George.

'So,' Keith continued, 'he ties them up, gags them, whatever. But then, don't tell me, there were no marks on them either, no rope burns, no gag marks ...' He looked at George for confirmation who nodded his head in agreement. 'So while sitting together on the beach, making polite conversation, he sews stones into their pockets, then makes them put their coats on and walk into the sea? Oh and incidentally, he does all of this with a gap of six years between the two deaths?'

'It's the gap which has got you involved,' said George.

Keith frowned. 'I don't know what you mean?'

'There was a big gap, wasn't there, in that Johnson case but you managed to find the link? Upstairs are hoping you are going to do it again.'

'So they want me back on the force?' Keith asked.

'Ah, no, this is the rather unpalatable part,' George hesitated. 'They want you back, they want your expertise, but they are not prepared to pay for it. They will give you generous expenses and a sergeant.'

'Can I have Jack Curnow?'

'No, of course you can't. He's being groomed for higher things. I've got a sergeant for you, his name's David Sterling, a bit green but decent enough.'

'Oh, great,' said Keith, 'so I have to train in yet another sergeant. Tell me something about him.'

'He is a rugby player, plays for Cornwall as a matter of fact, sports a fine cauliflower ear. The good news is he is built like an ox. You'll certainly be safe with him watching your back. Having said all that, he is a pussycat underneath.'

'But needs training in?'

'Totally,' said George, with a trace of a smile.

'OK, so let me get this straight. I get no wages and I've got to train in a rookie sergeant! Is there anything else I need to know?'

'Yes,' said George, 'and it's probably the deal breaker.'

'Go on,' said Keith.

'You don't have any power any more, Keith. Everywhere you go you have to take your sergeant. You can interview people but you won't have a warrant card and you can't do anything without your sergeant tagging along waving his.'

'Can I arrest people?'

'Only as much as any citizen can,' said George, 'but of course your sergeant can make an arrest.'

'Right,' said Keith, 'I can handle all that, but there's more, I can tell.'

'Obviously, as you are not a policeman any more you have to be able to report to someone senior.'

'OK,' said Keith, slowly.

'And in this case,' said George, 'it is DI Neil Mavers.'

'No!' said Keith. 'Anyone but him.'

'I knew you were going to say that,' said George. 'Are you sure I can't tempt you to a little more wine?'

'Unless you are suggesting a second bottle and staying the night in Truro,' said Keith, 'no, no I'm sorry, you can't seriously expect me to report to Neil? He is the biggest …'

'Stop!' said George, 'I don't want to hear what you think of Neil Mavers in case I am forced to agree with you.' The two men exchanged a smile.

'He is a complete plonker,' said Keith, after a moment's silence.

'No comment,' said George. 'If you want the job, this is what has to happen.'

'So do I have to ask his permission to do things?'

'No, I've given you the job. You have the authority to investigate the cases as you think fit but your findings have to be reported back to Neil.'

'And if he doesn't approve of what I am doing?'

'Then presumably he will tell you and suggest you move in another direction.'

'And if I refuse to move in another direction?'

'Knowing you and your customary tact, Keith,

I imagine you will agree with his suggestions and then do exactly what you want. Just like always.'

'And will you back me if we end up in some ghastly confrontation?'

'Absolutely not,' said George.

'Fine, it is good to know where I stand,' said Keith. 'How long do I have to make up my mind?'

'I need an answer now,' said George. 'Everybody is breathing down my neck. It's an odd one, this case; nothing about it feels right. There is something we missed last time. Let's hope that this time you'll get lucky.'

'I ought to talk it through with Felicity ...' Keith began.

'Oh, come on,' said George. 'That is one sensible woman, she knows you've been bored to tears ... you have, haven't you?' Keith didn't answer. 'This will give you something to do, get you out from under her feet. I bet you're driving her mad.'

'She seems to like having me around,' Keith said, defensively.

'Fish, house guests and stay-at-home partners are all very unpalatable after an extremely short time span. She will be thrilled to bits for you, you know she will.'

'She has a few problems at the moment,' Keith murmured, studying his plate.

'Not health problems, I hope?' said George.

Keith shook his head. 'No, nothing serious, just family stuff.'

'Enough to make you think she shouldn't be on her own?'

Keith thought about it for a moment, remembering the vehemence with which Felicity had said she could cope with her mother's death.

'No,' he said, 'no, not enough for that.'

'Well then,' said George, 'can I take it you're on board?'

Despite himself Keith felt a surge of excitement. 'Yes, sir ,' he said, 'but I do expect you to put in a good word for me when I go to trial for the murder of Neil Mavers.'

'Consider it done,' said George.

4

Horace Greenaway, the pathologist, was sitting at his desk drinking a cup of coffee when Keith Penrose walked into his lab. He spluttered over the coffee and put his mug down with a thump, spilling more.

'Good God, Penrose, not you again, I thought we had finally got rid of you.'

'And it is very nice to see you too, Horace,' said Keith.

The two men shook hands and then embraced. They had known each other since boyhood and had spent many happy years since annoying one another intensely. Horace sat down heavily in his chair and motioned to Keith to sit down too on a rather flimsy-looking stool on the other side of the desk.

'Is this a social call?'

'Afraid not, Horace,' said Keith.

'Oh Jesus, you're not back as some God-awful crime-busting private detective, are you?'

'I am back, but working with the police. I've just had lunch with George Staple. I'm a cold case officer I think, but I have no power which is a bit of a weird feeling, to tell you the truth.'

'I can imagine,' said Horace, raising an eyebrow, 'No power, eh, so bye-bye Superman?'

Keith ignored him. 'I'm getting a sergeant; I don't know if you've met him? His name is David Sterling.'

'Not "the" David Sterling?' said Horace.

'I don't know,' said Keith, bewildered.

'The rugby player, the prop, indeed the finest prop in all of Cornwall, in the whole damn world I shouldn't wonder.'

'Very probably, cauliflower ears were mentioned.'

'Dear God, the man is a legend, you'll be safe in his hands, Penrose, he's built like a brick shithouse.'

'George Staple suggested he was built like an ox.'

'Well, George would, wouldn't he, very proper and correct. You lucky sod, Keith, what an honour to be working with him.'

'Can I just remind you, Horace, that he is actually my sergeant. He is working with me, I'm not working with him.'

'Ah yes, but then he is a proper policeman,

isn't he?' said Horace, with a sly smile.

'Shut up could you, Horace, you are really starting to annoy me.'

'That's excellent! Business as usual!' said Horace. 'It's good to see you, Penrose. Now what can I do for you?'

'This woman who died in Gunwalloe?'

'Oh yes, Adrianne, spelt the girl's way, double n e,' he said. 'I've got her through there. Do you want to have a look.'

'Just tell me about her first, could you?' said Keith.

'Not much to tell, that's the problem,' said Horace. 'She drowned. It looks like she did it on purpose because she had stones, not just put into but sewn into her coat pockets.'

'Was it a long coat?'

'No, a short jacket, a tailored jacket, well-fitting so it didn't float away.'

'Was it one of hers?'

'The husband says so.'

'Where did the stones come from?'

'Pebbles off the beach, nothing special.'

'Any fingerprints, or DNA, or anything at all? If I sound desperate it's because I am.'

'Oh, come off it, Penrose, the woman had been in the water for two days, of course there is nothing.'

'Was she was alive when she went into the water?'

Horace nodded. 'Yes, and there are no signs of alcohol or drugs and no suggestion that she was restrained before she went into the water. It looks like a suicide, it looks like she walked down the beach and kept on walking until she drowned.'

'And were the stones heavy enough to pull her down?'

'Yes,' said Horace, 'but not immediately. However as her clothes became sodden and she got tired, the stones would have dragged her under, no doubt.'

The two men were silent for a moment. 'What a way to die,' said Keith, at last.

'We've seen much worse,' said Horace.

5

Felicity was peeling potatoes when Keith arrived home. She still looked pale but was very pleased to see him; she embraced him warmly and held him tight.

'How did the meeting go?' she asked.

'I'll tell you in a moment. Shall I put on the kettle?'

She nodded. 'I've got some black market sea bass for supper.'

'Black market?' Keith said. 'Remember I'm an ex-copper!'

'Well, I don't know that they're black market, to be honest. They came from Annie,' said Felicity, 'and she refused to take any money for them so they must have fallen off the back of a trawler or something. Anyway that is what we've got. I'm just doing some potatoes and a salad. Is that all right?'

'Perfect,' said Keith, 'I will pretend I have no idea as to their origins. What a treat!'

Keith poured the tea and then sat down at the

kitchen table. 'They want me to do a job for them,' he said.

'They?' Felicity asked.

'Well, George Staple does. It's a cold case.'

'It just proves my point. They can't do without you, Chief Inspector.'

'Chief Inspector no longer,' said Keith. 'That's the big difference. I don't have any power or authority. I have to take a rugby-playing sergeant around with me all the time. I've no rank and worse still, no wages.'

'What, nothing?' Felicity asked.

'Well, generous expenses I'm told, but certainly I'm not back on the payroll, and I don't feel up to training yet another sergeant, there have been too many of them over the years. This one is some sort of rugby star. He's called David Sterling and he has cabbage ears.'

'Anything else?' Felicity asked.

'Oh yes,' said Keith, 'I will be answerable to DI Neil Mavers, would you believe?'

'And he is?' Felicity asked.

'A complete idiot,' said Keith. 'He thinks he knows everything and in fact knows nothing. I can't stand the man.'

Felicity regarded him with a smile, leaning back against the Aga rail. 'And having listened to all this grumbling,' she said, 'I take it you can't wait to start the job?'

He started to protest and then saw her smiling. He shrugged in defeat, grinning back a little self-consciously. 'I suppose you're right,' he admitted.

'Of course I'm right,' said Felicity, getting up from the table and putting her arms around him. 'This is so what you need.'

'Is it?' said Keith. 'I thought we were happy as we are.'

'You *are* happy, we *are* happy,' said Felicity, 'but you need something in your life apart from our relationship and walking Harvey. You are a highly intelligent man and you look and behave years younger than your age. This sort of life will be perfect for you in ten or fifteen years' time, but not now.'

Keith smiled at her. 'I'll take that as a compliment.'

'So you should, and it happens to be true. The stupid rules in today's police force mean that just when a professional policeman reaches his prime, he is put out to grass – it's madness after all those years of training and expertise.'

'It's a young man's world,' Keith said.

'Yes, it is,' said Felicity, 'but it is also wrong to force people into retirement before their time and it was certainly wrong for you. There is no way you are ready for retirement yet. I am so excited for you.

Is it an interesting case?'

Keith picked up their mugs of tea and took them to the sink. 'Yes, and a baffling one. It begins with a cold case I worked on about six years ago. A woman named Morwenna Nicholls apparently sewed stones into the pockets of her jacket, then walked into the sea at Porthminster beach and drowned.'

'How awful, how old was she?'

'Only in her mid-thirties,' said Keith, 'she and her husband Colin lived in Marazion and she worked in Penzance at an old people's home. She was a carer and very good at her job apparently. They had two boys, the younger one was only six.'

'And what was the cause, why did she do it?'

'That's just it,' said Keith. 'There wasn't any reason for it to happen. The marriage was happy, she was happy in her work, she loved her boys. Her family, her friends, the patients at the care home – everyone said she was a very cheerful soul.'

'So why is the case being reopened?'

'It's not officially. It's just that there is a link. Another woman has just gone into the sea, this time at Gunwalloe on the Lizard and the scenario is exactly the same. She seems to have been a happy person with a contented marriage and a good job working as a doctor in A & E at Treliske Hospital.'

'Good maybe, but hardly a stress-free one,' said

Felicity, 'I imagine working in A & E is enough to make anybody suicidal.'

He smiled at her. 'I know what you mean. It is odd though, that there should be another woman also with apparently no reason for committing suicide and the really weird part is there were some stones sewn into her jacket too.'

'So what are you saying,' said Felicity, 'is that this is now being viewed as murder?'

'I honestly don't know,' said Keith, 'I've already been to see Horace. He has done the autopsy on the recent victim and he can find absolutely no suggestion that there was any criminal activity. She was alive when she went into the water and there were no signs of a struggle.'

'And they are asking you what ... to make a link?'

'Yes and quickly. I think this family, reading between the lines, are probably going to make more fuss than the Nicholls. The husband is a solicitor and he simply does not believe that his wife could have committed suicide. The powers that be are hoping to solve this second death by reference to the first.'

'Poor man, there must be an awful guilt thing going on,' said Felicity. 'Just imagine if someone really close to you committed suicide and you didn't see it coming, or worse, you were aware of their unhappiness but didn't take it seriously. You'd go into instant denial, wouldn't you and immediately look for someone else to blame?'

'I suppose so,' said Keith, 'certainly I can't imagine living with somebody and not recognising they were a suicide risk.'

'So, logically,' said Felicity, 'either the husband is lying or there genuinely is a reason to suspect some sort of foul play, to coin a phrase. Goodness, it's fun talking about one of your cases again.'

'Oh, I see,' said Keith, 'I've clearly been boring you rigid ever since I retired.'

'Bored to tears,' said Felicity, 'as you well know.' They smiled fondly at one another.

'So how has your day been?' Keith asked.

'OK.' She avoided his gaze, stood up abruptly and started fussing around a saucepan on the Aga.

'Did you get any work done?'

'No,' said Felicity. 'I didn't seem to be able to concentrate today.'

'Hardly surprising,' Keith suggested.

'You promised!' Felicity turned to him, the tenderness of a moment before gone in an instant. 'You promised we wouldn't discuss it again.'

'So are you truly telling me that you didn't think about your mother at all today?'

'Of course I thought about her, but I don't want to talk about it.'

'Even to me?' Keith persisted.

'Even to you.' She relented slightly, seeing the forlorn expression on his face. 'Talking about it makes it real.'

'But it is real,' said Keith.

'Not to me,' said Felicity. 'The woman who died yesterday was not my mother. She gave birth to me yes, but she rejected me and I in turn have rejected her and the memory of her. That's an end to it. Please, please stop talking about it. We were having a good time just now, talking about your case. I don't want to go there, Keith, I just don't want to revisit that period of my life – it's even a relief in a way that she has died.'

'Why?' Keith asked.

'Well, it means I ...' Felicity ran out of words, turned her back on him and walked over to the French windows. 'I said I didn't want to talk about it,' she repeated with her back towards him, rigid with tension.

'I just think that you should hear her side of the story.'

'Well I can't do that now, can I?' said Felicity. 'She's dead.'

'Through Otto?' Keith suggested.

'I am never going to speak to that man. I thought I made that quite clear last night.'

'It's just ...' said Keith.

'I don't want to talk about it,' Felicity shouted. 'Please, Keith. Stop.'

'Just let me say one thing,' said Keith, 'and then I will drop the subject, I promise.'

'As long as it is a very brief one thing,' said Felicity, wearily.

'You assume she didn't love you,' said Keith. 'You assume that a little lost boy meant more to her than her own child.'

'It is not an assumption,' Felicity burst out, 'it's a fact.'

'You don't know that, you don't know all the circumstances and if you want to know the truth, I think you should find out without delay. I don't think Otto Juniper is going to live very much longer.'

'What on earth makes you say that?' Felicity asked. She had come back to the table and was sitting down again, her head in her hands, scowling.

'They say in today's papers that he will never play again without your mother. He has a weak heart and he is not far off eighty himself. If you want to know the truth about what really happened then surely this is the moment to find out. I am absolutely certain Otto would be so pleased...'

'Oh, stop it, Keith,' said Felicity. 'You just don't get it. I don't want to know what really happened, because I know what happened to me. I had a seemingly devoted mother who I loved very much and one day she simply walked out of the house and never came back. She went to live with a man years younger than her and gave me not so much as a backward glance.'

'There you go again,' said Keith. 'That statement is an assumption. You are seeing the whole thing through the eyes of a desperately unhappy six-year-old. I think you need to know the truth, now you are old enough to cope with it and maybe even understand it.'

'I know the truth,' Felicity thundered, 'as it happened to me and stop lecturing me. I'm going out.'

'Where?' Keith asked. 'It's nearly dark.'

'I need some fresh air, I'll be back in a bit.'

'Do you want to take Harvey?' Keith asked.

'No.' She thundered down the stairs, picking up a coat from the banister rail as she went, slamming the front door behind her, none too gently.

'A bit like a teenager,' Keith thought. 'Well, that went well, didn't it, Harvey?'

With head down and moving very fast, Felicity walked along the wharf and then almost ran down the steps, across Porthgwidden beach and from there up on to the Island. She walked around its perimeter and when she reached a bench looking straight out to sea and Godrevy lighthouse, she sat down wrapping her coat tightly around her. Why couldn't he just leave it? Why couldn't he see that the kindest thing he could possibly do was to drop the whole subject? She wondered how many different ways she had tried to tell him to stop. She loved him so much but now regretted telling him anything about her mother. If she had just thrown the newspaper away, he would have been none the wiser.

She felt tears welling into her eyes but they were not for her mother, they were for her six-year-old self. When her children James and Mel, in turn, had each reached their sixth birthdays, she had tried to imagine any circumstances which would have made it possible for her to leave them. She knew it would be quite impossible and she could not understand how any woman could do such a thing. Whatever reassurance she had tried to communicate to Keith, in truth Felicity knew her mother's abandonment had affected the whole of her life. In her childhood and adolescence it had sapped her confidence. It was why she had been so attracted to Charlie Paradise, her late husband. Charlie was flamboyant, a complete extrovert – all she had to do was follow in his wake. Being surrounded by his confidence every day gradually enabled her to build a confidence of her own, but it never stopped her wondering what was wrong with her that her mother should have left her. Charlie had loved her in his own way; her children loved her; she had good friends and at last she felt a whole person again. Although the terrible blow of Charlie's sudden death had knocked her sideways, his legacy to her was that unwittingly he had restored her faith in herself to the point where ultimately she was able even to cope with being a widow.

This second chance of happiness, with Keith, was more than she had ever dreamed of being possible. Comparisons should not be made between the two major men in her life, she knew, but in her heart, although she had loved Charlie, she knew that Keith was her soul-mate. They were close in a way she had never been with Charlie, of whom she had always been slightly in awe. Not that she didn't respect Keith and was enormously proud of his achievements. It was just that his interest in people, in her, his kindness and his compassion led to a much more intimate relationship than the one she had enjoyed with Charlie. Here, she supposed, was where the problem lay. She blew her nose, stood up and started to walk again, heading towards Porthmeor beach. Charlie knew only that her mother had died when she was very young. It was the cover story that she and her father had concocted over the years. It stopped speculation and awkward questions. He was a widower who was bringing up his little girl alone. If she had told Charlie the truth about what had happened to her mother and then said that she did not want to talk about it, he would have accepted it and never raised the subject again. Keith's persistence was the price she had to pay for the bonding of minds and emotions in a way that had never happened with Charlie. She had no right to be angry with Keith. He was only trying to help, to ease her sense of hurt. She tried to imagine what it would be like if the roles were reversed and Keith had suddenly blurted out the secrets of his childhood. How would she have reacted? The same as him, of course – she would have wanted him to talk about it, for him to tell her everything, to unburden himself, to try and relieve the pressure of the years of secrecy. She climbed down the steps and began walking across the beach. Then she changed her mind. She needed to go home and apologise. Instead she walked up the slipway and headed back into town.

Keith had finished off the potatoes, laid the table for supper and was just opening a bottle of wine as she walked through the door.

'I am most terribly sorry,' she said.

He put down the wine and held out his arms. 'I'm sorry too.'

'It's just that …'

'Stop there,' he said. 'I've taken on board everything you've said, I should have respected your wishes; I should have listened to what you said and frankly just shut up.'

They kissed.

'I was thinking,' said Felicity, 'when I was walking around the Island…'

'Stomping around the Island, I imagine?' Keith said.

'Yes, definitely.' Felicity managed a small smile. 'I was thinking that if this was the other way round, if it was you who had told me the story of your childhood, I would have reacted in exactly the same way as you have done. I would have been so anxious to help and also I would have been kind of …' she struggled for the word.

'Greedy,' Keith suggested.

'What do you mean greedy?'

'Just that, I want to know everything there is to know about you, every single thing and this is such a big thing.'

'I understand that.'

'And I do so worry about suppressed emotions, it can't be good for you.'

'I'm not going to sew stones into my pockets and jump into the harbour, I promise,' Felicity said, slipping her arms around him.

'I should hope not,' said Keith, 'that would increase my case load to an unacceptable degree.'

6

Keith felt extremely disorientated as he drove into Police Headquarters in Truro the following morning. Firstly he struggled to find a car parking space, his designated space long gone, then the duty sergeant did not recognise him and admittedly he did not recognise the duty sergeant either. He had no warrant card, he just had to explain who he was and wait. It felt extremely undignified to wait for his presence to be acknowledged by DI Neil Mavers.

He was not looking forward to the meeting with Mavers; they had never got along, and he had realised during the night that his sergeant was going to be a Mavers man. Neil Mavers had been a big rugby enthusiast during his youth, but had gone horribly to seed. There was now a coarseness about him, all the muscle tone he must have had once was long gone, leaving him flabby with an enormous paunch. Only his face bore witness to his past, a broken nose that had healed crooked. The sergeant who had been picked to accompany Keith everywhere probably played at the same rugby club which would mean that everything he did, both orthodox and unorthodox, would be reported back. It was not a pleasant thought.

The passage that took him to Neil Mavers's office also took him past his own old office. The door was shut and there was no name on the door. He was tempted to look in and then pulled himself together. What was past was past, he was no longer a Chief Inspector, he was a member of the general public with specialist knowledge who had been pulled in to help on a cold case. Rank, seniority were no longer relevant and if he didn't like the job and didn't like the people with whom he was working, he could leave. He had no contract signed and so there was no requirement to continue doing something he didn't enjoy. This was the pep talk he had given himself on the drive into Truro, but it didn't stop him feeling extremely apprehensive, like a new boy on his first day at school. It was ludicrous.

As soon as he entered the office, Neil Mavers got up from behind his desk.

'Keith,' he said, 'welcome back. I gather you were finding retirement a little tedious and wanted something to do.'

This was typical Mavers, he instantly had

Keith bristling.

'On the contrary,' he said, 'I'm finding retirement delightful.'

'Ah yes, you have a new lady in your life, I understand?'

'Neil, let's not mess about with niceties,' said Keith, 'I'm sure you're very busy and as we know, the first forty-eight hours of an investigation are all-important. Time is ticking by.'

Neil frowned which brought his hairline almost to his eyebrows. 'All right Keith,' he said, 'if that is how you want it.' He sat down heavily, indicating to Keith the chair opposite him.

'Sorry,' Keith felt obliged to say, 'I'm just finding this all a bit strange and I'd just like to get on with the job.'

'I gather the "Super" wants you to try to establish a link between the two deaths other than the stones in the pocket business. Very bizarre! I have to be honest, Keith, I really can't see the point of bringing you in. I know you were involved in the original investigation but we have already established there is no link between the two families, no friends in common, nothing, so what you can bring to the investigation, I have absolutely no idea.'

'Me neither,' said Keith, cheerfully, 'but I'm not going to know until I have a look. I gather I have a sergeant, well no, it's not a sergeant is it, he's more a minder.'

'He's a good lad actually,' said Neil. 'He's the son of a friend of mine,' he patted his corpulent belly, 'from my rugby days, a real leading light, excellent player, could get an England cap, if he keeps up his current standard of play.'

'I hope he's not so covered in glory, he won't be able to keep his mind on his job?'

'He'll be fine, I'm sure,' said Neil. 'Now you understand, don't you, that you have no powers at all? You don't have a warrant card, you can't interview anybody without David alongside you, ditto arrest, ditto searching people and premises.' He smirked, 'and I understand that you are doing this for love rather than money.'

'Thanks to my police pension,' said Keith, 'I am able to do just that and I understand the expenses are generous.'

Neil shrugged his shoulders. 'Well, each to their own. I can tell you this for nothing Keith, when my retirement comes up, you won't see me for dust. There is no way I'm going to be dragged back into investigating cold cases for no wages. When I am out of here, I'm out of here, with no looking back.'

'Well, that is one of the many ways in which

we are different,' said Keith, smiling to try to soften his words. 'Now, can I meet my sergeant?'

Neil stood up. 'Yes, I'll fetch him, he's only next door.'

'How's Jack?' Keith asked.

'Jack?' Neil frowned.

'Jack Curnow, my old sergeant.'

'Ah, he's destined for great things, he is up at Bodmin at the moment.'

'His wife can't like that very much,' Keith said.

'I wouldn't know,' said Neil, dismissively.

David Sterling was in many respects a caricature of a rugby player but meeting his eye for the first time, Keith immediately liked him. Despite his rugby stardom, he was not pompous. He looked cheerful, friendly and anxious to please, rather like a overgrown puppy.

Keith shook his hand and grinned. 'I don't think I'm going to get away with calling you Mary.'

'Mary?' said David, looking very confused.

'I mean as in Poppins, you're my nanny I understand?'

'To be honest, sir, it's an absolute privilege, you're quite a legend at this station.'

Out of the corner of his eye Keith could see Neil Mavers bridle at the remark, which was enormously satisfying.

'We've no time to waste so shall we go?' said Keith.

'Where are you going?' Neil asked.

'I'm going to sit down with David, get to know him and work out our strategy.'

'As I understand it, I am to be involved in your decision-making, in fact I have some ideas as to what you should do first.'

'One of the conditions George Staple agreed upon in order for me to do the job was that I would be my own man. I won't tread on anyone's toes but I have to make the decisions as to who we see, when we see them and why. If this is something that can't be accommodated then I am afraid I will have to tell the "Super" that I don't want the job. However, he seemed to think that it was a perfectly reasonable demand. I will, of course, report to you when there is anything to report.'

'I'm not happy about this, Penrose,' said Neil, standing up. 'Someone has to be in charge.'

'I agree,' said Keith, 'and I'm in charge of my investigation, my part of it. That's how it has to be. I'll come back to you as soon as we have any news.' Keith nodded in the direction of the door and David went straight through it without a backward glance. Once outside the building Keith said. 'I can't think straight in there with Mavers breathing down my neck and no office. That's my car, let's drive out to Malpas and talk things through.'

'I'm really impressed, sir,' said David, as they fastened their seatbelts.

'Impressed?' Keith said, concentrating on reversing the car.

'I know I shouldn't say it, I know it is not a very professional thing to say but I loved the way you dealt with Inspector Mavers, it was great.'

Keith gave him a quick smile. 'You know what, David, I think there is a chance that you and I might get on rather well.'

Ten minutes later found the men sitting on a park bench looking out over the estuary where a heron flapped lazily across the water.

'We should probably spend some time discussing our respective life histories but to be honest, David, I don't think we have the time.' David nodded. 'Have you had any contact with any of the parties involved in the current murder?'

David shook his head. 'I think I know no more than you, sir, I've simply read the files, that's all.'

'The problem we're facing,' said Keith, 'is that the original family is unlikely to be able to provide any new evidence.'

'How can we be sure?' David asked.

'The victim, Morwenna, was cremated so we have absolutely nothing to go on other than taking her husband and their boys through the whole tragedy again.'

'Are you saying you believe there is no link between the two families?' David asked.

'No, I'm not. That is what we are going to find out. We will have to re-interview the Nicholls, which is tricky, that's all.'

'Tricky in what way?' David asked.

'They were very embittered by what happened. The boys were only thirteen and six and very traumatised but at the time their father was no help to them because he was so angry about the whole thing.'

'Maybe he murdered her?'

Keith shook his head. 'I don't think so. He had a cast-iron alibi. His anger wasn't the sort that led to violence. He was one of those people that always think that life has got it in for them, that nothing's fair, that they've drawn the short straw.'

'If his wife committed suicide, it must have been a dreadful thing to cope with,' David said, not unreasonably.

'I agree,' said Keith, 'but somehow he wallowed in it. He should have been trying to make an effort, if not for himself, for his sons. Anyway,' said Keith, 'this is what I think we should do. I think you should go and visit the new family, the Becketts in Truro and I should go and see the

Nicholls since I know them. They have moved up to Exeter, I understand.'

'I'm really sorry, sir, but you can't do that,' said David.

'Why ever not?' Keith asked.

'I have to go with you whenever you interview anybody.'

'Oh, for Christ's sake,' said Keith. 'I'd forgotten all about that. I was planning to drive up there now. I don't know whether it's still his job, but Colin Nicholls was a plumber. I have his address and thought I could catch him when he gets back from work, which used to be about half-past-four. If you come too, it will mean you'll be late home.'

'That's no problem,' said David. 'I've no one waiting at home for me.'

'Not married?' Keith asked.

'No, I'm married to the job and married to rugby so there isn't too much room for anything else.'

'I can quite see that,' said Keith.

It was just after three o'clock by the time they reached Exeter Services, where they filled up with fuel and grabbed a tasteless garage sandwich. Half an hour later they pulled into the street in which the Nicholls lived. It was a mean little street, the houses small, drab and neglected. There was a dispiriting air about the place, litter was strewn all up the street and it looked as if no one cared about anything very much.

'Number twenty-three,' Keith said.

'Just up here on the left, I think,' said David.

'I'll pull in here and then we'll get a good view of the comings and goings.'

'So you're not just going to knock on the door then?' David asked.

Keith shook his head. 'I don't want to confront the younger son on his own. He's only twelve and it's likely he is already home from school. His father is an edgy sort of character, he would take it badly if we were talking to his son while he was not there, and I don't blame him.'

'I could just go and knock on the door and if the boy is alone say I'll come back later when his father is in,' David suggested. 'They don't know me – it will only be seeing you which will raise alarm bells.'

'That's true,' said Keith, 'but I'd rather we waited, David. Let's just sit here for a moment or two.'

'I hope we haven't come all this way to find they're not even in,' David said, after a few minutes silence, 'or moved away.'

'There's a newsagent's on the corner,' said Keith, 'you sit tight, I'll wander over and see if I can find out anything about the family.'

A cheery-looking woman in her early forties was standing behind the counter in the small well-stocked newsagents. There was no one else to be seen.

'Hello,' she said, 'what can I do for you?'

'I'd like a paper for a start and a bottle of water, but also I'm trying to find some old friends of mine from Cornwall who I believe live in this street. Their name is Nicholls, a father and two sons.'

'Oh, you mean Colin?' said the woman. 'Yes they live at number twenty-three. You're from Cornwall too, aren't you? I'm good on accents.'

Keith brought his newspaper and water to the counter. 'Yes,' he said, 'I live in St Ives. Colin and his family used to live in Marazion.'

'I know they came from that way, but I don't know much about them. Your friend, he's not an easy man to talk to.'

'No, he's not,' Keith said, with a smile. 'I was passing through Exeter and I suddenly thought about him. What time does he get back from work, do you know?'

'Normally, any time now. His older boy is away at University but the younger one needs his tea.'

'So Colin's not remarried?'

'No, I don't know what happened to the wife, none of them ever talk about her. Run off, did she?'

'Probably best I don't gossip,' said Keith, mildly.

The woman was silent for a moment as she took his money and gave him his change. 'I don't gossip either,' she said, with a slight smile. 'Like I know you're not really a friend of his, I know you're a policeman, but I am not going to say anything to anyone, especially not the neighbours, so don't worry.'

'He is not in any kind of trouble,' said Keith, 'he has been a law-abiding citizen all his life.'

'I'm sure he has,' the woman replied.

Keith turned to go and then turned back. 'How on earth did you know I was a policeman?'

'You just look like one,' she said. Keith laughed. 'Why do you find that funny?' she asked.

'I've been retired for a year now, well nearly a year. I thought maybe it had worn off, the look, I mean.'

'I don't think so,' she said, laughing too, 'once a policeman, always a policeman I would imagine.'

'Maybe,' said Keith. 'Anyway thanks for your help.' He got as far as the door and then paused. There was a poster attached to the inside of the glass. 'Otto Juniper at Exeter Cathedral' with a sticker across it saying 'Cancelled'. Keith turned. 'Was Otto Juniper due to play here?'

'It's not so surprising,' the woman said. 'He has

a house in Exeter and spends much more time here these days than he does in London. He often plays at the cathedral, usually for charity. I always go along, I love to hear him and I'm lucky because my son is a chorister, so I usually manage to wangle a ticket.'

'It's sad, isn't it?' said Keith, nodding towards the poster, 'they say he may never play again.'

'I would think that's possibly true,' the woman said. 'His lady, Sophia, she was always there you know, at Otto's concerts, never missed one. He will be lost without her. They're having the funeral here, of course.'

'What, in Exeter?' said Keith. 'I had imagined it would be up in London.'

'No, she died down here, just keeled over apparently, heart failure. Mind you, she was very old, but even so it must have come as an awful shock for him. The funeral is next Wednesday.'

'What, tomorrow?' Keith said.

'No, no, the Wednesday after. My son is singing at it. Eleven o'clock it is, in the morning.'

'And is Otto in the city at the moment?'

'As far as I know. She's here, God rest her soul, so I can't imagine there is any reason for him to go up to London.'

'I see,' said Keith.

'You're a funny sort of policeman,' the woman

said, 'fancy being interested in both Colin Nicholls and Otto Juniper, there's a mystery in itself, if ever there was one.'

Keith laughed. 'Thanks again, you really have been extremely helpful.'

'What took you so long?' David asked, when Keith climbed back into the car.

'Oh, just chatting to the newsagent, nice woman. Colin should be home any moment now. It sounds like he hasn't changed much, still a bit of a recluse. Let's just wait and see.'

'Patience is one of the things I'm not blessed with,' said David.

'It's a skill you are going to have to acquire if you are going to make the police your career.'

'That's just it,' said David, 'I don't know if I am.'

'Why would you not?' Keith asked.

'It's rugby, you see. If I get the chance to turn professional, I have to admit that will take precedence over the force. I just don't know if I'm good enough, yet.'

'Well, according to my pal, Horace, in the pathology lab, you are the finest prop in the whole world.'

'I wish that was true,' said David.

'He is not known for flattery is Horace, in fact

he is usually bloody rude to me,' said Keith. 'Trust me, you must be pretty good to be on the receiving end of any praise from him.'

'I am pretty good,' David admitted, 'but whether I am good enough … hey, is that the man you're looking for?'

Keith looked up. 'Yes, yes that's Colin. God, he's aged; still I suppose I have too – poor bloke.' They watched as Colin Nicholls unlatched the gate and walked up the path to his front door. His shoulders were stooped, his hair grey and thinning. Like the street itself, there was a defeated air about him. He put his key in the lock, opened the door and went inside.

'He looks so sad,' said David, 'almost like he has just lost his wife, not had six years to come to terms with her death.'

'I was talking about him last night with my ...' – Keith never knew how to describe Felicity – 'with my partner,' he said at last. 'We were wondering how on earth you cope when someone you love takes their own life – the guilt must be awful.'

'But we are here to prove that she didn't take her own life, aren't we?' David asked. 'That is going to be a good thing for Colin Nicholls, surely?'

'Certainly if we could do that,' said Keith, 'we would make all the difference to this family. The trouble is, I couldn't prove anything when it happened so God knows how I am going to change things now. The key, of course, has to rest with there being some sort of link with the Becketts.'

'But I thought it had been established that there was no link?'

'There has to be,' said Keith. 'As I understand it, Mavers has established that the Becketts had never heard of the Nicholls, that there is no common ground, children at school, work anything like that. What no one has yet done is ask the Nicholls whether they know the Becketts and that is one of the reasons we're here.'

'So,' David said, 'Colin Nicholls doesn't yet know that there is another woman who has drowned like his wife?'

'No,' said Keith, 'that's what we are here to tell him.'

'It's going to come as quite a shock then?'

Keith looked at him, his face suddenly creased with concern. 'Yes, yes it is, which is why I wanted to make sure he got home and had a chance to make himself a cup of tea before we blow his life apart again.'

'Do you think it is going to be that serious for him?'

'Yes, I do,' said Keith. 'I was the one who told him his wife was dead, I'll never know what sort of man he was before I walked into his house that day but I certainly know what sort of man he became afterwards. Obviously, he has made some sort of life for himself and his boys but I can't imagine him ever fully recovering from the death of his wife.'

'Did the coroner record suicide?'

Keith shook his head. 'No, thank goodness, we managed to persuade him otherwise, it was an open verdict. She left no note and her family and friends swore she was not the suicidal type, so he was relatively easily persuaded – that and the fact he was a decent bloke who understood the importance of avoiding the suicide verdict so far as the surviving family were concerned.' Keith glanced at his watch. 'Right, let's go and talk to him.'

The boy who answered the door was small for his twelve years but looked cheerful enough. He had bright red cheeks and a shock of red hair which seemed to clash with them. His grin of welcome was genuine.

'Hello,' he said.

'Is your dad in?' Keith asked.

'Yeah, I'll get him.' He turned and walked back down the passageway. 'Dad,' he yelled, 'two men to see you.' He then turned into what was obviously the sitting room where they could hear the sounds of a television. He was evidently not even slightly curious as to who the two men might be who had come to see his father.

'That's Graham,' Keith said quietly.

A moment later the stooped figure of Colin Nicholls appeared at the end of the corridor. For a moment he looked puzzled; then recognition dawned. 'Inspector Penrose.'

'Hello Colin,' said Keith, and stretched out a hand. Colin shook it. 'This is my sergeant, David Sterling.'

Colin nodded in greeting to David and then turned to Keith. 'Why are you here?' he asked immediately. 'What's happened?'

'Can we talk?' Keith said.

Colin jerked his head towards the sitting room door. 'The boy is in there, you'd better come through to the kitchen. Did he recognise you?'

Keith shook his head. 'No, not a clue. He wasn't interested.'

'And you didn't tell him who you were?'

'No, of course not, Colin.'

'OK, come on through. I'll just tell him you are here to talk about insurance, right?'

Keith and David walked through to the small cramped kitchen which definitely lacked a woman's touch. Cheese on toast was being prepared, there were crumbs everywhere. Colin joined them a moment later.

'Would you like some tea?' he said. 'I've just made a pot.'

'That would be great,' said Keith. Colin poured two mugs of tea and Keith noticed his hand shook a little. He wished suddenly that he could be anywhere but here, that he didn't have to stir up this man's life again. 'Still in the plumbing business, Colin?' he asked

Colin nodded. 'Yeah, but can we cut the polite conversation please, Inspector Penrose. Can you tell me why you're here.'

'May we sit down?' Keith asked.

'Yeah, help yourself.' The three men sat round the grubby Formica table.

'I'm here,' Keith said, 'because another woman has apparently drowned in very similar circumstances to your wife's drowning.'

'How do you mean?' Colin asked. He had gone very pale and ran a nervous hand through his hair, what was left of it.

'A woman named Adrianne Beckett drowned at Church Cove in Gunwalloe, on the Lizard.'

'I know Gunwalloe,' said Colin, 'but what has that got to do with my Morwenna?'

'Adrianne had stones sewed into the pockets of her jacket.'

Colin shrugged. 'Isn't that what people do when they commit suicide?' His voice was challenging.

'Maybe, though I have never come across it before except on these two occasions,' said Keith, 'and there is another thing – the stitching is very similar, a very distinctive cross stitch. The coats are different, the thread is different, I imagine the stones are different, pebbles off the beach, nothing particularly special about them. The other similarity is that, like Morwenna, Adrianne had everything to live for … a good job, a happy marriage, a child … her death, or rather her suicide, seems as unlikely as Morwenna's.'

Colin was silent for a long moment, staring at Keith. 'So are you saying that because some other woman has drowned, at last you are prepared to accept that my Morwenna didn't kill herself? Is that what it takes, another death?'

'Oh, come off it, Colin,' said Keith, 'you know I did my very best for you. We got an open verdict, we managed to persuade the coroner that none of us really believed it was suicide but the fact remains we could find no other explanation.'

'If you just did your job …'

'I did try,' said Keith, 'the only good thing to come out of this second terrible death is that I now have permission to reinvestigate both cases.'

'Jesus!' Colin got to his feet abruptly and began striding around the small kitchen. 'So what does that mean? You're going to be asking the same bloody questions over and over again, like you did before, making me feel like I'd killed her, upsetting my boys … are you going to be talking to them too?'

'No, no,' said Keith. 'It is not going to be like before, Colin. I am not here to complicate your life or make it even more difficult than it already is.'

'You've just done that. We've managed to put our lives back together, me and the boys, and then you come here …'

'I know, I know,' Keith stood up too, 'but there are two things to consider here. If we could find out what really happened to Morwenna it would be a good thing, wouldn't it?' Colin turned away from him, but not before he had nodded. He was close to tears, Keith could see. 'And secondly, accepting for a moment that these two deaths weren't suicide then by definition, they would have to be murder. If we could find who did this then we could make damn sure no other family has to go through what you and your boys have been through, what the Becketts are going through now.'

With his back still turned towards the two men, Colin pulled a handkerchief from his pocket, blew his nose and wiped his eyes. Then he turned around to face them. 'Do you really think she was murdered, Inspector Penrose? Do you really think my Morwenna was killed by someone?'

Keith put his hands in his pockets, sighed and

studied the floor between his feet for a moment trying to collect his thoughts. 'What I truly believe, Colin, is that your wife didn't commit suicide.'

'That was quite a bold thing to say,' David said, when they were back in Keith's car.

'What was?' Keith asked.

'That you didn't believe Morwenna Nicholls committed suicide.'

'I don't,' said Keith. 'He asked me the question and I gave him the honest answer.'

'But …'

'No buts David,' said Keith. 'As anticipated I have just blown his world apart again. The least I can do is offer something, even if it is no more than a sticking plaster.'

'And giving him something to do will help,' David conceded.

'Yes, I think it will.' They had given Colin Nicholls the names of the Beckett family, they were all over the papers in any event.

'Talk to your boys when you are ready. All of you think about any possible connection. Google the Becketts, try and find a common link with them if you can, anything, however trivial.' Keith had said.

'I don't know about Googling them,' Colin said, 'I don't know how to do that, but I guess

Graham can, even though that means telling him everything.'

'I think you should tell both boys,' Keith had said. 'Inevitably at some point, the press are going to pick up on the similarities between the two cases. We have kept it quiet so far, but some bright spark is going to make the link and it is far better the boys hear it from you than read about it in the paper or see it on the television.'

'Do the Becketts know anything about us?' Colin asked.

'We've told them about you,' said Keith, 'and they can think of no possible link between their family and yours but they are also racking their brains and we are checking some possible links between your two families. So far nothing has come up.'

'What sort of people are they?' Colin had asked.

'She was a doctor at Treliske Hospital, he is a solicitor.'

'Oh, posh then. They'll have nothing in common with us, will they?'

'He's got a chip on his shoulder, hasn't he?' said David, as they drove down the street away from the Nicholls' house.

'Yes, but that is hardly surprising, is it?' said

Keith. 'As I've already said to you, I have no idea what the man was like before this terrible thing happened to him, but inevitably the finger was pointed at him, he was the most obvious candidate if there had been any criminal activity connected with Morwenna's death. Once we had established his alibi, even though there was no way he could be accused of murder, there was still "the insensitive sod" label hanging over him.'

'It's good working with you, sir,' David said after a moment.

'Is it?' said Keith.

'Yes, you care about people. I like the way you handled Colin just now. I hope you don't mind me saying so, sir, it's a bit cheeky but it was a bit of an inspiration.'

'Ah, good,' said Keith, 'so perhaps we'll get rid of all this professional rugby nonsense and turn you into a proper copper yet?'

'Who knows,' said David, with a grin.

'Actually,' said Keith, 'while you are feeling well-disposed towards me, I was wondering how you would feel if I put you on a train back to Truro?'

'You're not going to go and see Colin again without me?' David asked, anxiously.

'No, no, I'm not. It's a personal family matter. There is just someone I ought to see while I'm in Exeter, not tonight but maybe tomorrow morning.

It just seems silly to miss the opportunity. Where is your car?'

'I couldn't get into the car park this morning,' he said, 'so I am parked in the city car park next to Tesco.'

'Get a taxi from the station, I've got generous expenses apparently. I'll pay for your train ticket and you charge the taxi out to me.'

'Oh, I don't need a taxi,' said David. 'I'll run.'

'Run?' said Keith.

'Yes, I always keep trainers in my bag.'

'I wondered what that bloody great briefcase was all about?'

'Tracksuit and trainers, I'm never without them. If there is an opportunity to run I always take it.'

'So do I even need to buy you a train ticket at all then?' Keith asked, with a grin.

'Exeter might be a little bit far,' said David, 'now if we were at Bodmin Parkway ...'

Keith laughed. 'Enough bragging, young man, I'll drop you at the station.'

Having deposited David at the station, Keith parked his car and crossed the road to a large Victorian building which looked like a comfortable enough hotel. They had a room free. He checked in and then sat down thoughtfully on the bed, composing himself to tell Felicity a white lie.

'The interview is going on a bit,' Keith said, when he got through to her. 'So I am going to stay overnight in Exeter, I hope that's OK?'

'Is there some luscious woman involved?' Felicity asked.

'Yes, of course,' said Keith, smiling. 'You wouldn't want me to be lonely now, would you?'

'That's quite enough of that sort of talk,' said Felicity. 'How are you getting on with your sergeant?'

'I like him,' said Keith. 'He's a good bloke and amazingly he seems to like me too.'

'A good bloke and obviously an excellent judge of character, what more could you ask for?' said Felicity.

'Flattery will get you everywhere,' said Keith. 'I'm sorry I won't be home tonight.'

'Will you be back early tomorrow?' she asked.

'Probably not, I'll go straight to the station and interview the other family, the Becketts, before I come home. I will be back for supper but probably not much before …'

'This is starting to feel very much like old times,' said Felicity. 'I'll see you when I see you. You take care. Night, night, darling.'

'Night,' said Keith. He turned off his phone feeling a little guilty, but then what he was proposing to do was for her benefit ultimately. He truly believed that.

7

The following morning at ten o'clock Keith found himself standing at the bottom of some imposing steps leading up to a Queen Anne house situated just outside the cathedral close. It was a beautifully proportioned building and beautifully maintained too. Keith couldn't help thinking of the contrast between this magnificent house and Colin Nicholls's home and remembered the words of the newsagent – the incongruity of being a friend to both Colin Nicholls and Otto Juniper.

All through the night he had rehearsed what he was going to say, but he was aware that his most difficult task would be to actually gain access to the great man. There were bound to be obstacles placed in his way. The days when simply flashing his warrant card and announcing himself as Chief Inspector Penrose would get him in anywhere were over. It was a difficult adjustment and he was acutely aware that it might not be easy without the support of his title and position. He rang the bell. After a considerable pause, a woman answered the door. She had grey hair pulled back into a chignon, she appeared to be in her fifties, beautifully-groomed with an elegant, upright figure.

'Yes?' she said.

'I was hoping to see Otto Juniper.'

She raised one beautifully-plucked eyebrow. 'You and half the world! I am afraid he is not available to anyone, he is grieving as I am sure you understand.' She had a slight foreign accent, but so slight it was difficult to place.

'I really do need to see him, I will not take up much of his time,' Keith began.

'Are you a journalist?'

He shook his head. 'No, actually I am a retired policeman, but that is not why I'm here. You see, my partner is Sophia's daughter and I wanted to talk to Otto about her.'

'Sophia had no daughter.'

'Yes, she did,' said Keith, 'and Otto knows she did.'

'So you want money. You are hoping that this daughter will benefit from the will, I can assure you now …'

'No,' Keith said firmly. 'This is nothing to do with money. My partner is grieving for a mother who abandoned her when she was six years old, she needs some answers.'

'My employer is also grieving and his well-being is my only concern. I wish you good day.'

Keith took a step forward and placed a hand on the closing door. 'I'm not here to bully him,' he said. 'I am just here to ask for his help and advice, that's all. I have a feeling that if you refuse to let me see him and he finds out, he will be very angry, very angry indeed. At least before you slam the door in my face, make sure that you are doing what Otto wants, please, as much for your sake as mine.'

She studied him in silence for a moment, he found her scrutiny unnerving. 'All right,' she said. 'Wait there,' and slammed the door in his face. Minutes passed. Keith wondered whether the woman was even going to consult Otto, or whether she was enjoying keeping him waiting on the doorstep. Just when he was beginning to think it was the latter the door suddenly opened.

'You may come in,' she said, but with no air of defeat. It sounded more as if she was doing him an enormous favour.

'Thank you,' he said, graciously.

The hallway was beautiful; a spiral stairway led out of it and from the ceiling above hung a huge chandelier.

'This way, please,' she said, while he hesitated staring around him. 'Otto is in his morning room, you must not tire him. He has put no time-limit on your meeting, but I do. Fifteen minutes is all you have.'

'Fifteen minutes is fine,' Keith said.

An old man was sitting by the fireplace as Keith entered the room, but what an old man! Immediately Keith felt the vibrancy of his presence and then he turned his head to look at Keith. When asked to describe that moment, in the years ahead Keith could only say that he was an old man but that he was beautiful; it sounded ridiculous, an extraordinary way to describe another man but it was true. He had the cheekbones and the slightly aquiline nose that would have sat perfectly on a Roman coin – there were several thousand years of civilisation etched into his bone structure. His eyes were a bright clear blue, and he had a thatch of snowy white hair. Without a trace of difficulty he stood up and walked briskly towards Keith, holding out his hand.

'My name is Otto Juniper,' he said unnecessarily, 'but nobody has thought to ask you yours.'

'Keith Penrose,' said Keith, shaking his hand.

'And the name of your lady friend?'

'Felicity Paradise,' Keith said.

'Ah,' he said with a trace of a smile. 'I look at

you and I do not see an imposter, but how do I know you are not a journalist digging for dirt, trying to prove something unpleasant against my poor Sophia?'

Keith thought for a moment, frowning; then he remembered his wallet. He pulled it out of his inside jacket pocket and from it extracted a photograph of him and Felicity on Porthmeor beach. The picture had been taken by Felicity's daughter, Mel. They had their arms around one another, they were windswept and laughing.

'That is Felicity,' he said. For the first time Otto showed his age; taking the photograph he walked back to his chair, sat down and picked up some reading glasses which he perched on the end of his nose. 'She is very like her mother,' he said, after a moment. 'Not as beautiful, of course, but still very like her. How old is she now?'

'Fifty-six' said Keith.

'She doesn't look it, like my Sophia she ages well.'

'Yes, she does,' said Keith, 'I am a very lucky man.'

'Me too,' said Otto, 'me too.' There was a moment's silence between them but there was no tension. Already the two men were comfortable with one another. 'Oh dear,' said Otto after a while, 'my manners, have a chair. What would you like …

some coffee, some Madeira, a sherry?'

'Coffee would be fine,' said Keith.

Otto rang the bell and moments later the terrifying guardian of his front door appeared. 'Coffee for two please, Margot,' he said.

Margot managed to give Keith a ferocious look on her way out.

'She doesn't like me,' Keith said, by way of easing the tension between them.

'She doesn't like anyone except me and Sophia,' Otto said. 'She guards us, guards me now, like a lioness with her cubs.' He smiled. 'You did well to get across the threshold.'

'I used to be a policeman,' Keith said. 'I was thinking about it on the way to see you this morning. I have been so used to flashing my warrant card and gaining access to anyone, anywhere. I found it rather daunting to have to rely on my story being good enough for me to be able to speak to you.'

'Well,' said Otto, with a twinkling smile, 'for an amateur you did very well indeed.' Coffee was served along with another stern look from Margot. 'Don't worry about her,' Otto said, 'she is putty in my hands.'

'I imagine a lot of people are, with good reason. I'm sorry, that sounds wrong. I meant it as a compliment.'

'Then I shall take it as such,' said Otto. 'Now tell me what I can do for Sophia's daughter.'

'I don't know if there is anything you can do,' said Keith. 'I only learnt about her mother and you, and the circumstances, thirty-six hours ago. It came as a shock because up until then Felicity had told me that her mother was dead.'

'And what changed her mind?' Otto asked.

'She saw the newspaper headlines announcing Sophia's death. I could tell immediately that something was very wrong, that something had happened. Eventually she told me everything. Apparently, no one but a childhood friend has ever known about Sophia, not even her late husband.'

'Then she must trust you,' said Otto, 'and therefore must love you. So if I am talking to the man who Sophia's daughter loves then I must listen to what you have to say.'

'Thank you,' said Keith. He cleared his throat, aware that if he was not careful emotion would get the better of him. 'The way Felicity has coped without a mother over the years has been to blank out the whole episode. As I say, she never told her husband, Charlie, what truly had happened, nor her children. Now she has four grandchildren and none of them have the slightest idea that until the day before yesterday, Felicity's mother was still alive.'

'That is incredible,' said Otto.

'Denial has been her safety valve,' said Keith, immediately defensive. 'She was six years old, the mother she adored walked out and left her and she was never able to get close to her father so as an only child, it was a pretty bleak existence.'

'She believed her mother walked out and never tried to come back?'

'She doesn't just believe it,' said Keith, frowning, 'she knows it.'

'I don't know how much you know, how much Felicity knows of the circumstances,' said Otto, 'Sophia came to a concert at the Sheldonian Theatre in Oxford. I was playing, I was not so famous then but it was a good gig, I think is the expression you use today.' Keith smiled in agreement. 'She was sitting there listening to me playing and suddenly she realised who I was – the little boy she had rescued from the streets of Berlin.'

'Yes,' said Keith, 'yes we know that much.'

'The family lived in North Oxford only ten minutes walk from the Sheldonian Theatre. Sophia told her husband that she wanted to stay behind after the concert because she wanted to talk to me. She said she thought she knew me from her time in Berlin. I don't think she had told him the details at that stage. He was impatient, he said he was tired and didn't want to stay so he suggested he left her to come home later. That was a grave mistake on his part. She burst into my dressing room and I knew immediately who she was – my beautiful lady.'

'Your beautiful lady?' Keith asked.

'That's what I called her when I was a little boy in Berlin and she saved me. I had always wondered why we had never met again. She had promised me, you see, that she would look after me, find me in England but I had not seen her since she put me on the Kindertransport train. We talked for hours. It turned out she had searched high and low for me, but as soon as I arrived in Dover I was taken in by a very kind family and within a matter of a few months they had decided to adopt me. Their names were Hugh and Sally Juniper, they already had two children by birth much older than me but they were all so very kind. There was no sibling rivalry, no problems at all, I had an idyllic childhood from that moment on. Of course I thought about my real mother and father and my life in Germany, but the memories faded. What I could never get out of my mind was the fact that my beautiful lady never came back for me.'

'So was it the change of name to Juniper which complicated her search?'

'Yes, I think so. My family name was Shillmann which she knew and so that was the name she was searching for. They were such chaotic times, it was not difficult to lose track of one little boy, especially one so young and confused.'

Keith hesitated. He did not want to upset this courteous old man but he felt he had to know everything for Felicity's sake.

'I understand all of that and I can quite appreciate the huge bond that must have existed between you, but what I don't understand is how a woman can just abandon her child.'

'She didn't,' said Otto.

'How do you mean?' Keith asked.

'That night she went back to the family home. She talked everything through with her husband, was totally open with him, told him how she had searched for me for years. Of course, there was no question of a relationship between us then but her husband, Bernard, forbade her to see me again. Already I suppose he could see, could tell how much I meant to her and was jealous, scared, I don't know. Well …' he hesitated. 'I don't know how much experience you have of women, Keith, but to tell a beautiful headstrong woman that she cannot do something is, how do you say – a red rag to a bull.'

Keith smiled. 'I have one of those at home.'

'Yes indeed,' Otto said. 'So she began to see me, she would come up to London. I did not have this house then but I had a nice flat in Kensington, easy access for the Albert Hall. It was inevitable, our relationship blossomed, we hardly felt we were in charge, it took us over completely and changed everything. I was an excellent violinist when we met again – forgive me if I sound pompous – but with Sophia in my life, I started to play like an angel.'

'I know that,' said Keith, 'I went to a concert of yours once in Plymouth. I was a pretty ordinary plodding policeman but you made me cry.'

'I'm sorry, Keith,' said Otto, 'we've only known each other for ten minutes but there is nothing ordinary about you.' The two men sipped their coffee in companionable silence.

'Go on with the story,' said Keith, after a while.

'In the end Sophia had to tell Bernard that we were in love and that we wanted to be together. She said she would ask nothing from him other than the fact that she obviously wanted to take her daughter with her. Up until then, Bernard had shown very little interest in the child. He was very involved with his work, he was quite a cold personality. I am not saying he was a bad man but he was not blessed with much depth of feeling as I understand it. Anyway, he agreed. The following day when Bernard had gone to work Sophia packed her things and Felicity's and she loaded the car and then went to Felicity's school to pick her up. When she got there she found Bernard had been there before her and that Felicity was gone. She assumed they had just missed one another, that he had taken Felicity home so that he could spend a little time with her before she went to live with her mother and me. We had agreed visiting arrangements, it had all seemed so amicable. However, when Sophia got home the house was empty, they had both disappeared. After frantic searching and enquiries she contacted the police but Bernard had anticipated that. He had already informed the police that his little girl's mother was planning to leave him for another man and that he had taken the child away on holiday to make sure that the trauma of her mother's leaving did not affect her.'

Otto sighed. 'When they say possession is nine-tenths of the law, that is indeed true, or at least it was in our case. Sophia battled for years through the courts but the fact is Bernard was the wronged party. Felicity was settled in school, she had friends in Oxford, she had her home and her mother had chosen to leave her for someone else. The fact that we did not marry, the fact that Sophia was older than me, the fact that we lived a rather bohemian lifestyle, that I travelled all over the world and Sophia went with me – all of these things counted against us and provided reasons why it was not a good idea in the eyes of the court for Felicity to live with us.'

'So Sophia did try to have Felicity live with her?'

'She tried, dear God,' said Otto. 'The agonies we went through, the time, the money: not that money is of any consequence in the circumstances. We did everything in our power, short of kidnapping her, to gain access to Felicity but it was hopeless and of course in those days, no one consulted the child. I am not saying we would have been brilliant parents and of course the courts were right, our life was a bit unusual, but at least she would have had warmth and love which we both felt she was not getting from her father.'

Keith smiled. 'I think it is a life she would have loved. She is a little unconventional herself, to put it mildly. She is an artist, you know.'

'Really, so was her mother, only in an amateurish way. Look, let me show you this.' Otto stood up and walked over to the bookshelf. There was a small portrait perched on the shelf in front of the books. It was a simple pen and ink sketch of him playing his violin but it caught him perfectly. He appeared lost in his music, there was such fluidity to his pose that you felt that any moment he might move.

'This is marvellous,' said Keith.

'Yes, it is rather,' Otto agreed, 'so that must be

where her talent comes from, your Felicity's.'

Keith, still looking at the drawing, asked. 'In the end you had to give up?'

'Yes, yes we did,' said Otto. 'We tried to contact Felicity direct when she was eighteen but she would have nothing to do with Sophia. It broke her heart but she understood why.'

'Maybe you should have gone to see her, persisted?'

Otto shook his head. 'You see, if we had explained the true position to her, not only would she have spent a childhood without a mother, she would have realised her father was not the man she had thought him to be, that there was this other side to him, this jealous side that had stopped her seeing her mother. We didn't feel it was right to push it, particularly during the turbulent teens. We just made sure that she knew we would love to see her if that is what she wanted.'

'A story with no happy ending,' Keith said, replacing the drawing and returning to the fireplace for his coffee.

'Yes, yes it is, and there is an added sadness but a personal one.'

'Oh?' said Keith.

'We never had a child, Sophia and I. When we got together she was just young enough to conceive but she wouldn't do it. She thought it was a betrayal of Felicity. I understood it completely, that if she'd had a baby it would have seemed like she was replacing Felicity, giving up on her.'

'That is so sad,' said Keith.

'Yes, yes, it is,' said Otto.

'I have tried to explain to Felicity, and I hope I am right in this, that the wonderful music, with which you have delighted the world, would not have been possible without her mother. Is that true?'

'Yes,' said Otto, 'as I said to you, I was good but I only became magnificent when I had Sophia in my life.'

'And now?' said Keith.

Otto smiled. 'Now it is over, but that is OK. She and I had talked about it, we knew this day was coming.'

'Will you play for yourself,' Keith asked, 'alone, in private?'

'I don't know,' said Otto. 'I have not lifted the bow since she died and this is the longest I have been without playing since I was a child.'

'It sounds as if you had encouragement when you were growing up,' said Keith, trying to ease the tension a little. 'The Junipers were musical?'

'Yes,' said Otto, seizing on the opportunity too. 'Hugh, my father, my adopted father was head of music at a boys' private school. He was delighted that his little protégé turned out to have a gift. They were very proud of me. I was so lucky with my childhood, ironically much luckier than Felicity.' He bowed his head, staring into the fire, clearly lost in thought. After a moment he rallied. 'So, Keith, what do you want to happen now?'

'What I would like to happen,' said Keith, 'is for Felicity to tell her children about her mother and that for her, her children and her grandchildren, Sophia's great-grandchildren, to come to the funeral. I would like over the months ahead for you and Felicity to talk and hopefully to heal the wound which, in my view, over all these years, has never been dealt with, never been confronted.'

'And Felicity, what does she want?'

'She doesn't want to meet you, ever. She doesn't want to tell her children about their grandmother, she doesn't want to go to the funeral and she doesn't want to talk about it, any of it, ever again, not even to me.'

Otto gave Keith a sad smile. 'Then, my friend, we have quite a task ahead of us, don't we?'

8

It was after midday by the time Keith drove his car into the Truro police car park only to find there were no spaces. Cursing he remembered David saying he had found space in the city car park, so he rejoined the roundabout traffic and drove up towards Tesco. He had to drive around the car park three times before he finally found a space and then discovered he only had enough change for an hour's parking. He thought longingly of his private car parking space as he trudged back along the main road to the station. He found David in the canteen; he looked weary.

'What have you been up to?' Keith asked, sitting down heavily beside him.

'Staring at my computer screen with an increasing sense of frustration. Can I get you a coffee?'

Keith shook his head. 'Not here anyway. I'm hoping the Becketts might offer us one.'

'Is that where we are off to now?'

'Yes, if you're ready.'

'Can I just finish this piece of toast?' David asked, hopefully.

'If you're quick. So, why the frustration?'

'I've been trying to find a link between the Nicholls and the Becketts, I've gone right back to the parents' schooldays, even looked at the grandparents. The Becketts aren't Cornish, but they are very keen sailors, so when Adrianne became a registrar, they decided life in Cornwall would be preferable to life in London. Jerry, that's the husband, secured a partnership at a local firm of solicitors and they moved down here seventeen years ago. Evan, their son, was born the following year.' He finished his toast and drank the remains of his coffee. 'He is at Truro School, a bright boy apparently, Oxbridge candidate possibly.'

'I can't think what has happened to his mother will do his exam chances much good,' Keith said, gloomily.

'No,' said David. 'I imagine not.'

'So no links yet, no clues at all?'

David shook his head. 'I thought I'd have another session tonight.'

'Shouldn't you be out training or dating pretty girls?' Keith suggested.

David smiled and shook his head. 'I've got bitten by this case. Colin Nicholls just knows his wife didn't kill herself and to learn the truth would make a huge difference. That boy, Graham, he is still so young, he doesn't need to live under the shadow of his mother's death.'

'I agree,' said Keith. 'Let's go then, shall we?'

The Becketts' house was only a couple of streets away from where Keith and his wife, Barbara, had lived and brought up their children. It was a much a bigger and more imposing house than the Penroses' had been – it was modern, stylish with wonderful views looking out over the city, dominated, of course, by the Cathedral. The two men got out of Keith's car and stood for a moment admiring the view.

'This is very similar to the view from my old house,' Keith said.

'You used to live in Truro?'

'Yes, until I retired. My house was a little higher up than this and not nearly so grand but the view is very similar. It's all very familiar.'

'Do you miss it?' David asked.

Keith shook his head. 'Not at all. St Ives is far more my sort of place, more relaxed and full of weird and wonderful characters. It suits me very well.' They walked towards the front door.

'I'm not looking forward to this interview either,' David said.

'Nor me,' Keith agreed.

The man who answered the door was tall, considerably taller than Keith and almost as tall as David though, of course, not as broad. He had a full head of dark hair which was going attractively grey at the temples. He was a good-looking man but his complexion was very pale and there were dark rings under his eyes.

'Yes,' he said, aggressively, 'if you're the press again ...'

'We're not press,' said Keith, 'we are police. I am a cold case investigator and this is my sergeant, David Sterling.'

David offered his warrant card.

'Cold case?' Jerry Beckett frowned. 'Oh yes, there was talk of another woman, I remember now. Come in then, not that I have anything to tell you that I haven't already told all the other officers several times over. I am worn out by it all. What my son and I need is some peace.'

'I appreciate that.' said Keith, 'We won't keep you long, I promise.' They were shown into an elegant sitting room, all in cream and pale green, with floor to ceiling windows which opened out into a conservatory beyond which was the marvellous view of the city.

'I could brew up some coffee, I suppose,' Jerry

Beckett said.

'Don't worry,' said Keith, trying to keep the longing out of his voice. 'May we sit down?'

'Yes, of course.'

'Where is your son?' Keith asked.

'He's at school. He went back today.'

'How is he doing?' Keith asked.

'As well as can be expected, I suppose. His form teacher rang me just now to say that he seemed to be settling in all right. He is sixteen, not a baby.'

'Sixteen is a pretty vulnerable age,' Keith suggested.

'Yes, I suppose it is. Now, can we talk about whatever it is you have come to say and then I would be grateful if you could leave.'

'I understand ...' said Keith, 'that you don't believe your wife committed suicide?'

'Wrong,' said Jerry Beckett, clearly agitated.

'You do believe she committed suicide?'

'No,' he thundered, jumping to his feet and starting to stride around the room. 'I don't *believe* she didn't commit suicide, I *know* she didn't commit suicide.'

'My experience of suicide,' said Keith, 'after a long career in the police force is that people who regularly threaten it are the people who never actually do it. The people who sadly die keep whatever sadness or hopelessness they feel about life to themselves, which is why so often suicide comes as such a tremendous shock to their nearest and dearest.'

'I really don't need a lecture, what did you say your name was?'

'Keith Penrose,' said Keith. 'I'm sorry, I should have introduced myself.'

'I really don't need a lecture, Mr Penrose. My wife did not commit suicide and I know that for certain.'

'So have you got a theory as to how she drowned?' Keith asked.

'That is your job,' Jerry Beckett spat out, his anger clearly mounting.

'Was she happy in her work?' Keith asked. 'It must be very stressful working in A & E.'

'Oh, for God's sake,' said Jerry. 'Of course she was happy in her work but of course she was stressed by it. I can't go all through this again. She loved being a doctor, she loved making a difference, yes she was frustrated by the NHS, by the lack of facilities, by the lack of beds but she got such a buzz when she was able to save people and change lives. We went out to dinner with friends the night before she disappeared, they will tell you what fun she was, we had a great evening.'

'Could I have their names?'

'I've given their names to you people, I'm sure they've already been interviewed,' he sighed.

'I appreciate that,' said Keith, 'and I am sorry, but for speed's sake could you tell us as well, we are looking at the investigation from a different angle.'

Jerry raised an eyebrow and gave Keith an extremely unfriendly look. 'Jane and Roger Cleaver,' he said, 'they live just down the road.' He rattled off an address which David wrote down in his notebook. 'Roger was a colleague of Adrianne's, he is an orthopaedic surgeon so although they worked in different parts of the hospital, as Adrianne was in A & E, she quite frequently came in contact with Roger over a patient – we've known them for years.'

'That is very helpful,' Keith said. 'Thank you.' He stood up and wandered over to the window to gaze out at the familiar view. It made him think of his family growing up. Although he and his wife, Barbara, were very different in very many ways and although theirs had not been the best of marriages, it had been a partnership and they were absolutely joined at the hip when it came to the raising of their children. It was hard to imagine what it would have been like if ten or fifteen years ago, Barbara had died in similar circumstances to Adrianne Beckett leaving him with his children as teenagers – the shock, the manner of her death, the responsibility for the children, it was an absolute nightmare. He turned to Jerry Beckett. 'I have been brought in because I was the officer in charge of the very similar incident that occurred six years ago, you've been told all about it, I understand?'

'Yes,' said Jerry, 'and it doesn't make me feel very confident, though. If you couldn't solve that death how can I expect you to have any more luck with this one?'

'That's true,' Keith admitted, 'but investigating two such similar deaths might mean that the pooled information from both crimes, if crimes is what they are, will lead us to an answer.'

'If crimes is what they are?' Jerry mimicked Keith. 'My wife did not kill herself, I don't know how many more times I have to say this, but I can assure you that it is the case.'

'And I stood in a sitting room at Marazion six years ago when a man called Colin Nicholls said exactly those words to me. He has had to live for the last six years with not knowing why his wife died and I am very anxious, Mr Beckett, that you do not suffer the same fate. In both cases the sea was relatively calm, no big waves which could have sucked either victim off the beach and in both cases husbands, friends, family, work colleagues believe that there was no way the victim would have committed suicide.'

'So that leaves us with murder,' Jerry said.

Keith nodded.

'And you think they were murdered, my wife and this other woman?'

Keith put his hands in his pockets, shifting from one foot to the other, knowing he should respond with some bland answer. He straightened up and met Jerry's eyes in a steady gaze. 'Yes, ' he said, 'I believe it was murder.'

'Thank God for that,' said Jerry Beckett, groping for the nearest chair he sat down. 'A policeman with some sense, now all you've got to do is find the bugger.'

Keith nodded.

'And the how and the why,' said Jerry, 'how could he fill up the pockets of my wife's jacket with her consent and how could he persuade her – I am presuming it is a he – to walk into the sea and kill herself. I understand from the autopsy that there is no obvious suggestion of any struggle or injury other than ...' his voice cracked slightly, 'other than being in the sea for two days.'

'That's true,' said Keith, 'I have been to see the pathologist myself. He is a good man and we have worked together for many years, he is unlikely to have missed anything.'

'So,' said Jerry, 'a murder with no suspect, no motive that I can think of, no weapon and to cap it all apparently no practical way of committing the deed – and please don't ask if my wife had any enemies, she didn't.'

'I can't make you any promises, Mr Beckett, but I will do my utmost to solve this. There must be a link, we just have to find it. You've had no more thoughts in that direction?'

'No,' said Jerry, 'but now there is somebody sensible taking an interest in the case, I will think again.'

'And so will we,' said Keith. 'Come on David, we have stayed long enough.' The two men walked to the front door, Jerry Beckett following them. Keith turned. 'I should have said before, I am so sorry for you and your son. It must be awful.'

Jerry Beckett eyed him for a moment. 'Do you know I have been on the receiving end of a lot of insincere sympathy over the last few days, but not from you, I think.'

'There you go again,' said David, once they were outside in the driveway. 'I know it is good to reassure them, but is it good to make them promises?'

'I didn't make any promises,' said Keith, 'I just said I would do my best and I will.'

'But this business about saying you thought it was a murder, is that what you really think?'

'Of course,' said Keith, 'it can't be anything else.'

'I don't see how you can be sure,' said David as they climbed into the car.

'Hang on a moment, I can't do two things at once, I'm not a woman,' said Keith, tersely. 'Let me reverse out of this bloody awful drive before arguing with you.' After a five-point-turn he managed to get the car out onto the road. 'Well,' he said, as he let the car into gear, 'if it isn't suicide and it isn't an accident, what else can it be, David?'

'I suppose so,' David said.

'Look at the cross-stitches on the coat pockets. Horace Greenaway is getting Morwenna Nicholls's coat up to the lab so he can compare the two, but neither he nor I are in any doubt that the similarities are considerable.'

'Maybe Adrianne Beckett read about the details of Morwenna Nicholls's death, remembered what she had done and thought it was a good idea to sew stones into her pocket when she'd had enough.'

'I think you're now moving into the realms of fantasy,' said Keith.

'You're probably right, I am just concerned about you being so adamant to Jerry Beckett. You saw how he reacted, he was so relieved.'

'I know, I know,' said Keith, 'but I have never

been much good at withholding information and playing clever blighters with grieving relatives.'

'But if it is murder, he could be the murderer.'

'He could,' said Keith, 'but I rather doubt it though, don't you?'

'I don't know,' said David.

'Well, he has a cast-ron alibi for a start.'

'Has he?' David said.

'Yes, I've already checked,' said Keith, 'so if it is all right with you I will drop you back at the station to go on playing on your computer and I am going to see Horace, to see if he has anything else to tell me.'

'I'm still looking for the link, am I?'

'Yes,' said Keith, 'we just need a break, just a little one to get us started.'

When Keith reached the lab he sat outside in the car park for a few moments thinking over what his sergeant had said. David was right of course, he should not have been so categoric in front of Jerry Beckett about his thoughts on the case. Maybe, before he retired, he would have been more reticent and maybe he felt that now he was no longer a policeman, the rule book didn't have to be followed so slavishly. What had happened to these two women? Was it a premeditated act by someone who knew them and wanted to punish them or their loved ones or was it a random encounter that had led to their deaths? Surely it had to be the former. Nobody walked around with a needle and thread in their pockets in the hope that they could sew some stones into a random person's coat. Maybe they had been stalked, maybe somebody had followed their routine going to and from work and then made their move, but how, as Jerry Beckett had said, had the murderer persuaded them to walk into the sea?

With a sigh he climbed out of the car and ran up the steps to Horace Greenaway's office.

'Oh, not you again alread, Penrose?'

'Afraid so,' said Keith.

'You look a bit peaky, what's up?'

'I've had a harrowing couple of days,' said Keith, 'and I am getting absolutely nowhere.'

'The Beckett case?'

Keith nodded. 'Yes and of course the Nicholls cold case.'

'I've received the jacket from Morwenna Nicholls. Come and have a look.' The jacket was stained and rigid with dried sea water. Horace placed it next to Adrianne Beckett's jacket and pointed with a pencil towards the two sets of stitching.

'They look very similar. This one,' said Keith, pointing to Morwenna's, 'is with a thicker thread.'

'And bigger needle,' said Horace, 'but the

interesting thing is that in my view, whoever did the sewing is left-handed in both cases.'

'Really?' said Keith.

'Yes, see how these crosses are made they wouldn't be easy to do if you were a right-handed person, the natural flow for this sort of sewing is to hold the coat in your right hand and sew with your left.'

'I'll have to take your word for that,' said Keith.

'Well you should because I am sure I'm right,' said Horace, 'and the further interesting thing is that neither Mrs Nicholls nor Mrs Beckett were left-handed, I've checked, they were both right-handed. A further indication that neither of them did the sewing, and by inference, the suicide.'

'What about their husbands?' Keith asked.

'I thought you would ask that,' said Horace, 'and I've checked, both husbands are right-handed too. It is certainly an odd one, Penrose, very odd.'

'If you were going to sedate or kill someone with some kind of drug, could you administer it and be fairly confident that the seawater would destroy any remnants of it in the body, when found?' Keith asked.

'There are a few things,' said Horace. 'There is a muscle relaxant, it's called Suxamethonium Chloride, it is a neuro-muscular blocker.'

'What does that mean?' said Keith.

'It means that while the patient remains conscious they can no longer move. It is used sometimes when a tube has to be kept down the throat of a patient. Actually they also use it on death row in America, I understand, to stop the patient wriggling around when they administer the deadly dose.'

'And it can't be detected?' said Keith.

'Not really,' said Horace. 'You would have to take a specimen of blood within thirty minutes of it being administered, after that the enzymes in the body break it down and it becomes almost undetectable unless you were looking for it.'

'So would you be able to find it now?'

'Possibly,' said Horace.

'Anything else?'

'Well the thing about Suxamethonium is that it is not readily available. You could go for something like Propranolol, now that is something which is prescribed in cases of anxiety, migraine, high blood pressure and fast heart rate. That is a drug the general public could get hold of more easily.'

'And difficult to detect?'

'Yes,' said Horace, 'but normally it is prescribed in tablet form. I don't know how the potential victim could be persuaded to swallow enough tablets to induce a coma. It would not be entirely impossible to force someone into swallowing, I suppose, but I would have thought that if it had been administered in such a way I would have been able to spot it. There would have been some signs of the violence that would have been necessary in the administration, a chipped tooth, abrasions to the mouth something like that. In this case, there was nothing.'

'There must be something,' said Keith, 'something that people can readily obtain and which can be easily administered, that you can't detect but that makes it possible for the victim to be pushed or dropped into the sea while they are unconscious or semi-conscious?'

Horace stood up and began pacing; then he frowned and stopped. 'I had a case a number of years back, actually it was a mercy-killing. It wasn't one of yours but you may remember it. The son in his forties killed his elderly mother because she was in so much pain from cancer. She was riddled with it and his view the morphine they were giving her was inadequate – the Shipman factor again, of course. The whole situation was miserable. Anyway she died and everybody was expecting her to die so I did a routine post-mortem and found nothing wrong. Then the son had a terrible pang of conscience and couldn't live with what he'd done, he was quite religious.'

'Couldn't live with what?' Keith asked.

'The fact he had murdered her, of course. Keep up, Penrose.'

'And how did he do that?' Keith asked.

'He was a diabetic, he injected her with enough insulin to kill her. She was very frail and I don't expect it took very much. Because it was a routine post-mortem and because we were busy at the time, I didn't get to her for several days.'

'So insulin injected into somebody who is not a diabetic can be lethal?'

'It could in the case of this woman,' said Horace, 'but in a strong fit young woman an insulin injection would probably not be a killer but within two or three minutes they would start to feel sweaty, sick and confused and probably slip into a coma or a semi-coma. Certainly, they would not be in a fit state to battle with the waves.'

'And you wouldn't be able to pick it up now if that was what had happened to Adrianne Beckett?'

Horace shook his head. 'Not after a couple of days in the water, no I wouldn't.'

'And there are no obvious needle marks?'

'No,' said Horace, 'but then the thing about insulin you can inject it anywhere, and her body is very bruised and battered. However, on the strength of this conversation I will have another look but I did have a search and found nothing.'

'It's interesting but I don't know where that leaves me,' said Keith, 'no further forward, I suppose?'

'I think you are being unduly pessimistic, Penrose,' said Horace, 'it's obvious you are looking for a left-handed diabetic – there can't be more than a few million of those.'

'Thanks Horace,' said Keith, with a grin. 'Do you fancy a pint before you go home?'

'I thought you weren't a beer man. Has visiting Australia changed you?'

'It was a euphemistic term,' said Keith. 'I'm offering to buy you a pint, I'll have a glass of red wine, as usual.'

'You're not in a hurry to get back to the fair Felicity?'

A shadow chased Keith's face.

'Oh, my God,' said Horace, 'it's not gone wrong already, has it?'

'No, no,' said Keith. 'We are very happy.'

'Well something is clearly upsetting you. Come on then, young man, let's go to the pub.'

9

An hour later Keith drove slowly down the A30 towards St Ives. Horace Greenaway was one of his oldest friends and he longed to ask his advice and talk through the problem surrounding Felicity's mother, but he couldn't. He had been sworn to secrecy. He could talk to no one. The decision as to what to do next was his and his alone. Horace had gently probed and then recognising that there was no way Keith was going to discuss his problem, had veered off and been his usual entertaining self, full of anecdotes most of which concerned cadavers. It had made Keith feel awkward – the two men had shared much over the years. If they had not been boyhood friends, their work alone would have brought them close, but they shared a lifetime's friendship and understood one another perfectly. Keith remembered suddenly the evening he had spent with Horace when Horace's first child had been stillborn – they had been through so much together, it felt disloyal somehow not being able to confide in him.

Keith sighed and having overtaken a tractor pulled into the slow lane. He was painfully aware he was avoiding going home, that he was ducking the issue, shying away from the inevitable. Frankly he was terrified, terrified that what he had done in talking to Otto Juniper could seriously damage his relationship with Felicity. She had been adamant. He had lost count of the times she had told him she wanted nothing more said about her mother, that the subject was closed, yet here he was, on his way home, to tell her he had ignored her dearest wish and rejected her pleas.

As the turning to Camborne and Pool came into sight, it occurred to him that he could just pretend that he had never seen Otto Juniper. I don't have to take this any further, he thought, surely that was the best way – to say nothing. The old man would like to meet Sophia's daughter but his main preoccupation had to be with the death of Sophia, not Felicity. Felicity wanted the subject dropped, so drop it. In his heart though he asked how could he keep quiet, now he had met Otto, now he knew the truth, knew that far from being rejected by her mother, Sophia had tried desperately to reconnect with her child but had been stopped from doing so by Felicity's father. Had Otto got a point when he had said this information could be terribly hurtful? Felicity had one parent she trusted. By telling her that her father had gone to enormous lengths to ensure that her mother stayed out of her life, would she end up feeling even worse, feeling she had been betrayed by both parents, not just one? It was all such a mess.

He turned off the A30 and headed for St Ives. As always as he dropped into the town, the sight of the harbour in the growing dusk calmed him but he knew he was not ready to go home yet. He drove to Barnoon car park, parked his car and walked down through the streets to the wharf and on impulse went into the Sloop. He always favoured the small public bar. He unlatched the door and walked in, going straight to the bar and ordering a glass of red wine.

'Inspector Penrose,' came a familiar voice from behind him. He turned to see Annie sitting at one of the long trestle tables. He was very fond of Annie but just at this moment he felt he couldn't cope with her.

With a huge effort he managed a smile. 'Hello Annie, how nice to see you. Can I get you a drink?'

'No, no, I'm all right. I'm not a drinker as you know, boy. I'm just nursing this half of cider while my son attempts to sort some wiring out in my house. A right bloody mess he is making of it, I can tell you.'

Keith paid for his wine and went and sat beside Annie. 'That fish pie went down very well, Annie.'

'Did you admit that it was mine not yours?' she asked, with a wicked grin.

'I was a policeman, Annie. I have to tell the truth, besides which she knew immediately. She knew I couldn't produce anything as good as that.'

Annie sipped her drink and frowned at him. 'You look well blathered, Inspector Penrose, if I may say so?'

'I'm fine,' he said, 'just tired. I don't know whether you know …'

'That you've got your old job back?'

'No, not my job back but I am doing some investigating on a cold case.'

'And enjoying it I wouldn't be surprised!'

'I am,' he admitted.

'So if it's not your job worrying you, what is it – are you and Felicity all right?'

'Yes, we're fine, Annie, thank you very much.'

She continued to scrutinise him and suddenly he had the same feeling as he'd had with Horace, a longing to unburden the problem. After all, Annie in a way was the nearest thing Felicity had ever had to a mother, she had taken the newly-widowed Felicity under her wing when she had first moved , she was as bright as a button and marvellously astute when it came to life's problems. He couldn't betray a secret but Annie loved and understood Felicity – maybe there was a way to ask for her help.

'I've got a problem, Annie. I've done something that Felicity told me quite specifically not to do – nothing bad,' he added quickly, seeing Annie's face. 'The thing I have done, in my view, needs doing for Felicity's happiness but she disagrees, but I have done it anyway and now I've got to tell her and I don't know how to do it and I don't know how she is going to react.'

Annie gave him a critical look, popping her head on one side like a sparrow. 'So why did you go against her express wishes in this matter?' she asked.

'Because I believe I know best. I believe that she is wrong in not letting me do the thing I thought we needed to do to make her feel better.'

'You're talking in riddles, boy, but I'm doing my best,' said Annie. 'What makes you think you're right and she's wrong?'

'Because she is too close to it, she can't see the wood from the trees.'

'And what is your motive?'

'What do you mean?' Keith asked.

'Well, why are you going against her express wishes?'

'Because I love her and because I believe that what I have done is the right thing for her.'

'Even though she doesn't?'

'Even though she doesn't,' he agreed.

'Well,' said Annie after a pause, 'you can either decide that you were wrong and you should have listened to what she said, in which case perhaps pretend you haven't done the thing, whatever it is, or you will have to find the courage to tell her and brazen it out, persuade her you are right.'

'But it may damage our relationship?'

'Then you are a fool, aren't you boy? You shouldn't have started on this if you think it is going to damage your relationship. You're a lovely couple, you two, made for each other, what the hell are you doing putting that in jeopardy?'

'I don't know,' said Keith, miserably, 'when you put it like that.'

'The thing that you've done, can it be undone?'

'Not undone,' said Keith, 'but I don't have to pursue it, I don't have to admit that I've done it.'

Annie looked at him appraisingly for a moment and then shook her head. 'That's not going to work, is it?'

'Why?' Keith asked.

'Because you are an extremely honest and honourable man, foolish probably, but honest and she loves you and she understands you. You two are as close as a couple can be, she will know you are carrying a secret, she will probably know it the moment you walk through the door. I could tell something was wrong with you the moment I saw you.'

'Could you?' said Keith.

'Yes, of course I could,' said Annie.

'I thought I had spent all those years in the police force learning to be inscrutable.'

'That's work, it's completely different. You love her, she means the world to you and you're terrified of messing things up.'

'I am,' Keith admitted.

'Then all you can do is trust your own judgement,' said Annie. 'You're a clever man, you know what makes people tick. Search your conscience as to what the right thing is to do. Go on with you, stop messing about talking to the likes of me, walk round the Island and clear your head and then whatever you decide, just do it.'

Keith got to his feet leaving his wine glass half empty. 'Thanks, Annie,' he said.

She smiled at him and held out her hand which he took. 'Good luck boy.'

He smiled at her, squeezed her hand and walked to the door.

'Hello stranger.' Felicity came across the kitchen as he climbed the stairs and put her arms around his neck and kissed him. 'Oh, you smell of wine; what have you been up to?'

'I had a drink with Horace,' Keith said.

'And how is the old rogue?' Felicity asked.

'Good. He sends his love.'

'Is he being much help with the case?'

Keith smiled at her. 'His only suggestion to date is that I should be looking for a left-handed diabetic as a potential murderer.'

'There can't be too many of those in west Cornwall,' Felicity said, helpfully.

'Maybe not,' Keith agreed, 'but at the moment the whole case seems very daunting – there is absolutely nothing to go on. If the forensic evidence can't pick up anything, and it can't, I just don't know which way to go. No one saw anything, no one knows anything, I've got David working on links between the two families, links perhaps of which they themselves are unaware. I don't believe either husband was responsible in any way but I can't see beyond that.' He smiled at her. 'I'll just go and have a wash and brush up and then shall we have a drink?'

'Supper is ready,' said Felicity.

'Let's have a drink first,' said Keith. 'I won't be a moment.' In the bathroom mirror he stared for a long time at his reflection. Their happy loving bond, the marvellous way in which their relationship had developed and cemented. Was it all about to end? He shook his head as if to dislodge the thought which was unthinkable.

'Are you coming?' Felicity called.

'On the way,' he said and as he climbed the stairs he thought fleetingly that this must be how a man felt climbing the steps to the scaffold.

She had a glass of red wine waiting for him, there was a bowl of cashew nuts and a glass of white wine for herself. It was dark now and the kitchen looked cosy, domestic, a lovely setting in which to spend an evening with the woman you adored.

'So,' said Felicity, 'tell me more about the case, I'm dying to hear where you've got to.'

'Before I do that,' Keith said, 'I have a confession to make.'

Felicity took a sip of her wine. 'OK, you'd better come clean, with whom did you spend the night in Exeter – anyone I know?' She turned to smile at him and then seeing his expression, her face fell. 'Oh, no jokes,' she said. 'This is something serious. What on earth is wrong, Keith?'

He held her gaze steadily. 'While I was in Exeter I went to see Otto Juniper.'

The colour drained from her face. 'You did what?' she said.

'You heard,' said Keith. 'When I went to Exeter I had no idea that he lived there, but quite by chance I discovered he has a house in the city centre where he spends most of his time – in fact your mother's funeral is going to be held at Exeter Cathedral next Wednesday.'

For a long time no one spoke, but the tension was unbearable. Eventually Felicity said, 'How could you? I begged you to let this drop. I can't believe you went behind my back. I thought I could trust you, I thought you were the one person in the whole world I could rely on, no matter what, I just can't believe you've done this.'

Keith moved to put a hand on her shoulder but she turned away from him. 'I did it because I thought it was the right thing. It wasn't premeditated; I had no idea when I left home yesterday morning that this was going to happen but all seemed to just fall into place, felt like it was meant to.'

'Meant to!' Felicity screamed at him, 'So are you a clairvoyant now to add to your talents? Where were you when I was begging you to stop talking about my mother, to stop talking about Otto Juniper? It is just typical of you, you think you always know best, you think that because you were a policeman that you can decide what is going to happen. You're power-crazed! You think you have right on your side no matter what.'

'Oh, for heaven's sake,' said Keith, 'you know that's not true.'

When Felicity turned to him the expression on her face appalled him, it looked as if she hated him. 'I know no such thing,' she said. 'I am a person in my own right and this is my life we're talking about, not yours. How dare you try to interfere and tell me what is best for me, you know nothing about it.'

'Well that's just it,' said Keith, 'I do. Your mother …'

'Stop right there,' Felicity said. 'I don't want to hear another word. I'm going.' She pushed past him and started down the stairs.

'Going where?' he asked, bewildered.

'Away from you,' she said and again slammed her way out of the flat.

Keith sat down on a chair by the table. He felt shaky. What had he done? Was she right? Had his years as a policeman made him pompous to the point where he believed he was always in the right, always knew best? What were his motives for blatantly going against her wishes and making contact with Otto Juniper? How could he possibly judge what was best for her? If he had learned anything at all in the police force it was how different and varied human beings can be and how differently people cope with grief and loss. He had lost count of the number of times he had been forced to break terrible news to a stranger, trying carefully to pick his words so that he did not prolong the agony, but at the same time to try to prepare them for the shock. The reaction to terrible news could be so extreme – from complete hysteria, lack of control in every way, throwing furniture around, screaming and crying, to a quiet calm acceptance and a polite enquiry whether he would like a cup of tea.

He remembered one woman in her late fifties who, having absorbed the news that he had to tell her, which was that her husband had been killed at a freak level crossing accident, had been very concerned for him rather than herself. 'How terrible,' she had said, 'it must be for a young man like you to have to break this awful news. Would you like to sit down?' What could she get for him? By slipping seamlessly into the maternal role, focusing on his welfare rather than her own, she was able to deal with her tragedy.

So what right had he to say that it was in Felicity's best interests to know more about her mother's life, to know the circumstances in which she left her daughter, to get to know Otto Juniper, the man who took her mother away? Suddenly it seemed absurd to him that he could ever have thought it right for him to interfere. He must put it right, he must tell her. He searched around in his pocket, found his mobile and punched in her number. Her phone started ringing on the dresser making him jump. She had gone without it. Where had she gone? Was she all right? He looked wildly around the room wondering what she had taken with her. She had picked up her coat and her car keys were nearly always in the pocket. If she had driven off somewhere, was she being careful? In her state would she crash the car?

He was aware suddenly of a pair of eyes watching him, Harvey was hunched in his basket. 'She didn't even take you with her,' Keith said miserably. He tried to think for one moment what life without Felicity would be like. He felt his heart constrict with the pain of it. 'You bloody old idiot,' he said to himself. Harvey got out of his basket, stretched and came over to where Keith was sitting, putting his paws up on his knee. 'I don't deserve your sympathy,' said Keith, 'I really don't.'

By ten o'clock Keith was desperate. In his heart of hearts he knew that Felicity was not coming back that night but where was she and was she all right? It suddenly occurred to him where she would go – she would go to her daughter Mel's, of course she would. Taking a deep breath he picked up his mobile and dialled Mel's number; her husband Martin answered.

'Is she with you?' Keith asked.

'Yes, she is,' said Martin. 'What on earth is going on?'

'Is she all right?'

'In a manner of speaking,' said Martin. 'She arrived here about an hour ago, said she wanted to stay the night, refused to tell us anything and stomped up to the spare room. I took her up a cup of tea which she accepted gracefully enough but the moment I asked her what was wrong, she bit my head off. I assume you two have had a tiff?' There was a hint of amusement in his voice.

'It's not funny,' said Keith.

'Sorry, sorry,' said Martin, 'I have to admit, though, that Mel and I have been having a bit of a giggle about it, at your expense, I'm ashamed to say. It's like a total role reversal and it is slightly disorientating to have your mother-in-law behaving like a stroppy teenager. I suppose it is good practice for when Minty and Charlie grow up.' There was a silence. 'Sorry,' said Martin, 'I'm being tactless. It can't be serious though, not with you two, you are super-glued together.'

'It is serious,' said Keith, 'but I can't tell you about it, it's not my secret.'

'Secret, what are you talking about?' Martin said.

'I can't tell you what is wrong, only Fizzy can do that. Maybe she might confide in Mel?'

'She might,' said Martin, 'though usually when she's got problems Fizzy talks to me or Jamie. You know what Mel is like – she is my wife and I love her to bits but she is a bit like a bull in a china shop when it comes to emotional stuff. You and I have picked a couple of feisty women to spend our lives with, Keith.'

'Tell me about it,' Keith said. 'How are you and Mel and the children incidentally?'

'We're fine. I was going to suggest Sunday lunch over here this weekend but I suppose we better see what happens.'

'Yes,' said Keith.

'Couldn't you just give me a clue,' Martin said, 'something for me to start a conversation with her?'

'No,' said Keith, 'I've done enough damage as it is.'

'Is it such a big secret then?' Martin asked.

'Yes,' said Keith, 'it is a big secret and honestly Martin, it is no good picking away, I can't tell you anything more but if you could get her to talk to you, you are such good friends, maybe ….' his voice trailed away.

'I'll do what I can,' said Martin, 'try to get some sleep and we'll talk tomorrow.'

'OK,' said Keith. 'Oh incidentally can you tell Fizzy that I will take Harvey to work with me tomorrow so she doesn't have to worry about him.'

'Will do.'

Keith switched off his phone and went to the

Aga, lifted the lid and dropped the kettle on the hob. The relief that Felicity was safe and with her daughter was considerable – but now what, would Martin be able to talk to her? He doubted it. They had both known Martin Tregonning before he met Mel, in fact the three of them had met at much the same time over a particular gruelling case which had involved drug smuggling. Martin had been tragically widowed as a young man and was older than Mel, but both Felicity and Keith thought that was a good thing. Mel was headstrong, opinionated, a clever girl but not the easiest of people. Martin by contrast was calm, easy-going with a lovely sense of humour. He ran his own market garden business and the couple lived close by in Hayle. After two children and marriage to Martin, Mel had definitely mellowed. The four of them met often, not just because they were related, but because they wanted to, enjoyed each others' company. Felicity was very fond of Martin, maybe, just maybe, she might talk to him.

10

Keith met his sergeant by arrangement at nine o'clock at Truro station the following morning.

'Remind me I've got a dog in the car,' he said to David. 'He needs walking and feeding. God, you look terrible.'

'Thank you, sir!' said David. 'Actually you don't look that great yourself.'

'Not much sleep,' said Keith, shortly.

'Nor me,' said David, 'but I have had a bit of a breakthrough.'

'You've found a link?'

'It's a fairly tenuous one,' David said. 'Did you know the younger Nicholls boy, Graham, the one we saw briefly in Exeter, had heart problems at birth?'

Keith shook his head. 'No, I didn't.'

'He was born with a hole in the heart and he was operated on in Bristol twelve years ago.'

'And ...' said Keith.

'Adrianne Beckett was working at the hospital

at that time. She had decided on a career in paediatrics so she could well have met Graham Nicholls.'

'But I thought she was working in A & E at Treliske Hospital?'

'Yes, she was,' David said triumphantly. 'I rang Jerry Beckett this morning.'

'That was brave of you,' said Keith.

'I agree. Actually he was very helpful. She did start out planning a career in paediatrics but she found it too harrowing – sick children – but she definitely was at Bristol in that period and did deal with a number of heart surgery cases.'

'It's a coincidence,' said Keith. 'It's hard to imagine that this is the reason our two victims drowned.'

David looked crestfallen. 'I'm sorry, sir,' he said, 'but at the moment that is the best I can do.'

'And I'm sorry too,' said Keith. 'You've done well and it could be useful – let's face it, it's all we've got. What we need now is the name of Graham's surgeon and from there perhaps we can find some hospital staff who remember Adrianne.'

'We could talk to Colin Nicholls again too. He might remember who treated their son.'

'Agreed,' said Keith, 'but first we have an appointment with Jane Cleaver.' David frowned. 'She's the friend of the Becketts who Jerry and

Adrianne went to supper with the night before Adrianne disappeared. Come on, let's go.'

Harvey was very taken with David, there was a lot of wagging and licking. 'What a nice little dog,' David said, while trying to persuade Harvey to return to the back seat of the car.

'Yes, he is,' Keith said, obviously not anxious to be drawn on the subject. 'Now what do we know about the Cleavers?'

David fastened his seat belt and reached for his notebook. 'Jane and Roger Cleaver, best friends I think of Adrianne and Jerry. He is an orthopaedic surgeon at Treliske Hospital and so he and Adrianne worked professionally together some of the time. Jane is younger than the other three and still producing children – they have a seven and four-year-old and she has just had a baby, a little girl, so she is at home at the moment.'

The Cleavers' house was one of the few big houses left in Lemon Street which was still residential. Jane Cleaver answered the door, a pretty woman, blonde hair tied back in a ponytail making her look very young. However, there were dark circles under her eyes which clearly indicated a new-born.

'Come in,' she said. 'The house is in chaos I'm afraid, but at least for a moment it is quiet, the baby is sleeping and Roger has taken the other two off

142

to school.' She showed them into a big family kitchen. 'If we talk in here I can make you some coffee at the same time.'

'That sounds marvellous,' said Keith. 'I am so sorry about the death of your friend.'

Jane's face clouded. 'Yes, terrible, I still can't take it in.' She placed a cafetière and a jug of milk on the table. 'Do either of you take sugar?'

The two men shook their heads.

'Help yourself then.'

'I gather she and Jerry spent the evening with you the day before she disappeared.'

Jane came and sat down at the table. 'Yes, we had such a great evening too.'

'There were just the four of you?'

Jane nodded. 'It's something we do about once a month, take it in turns to go to each other's houses, or at least we did before our latest was born – recently it has been easier if they come to us.'

'And she was in good spirits?'

'Excellent, she was a very gregarious person, the life and soul of the party, very funny – I loved her …' Jane's voice cracked. 'I'm sorry, it's just so unbelievable.'

'So you, too, believe there is no way she could have committed suicide?'

'Absolutely not,' said Jane. 'We've known them for about ten years, I suppose. Roger and

Adrianne worked together but then I imagine you know that?' Keith nodded. 'Roger and Jerry are good friends, but they don't have a great deal in common. Jerry is a fanatic sailor and Roger feels seasick if his bath is too full. However, Adrianne and I, well, we were really good friends. If she'd had any problems, any worries, she would have told me. We've shared so much over the last few years, she was godmother to our son Paul, Roger and I thought the world of her.'

'And you reckon the marriage was a happy one?' Keith said.

'Yes, of course,' said Jane, 'I'd have know if there had been any problems.'

'And their son, Adam, no problems there?'

'None at all. He's a clever boy, he is in bits of course but he is doing very well in the circumstances, in fact he seems to be coping better than Jerry. They are both coming around for supper tonight, actually.'

'So,' said Keith, 'knowing what you do about the family, can you put into words why you know that Adrianne Beckett did not kill herself?'

'She just didn't,' said Jane, 'I can tell you absolutely categorically she did not, would not do such a thing.' A wail came from the baby alarm. 'Oh lord, that's Darcy, hang on a minute I won't be two ticks.'

Left alone David said, 'I find her a more credible witness than Jerry. I was brought up to believe it is better to trust a woman's judgement in all things emotional, rather than a man's.'

Keith let out a sigh. 'Yes,' he said, 'you're probably right there.'

Jane returned moments later with a small bundle wrapped in a pink shawl.

'I'm going to have to feed her in a moment,' she said. 'is there anything else I can help you with? I just don't know what to say. I was thinking about it just now as I was changing Darcy – someone must have done this to Adrianne,'

'And as far as you know,' said Keith, 'nobody had threatened her or stalked her, she hadn't upset a patient or anything like that?'

'Absolutely not,' said Jane. 'If there was anything like that going on in her life, I know for sure she would have told me.'

The Accident Department at Treliske Hospital was mercifully quiet on this particular Thursday morning. While David began talking to the staff on duty Keith went in search of Roger Cleaver. After becoming severely lost in the hospital corridors and various abortive trips to different wards, he finally tracked down Cleaver's office only to learn he was on a ward round.

'He won't be more than twenty minutes,' the sister in charge assured him. 'Can I ask what it is about?'

'Police business,' Keith said, shortly, then seeing the young woman's face pulled himself together. 'I'm actually enquiring about the death of Doctor Adrianne Beckett, did you know her?'

The sister shook her head. 'Not well, but I understand why you want to talk to Mr Cleaver. They were good friends … and colleagues,' she added. 'He is terribly upset by her death, everyone in the hospital is; she was much liked, a really nice woman, nobody can understand it.'

'That's what I hear from everyone,' said Keith. 'Would you mind if I waited?'

'Of course not,' she said. 'Would you like a coffee or anything?'

Keith shook his head. 'I'm fine thanks.' About ten minutes into the wait, David joined him. 'I'm waiting for Roger Cleaver to finish his ward round,' Keith said. 'Have you any news?'

David sat down beside him. 'Well, something a bit odd, might be something, might be nothing.'

'Oh, for heaven's sake, man, spit it out.'

'I'm sorry,' said David. 'I don't seem to be able to do anything right this morning.'

Keith looked up at David Sterling. 'It's me, not you. Apologies. What have you got to tell me?'

'Well,' said David, 'Adrianne would never work on Thursday afternoons.'

'So,' said Keith, 'maybe she went to the gym or did something with her son or husband?'

'Maybe,' said David, 'but it is a bit of a mystery. A few months back there was a really nasty pile-up on the A30 and they were desperate to get in every single A & E member of staff to help. No one at the hospital could raise her. Eventually they got hold of her husband but he didn't know where she was either, having assumed she was at work. She did not show up despite the severity of the emergency and despite the fact that she is normally a very conscientious worker. She is never late for her shift and often works long beyond the time she is supposed to clock off. However, Thursdays appear to be a different story.'

'Was she on call on Thursdays? It was a Thursday when she disappeared?'

'No,' said David. 'She was never on call on Thursday afternoons, though everyone had her mobile number. On the Thursday of the crash, her phone was switched off. She gave no explanation the following morning when she came in to work, other than to say she was very sorry and she didn't know there was an emergency. I don't know, obviously, whether her husband ever found her that day, but every Thursday afternoon she was never at work. Odd, don't you think?'

'Yes,' said Keith. 'Maybe this is the tiny inconsistency we've been looking for.'

Roger Cleaver was not an easy man to like. He was tall, elegantly and flamboyantly dressed and clearly had a very well-developed sense of his own importance. However, his handsome face was strangely devoid of expression. There was no kindness in his eyes, no sense of character or personality shone through. He was what Felicity called a 'plastic person'. The thought of Felicity made Keith inwardly wince. He shook hands and introduced David as his sergeant.

'I can't stay long,' Roger said, 'I'm due back in surgery shortly.'

'I appreciate you seeing us,' said Keith. 'It's obviously concerning Adrianne Beckett.'

'I've already been interviewed by the police about Adrianne, I have really nothing else to add,' Roger started to walk past them.

'I wanted to ask you about her Thursday afternoons,' Keith said.

'What do you mean?' Roger asked, turning abruptly.

'She never worked on Thursday afternoons and she was never contactable on Thursday afternoons. Do you know what she did?'

'We were friends and colleagues,' said Roger, 'but we didn't live in each other's pockets. I have absolutely no idea what she did on a day-to-day basis. So far as her home and social life are concerned, ask Jerry.'

'I intend to,' said Keith, 'but I understood that you two are good friends and I thought maybe you might be able to help.'

'No can do, old boy, I'm afraid,' said Roger, starting to walk away from them again.

'And there is one other thing, sir,' said Keith. 'Did you know Adrianne when she worked in Bristol?'

Roger stopped in his tracks and turned. 'No, of course not. We met ... we all met, the four of us, when we moved to Cornwall.'

'Only,' said Keith, 'I don't know whether you are aware but there was another death six years ago, not unsimilar to Adrianne's, and it seems that the son of the other victim was at Bristol Royal Infirmary at the same time as Adrianne was working there.'

'It's a very big hospital,' said Roger.

'I'm aware of that, sir,' said Keith, trying to keep his temper, 'but we are clutching at straws here. I am sure, as her friend, you would rather believe that Adrianne did not commit suicide. While nobody welcomes the idea of murder, I'm sure for her son and her husband and those close to her, murder would be preferable to suicide. If she killed herself it would mean that you had all missed something and presumably would all feel a sense of guilt for not helping her more in her life.'

'Have forensics come up with something then, to prove it's not suicide?'

'I am not at liberty to divulge anything that forensics have or haven't found, sir, as I am sure you appreciate,' said Keith.

'Anything else?' Roger Cleaver said.

Keith shook his head. 'That's all,' said Keith. 'Thank you for your time.'

'Isn't he awful?' said David, as they walked down the corridor towards the exit.

'I agree,' said Keith, 'and I can't help thinking about his poor wife. I like Jane Cleaver, a really nice warm person. How on earth did she end up with an idiot like that?'

'Lots of lovely women end up with awful men, in my brief experience,' said David, sagely.

Keith tried to believe, and failed, that this observation had nothing to do with him and Felicity.

11

While Keith was striding out of Treliske Hospital as if the hounds of hell were on his heels, Felicity was sitting in her daughter's kitchen nursing a cup of coffee. Mel had dropped the children off at the school and playgroup and then gone to work. Felicity, therefore, had the house to herself. She sat staring into space. For somebody normally highly-motivated and busy, a great planner, she felt deeply disorientated by a inability to think of what to do next. There was a commotion by the back door, the sound of boots being kicked off and Martin, her son-in-law, appeared in the kitchen looking windswept and dishevelled. Family life suited him. He looked years younger than he had appeared when she had first met him. He stood before her now, mud plastered down one side of his face, grinning like a naughty school boy.

'There you are,' he said. 'How are you feeling?'

'What are you doing here at this time of day?' she asked accusingly, feeling that his presence was an intrusion, even in his own home.

'I have to pick Charlie up from playgroup in half-an-hour so I thought I would come back and have a coffee before I go.'

'And to check up on me?' Felicity said.

'And to check up on you too, Fizzy. I can't deny it.'

'I could pick up Charlie,' said Felicity.

'If you could do that, it would be a big help,' said Martin, 'but let's have a coffee first.'

'I've had mine,' Felicity began.

'But I haven't had mine,' said Martin. 'Now sit down.' He made a coffee and then came and sat opposite her. 'What's up?' he said.

'Nothing,' said Felicity, 'I am sorry about last night.'

'So you and Keith have had a row?'

'Yes,' said Felicity, 'but I don't want to talk about it.'

'He's a lovely man, Fizzy,' said Martin, 'and he is worried sick about you. You should have heard him last night.'

'You spoke to him?'

'You know I did, I left a message outside your door to say he had taken Harvey to work.'

'Oh, yes,' said Felicity. 'Sorry, I didn't think.'

'Whatever you are arguing about, nothing can be as important as your relationship.'

'You can't have love without trust,' Felicity burst out.

'What are you saying? You don't trust Keith? He is the most trustworthy man in the world.'

'So, are you still trustworthy if you can't keep a promise, an important promise?' Felicity asked.

'I suppose you could be, if circumstances change to make that promise obsolete or inappropriate.'

'Circumstances haven't changed, so a broken promise is just that, a broken promise and that means he is untrustworthy.'

'I don't know Keith as well as you, obviously,' said Martin, 'but I have known him for some time now and I have to say that I cannot think of a more decent, honourable human being than Keith Penrose. He is a man, so like all of us men, he gets things wrong, but untrustworthy, Fizzy, I just don't believe it. Tell me why you think he is not to be trusted.'

'No,' said Felicity; she was vehement. 'No, I won't, I won't tell anybody, ever. It is my business and no one else's.'

'That's what Keith said last night,' said Martin.

'What do you mean?' Felicity burst out.

'I asked him the same question, what was wrong? He said it was your secret that nobody could tell me or Mel about except you, that it was not his secret to tell.'

Felicity stared at Martin. 'He said that?'

'Yes, so this untrustworthy fellow perhaps can be trusted after all? Forgive me, Fizzy, you know I love you but you are behaving very strangely, quite out of character.'

'I'm sorry if I am upsetting you,' said Felicity, 'I will do what I promised, pick up Charlie and look after him for a bit, but I won't stay here again tonight, I'll go off and stay in a hotel. I don't want to be an inconvenience.'

'Oh, stop it,' said Martin, 'you know perfectly well that is not what I meant. Mel and I want to help you in any way we can, but we can't if you don't tell us what is wrong.'

By the time Mel came back from court, Martin had the two children bathed, in their pyjamas and sitting in front of the last of CBeebies. He kissed her. 'Tea or wine?' he asked.

'Tea followed very rapidly by a glass of wine,' she said, smiling. 'How are they?'

'In good form,' said Martin. 'They've both had the most enormous tea and they've been very jolly.'

'You are a wonderful dad,' said Mel, 'and I am very lucky.'

'Yes you are,' Martin agreed, 'but so by God am I.'

'Where is Mum?' Mel asked.

'Gone,' said Martin.

'Thank God for that, Keith will be relieved.'

'No he won't, she hasn't gone home. She has gone to a hotel.'

'To a hotel! Martin, what on earth is going on?'

Martin handed her a mug. 'It's my fault I suppose, I should have been more tactful.'

Mel frowned. 'You're always tactful and Mum usually hangs on your every word. Tell me what happened.'

'I told her that we could only help her if she told us what was wrong and she blew up big time. She said she was sorry if she was an inconvenience and she would be leaving to stay in a hotel. Then she picked Charlie up from playgroup and came back here with him but she was in such a state, I didn't like to leave her with him for very long. I suggested she had lunch with us both but instead she said no, she would go ... and she went.'

'Did she give any clue as to where?'

'No, other than the fact that I know she wasn't going home.'

'You should have rung me,' Mel said.

'How could I? You were in court and what difference would it have made anyway? You wouldn't have been able to stop her, honestly. God knows what is wrong but maybe this is what she needs, maybe she just wants to be alone for a bit.'

'And she didn't tell you what poor old Keith has done?'

'No, not exactly, except that apparently he has betrayed a trust.'

'You don't think he is off with somebody else?'

'No, no, of course not,' said Martin. 'He seems to have broken a promise he made to her, though I have to say that she was slightly mollified when I said he had refused to say what was wrong, that it was her secret to tell, not his.'

'But she didn't give a hint as to what the secret was?'

'Absolutely not,' said Martin.

At that moment the home telephone rang and Martin reached for it. 'Keith,' he mouthed at Mel. 'No, I'm sorry,' he said, 'you can't talk to her, Keith. She's gone … no, not home, she said she was going to stay in a hotel … no, I don't know which one. I'm really sorry, she wouldn't say. Are you at home? OK, I promise if I get any news I will let you know. I think she's all right, Keith. I think she just needs to sort herself out and simmer down… No, no, she didn't tell us what it was about. Can you tell us yet? OK we'll speak later.' He returned the receiver. 'Keith is at home and of course she's not there, as we know. She has been back, he thinks, to pick up a few things but she has still left her mobile on the kitchen table so she clearly doesn't want to be in touch with any of us.'

'That is so irresponsible,' Mel burst out. 'Suppose something happened to one of her grandchildren.'

'Don't be too harsh,' said Martin. 'I don't think she is thinking straight about anything at the moment.'

'But what can be going on?' Mel wailed. 'She has always been a bit wacky, but never like this.'

'Keith sounded beside himself, poor man,' said Martin. 'I was wondering whether I should go round there and see him.'

'Do you know, I think that would be a really good idea,' said Mel. 'You might even find out what is going on.'

'I'm not going to try to talk him into telling me,' said Martin, 'but if nothing else, I can drag him out for a pint and try to cheer him up.'

' Let's get the children to bed and then you do just that,' said Mel.

Keith was sitting at the kitchen table trying hard to focus on the Becketts. He had fed Harvey and didn't feel like eating himself; the Aga created a false sense of comfort but there was nothing cosy about being at home without Felicity. He stared at his notebook; instinct told him that if he could discover what Adrianne Beckett did on Thursday afternoons, a lot of things would become clearer. He knew he was clutching at straws but long experience had taught him that this inconsistency in comparison as to how she ran the rest of her life was the chink in the armour that would give him the lead he so badly needed.

Roger Cleaver's reaction had been interesting too. He was a very slick operator but without any doubt the question about Thursday had shaken him. Tomorrow he would go and see Jerry Beckett again and see if he could throw any light on Thursday afternoons and he also wanted to have a talk to the boy, Adam, but he would have to be careful how he handled that. David meanwhile was searching for anyone who had worked at Bristol twelve years ago and who might be able to establish a link between the Becketts and the Nicholls. He could simply ring Colin, of course, and ask him but the chances are it would have been Morwenna who spent most of the time with her infant son while he was being operated on, with Colin in charge of their elder boy. To talk to him at this stage when the details were so vague seemed wrong. He felt strongly that it was only fair to Colin to contact him if he had something definite to say, the man had been through enough.

His thoughts were interrupted by a knock on

the front door. For one brief and wonderful moment he thought it was Felicity and then he realised how stupid he was being. Harvey was out of his basket and barking and in any event, Felicity had her keys, he knew that. He went down the stairs and opened the door. Martin Tregonning was standing on the doorstep.

'I've come to buy you a pint,' he said.

Keith smiled. 'That's really kind of you but why don't you come in instead and I'll open a bottle of wine. I don't really feel up to the pub right now. Would that be OK?'

'Perfect,' said Martin. Having established it was family not foe, Martin became embroiled in a heavy welcoming session with Harvey while Keith opened the wine.

'No news then?' Keith said.

Martin shook his head. 'And you?'

'No, nothing,' he nodded at the phone still on the table, 'and without her having that, there is not much I can do. You forget that only a few years ago people never expected to be able to get in touch with someone, wherever they were.' Keith poured two glasses of red wine. 'Let's go through to the sitting room and I'll light the fire.'

'No, no,' said Martin, 'don't worry, it's fine here in the kitchen, I like it.' They sat down companionably at the kitchen table. 'I know you're not going to tell me what is going on,' said Martin. 'I get that, but I am here because I am hoping there is something I could do to help, maybe act as a mediator, I don't know, anything.'

'You're doing something to help right now,' said Keith, 'just by being here. I'm very grateful.'

Martin lifted his glass and took a sip. 'Lovely,' he said. 'We can always rely on you when it comes to wine, can't we, Keith?'

'It is a minor passion, and one day, you never know, I might have time to explore the subject in more detail.'

'So is your argument about the fact you've gone back to work? Felicity told Mel all about it, but at the time she sounded very enthusiastic on your behalf.'

'Oh, she is,' said Keith. 'In fact, I think she's glad to get me out from under her feet. No, it's nothing like that and it is no good fishing, Martin, I am not going to tell you, not because I don't like you or trust you and to be honest, I would really value your opinion, it is just that I am in enough trouble already for my indiscretion, I daren't do anything more, or there will be absolutely no hope at all of us getting back together.'

'Do you really think things are that serious?' Martin asked, astonished.

'Yes, I do,' said Keith. 'I've been a blithering

idiot, I did it for the best of motives, but …' his voice trailed away.

'OK, I'll stop it,' said Martin, 'but just remember that Mel and I are here for you and Fizzy and will you promise to let us know when you hear from her and vice versa?'

'Of course,' said Keith. They drank in silence for a moment. 'Tell me, Martin, you're a sensitive sort of chap, can you imagine living with a woman, loving a woman and not be aware that she was contemplating suicide?'

'Good God, Keith,' said Martin, 'you don't think Fizzy …'

Keith held up a hand. 'Stop,' he said, 'I'm sorry, I've moved too swiftly from one subject to another. I'm now talking about the case I am working on. I'm really sorry. Of course Fizzy isn't going to commit suicide, I'm talking about the poor woman who drowned at Gunwalloe last week.'

'Oh yes, I read about that,' said Martin. 'That's the case you're working on, is it?'

Keith nodded. 'So to answer the question before I sent you into paroxysms of panic, would you believe it is possible?'

Martin was silent for a moment. 'I think if you are not a suicidal type, and mercifully most of us aren't, it is very difficult to imagine the state of mind one would have to be in, in order to contemplate taking one's life. That being the case I suppose it is possible, because while you might know that the woman you live with is unhappy, depressed, angry, dissatisfied with your relationship, you might not necessarily know that she was contemplating suicide, or was even capable of doing so.'

'I suppose that's right,' said Keith, 'and if that is so then maybe I am trying to read too much into the case.'

'Do you think your victim had a happy marriage?'

'I don't know,' Keith admitted. 'I don't like the husband much but then I've never met him in normal circumstances. Of course he is all over the place with his wife having just died – he is shocked, unhappy, angry. Who wouldn't be? What if you were aware you had missed the signs, what if you realised after her death that she was crying out for help and you had ignored her? Would you admit that to the police or would you say she can't have committed suicide, because you yourself couldn't face up to the fact that you hadn't taken her seriously?'

'What about friends, work colleagues?'

'They all back his view that she was a happy woman with absolutely no reason to take her own life. We've checked with her doctor and she wasn't ill.'

'Then given all that you've said,' said Martin, 'in my view somebody killed her and made it look like suicide.'

'That is the assumption we're working on,' said Keith, 'or at least I am.' He glanced at his mobile sitting beside his glass.

'Are you expecting her to call?' Martin asked. 'Sorry, I'm back to Fizzy.'

'I know that,' said Keith. 'No, I'm sorry it's rude of me. I put the phone on silent and I can't stop checking it, even though I know she is not going to ring me.'

'But she can't keep this up,' said Martin. 'She has to speak to someone.'

'If only Gilla was alive,' Keith said, 'not only would she talk to Gilla, but I would know where she was, that she was safe.'

'Gilla?' said Martin. 'She was her best friend, yes? The one who died?'

'That's it,' said Keith. 'She died of a brain haemorrhage. She was the only other person who knew about all this.'

'Oh God, Keith, you're driving me mad! Just spit it out whatever it is.'

Keith shook his head. 'I can't, sorry. Look I am very poor company, would you like another glass?'

'No thanks,' said Martin, 'I'm driving. I just wanted to see how you were. What will you do for the rest of the evening?'

'Try to keep my mind on my job,' said Keith. 'Try and worry around the facts and make some sort of sense of them. I've always found work to be the best medicine.'

Martin stood up. 'Take care now, we'll be in touch.'

Keith watched his departing back with something close to despair. Like Horace, Martin Tregonning was the type of man he could confide in; his opinion Keith valued but he knew he had no alternative but to say nothing to anyone.

12

The following morning when Keith and David drew into the drive of the Becketts' house, Jerry's BMW was still parked in the driveway.

'So it looks like he's not back at work yet,' said David. 'I still think we should have made an appointment though, sir. He was angry enough last time we came to see him.'

'It can't be helped,' said Keith. 'We're investigating a crime. We can't tiptoe round peoples' moods.'

David looked at Keith with surprise. He had not thought him the sort of man who would normally appear so insensitive. He had been terse ever since arriving at the station earlier in the morning.

Keith must have sensed his surprise. 'Sorry,' he said, 'didn't get much sleep last night. I just don't want any prepared speech. There is something about Jerry Beckett I don't like very much.'

They climbed out of the car and rang the bell.

It was several minutes before the door opened. Jerry Beckett stood on the threshold; he looked dishevelled and was not yet dressed, still in pyjamas and a dressing gown.

'What the hell do you want at this hour?' he said, and then stopped and thought for a moment. 'Have you any news?'

'Not as such ...' said Keith, 'but could we come in and talk to you for a moment?'

'I'm not even dressed.'

'It doesn't matter to us.'

'Well it matters to me, you can come in and wait.'

'I'm sorry, we would have come later,' said David, 'but it is nine-thirty and we thought you would be up and about now with your son back at school.'

'Adam hasn't gone to school today,' said Jerry. 'He doesn't feel well. It's all starting to catch up with him.'

'Poor lad,' said Keith. 'I'm so sorry.'

'It would help if we didn't keep having these bloody silly visits from the police. Take a seat,' he said, waving in the direction of the sitting room. 'I'll be with you in a minute.'

'I'm glad Adam is at home,' Keith murmured. 'I wanted to have a word with the boy. I'll just wander through to the kitchen and see if he's there.'

'You're not going to endear yourself to Jerry,' David said.

'I can live with that,' said Keith, 'you stay here and be the respectable one.'

The boy was sitting at the kitchen table spooning in a bowl of cereal at great speed.

'Sorry to interrupt you,' Keith said. 'Are you Adam?'

'Yeah,' the boy replied. 'Who are you?'

'Keith Penrose,' said Keith. 'I'm investigating the death of your mother. I am truly sorry.'

'So everyone keeps saying,' the boy said continuing to eat, his eyes now on his cereal bowl. He was dressed in a T-shirt, tracksuit bottoms and had bare feet. His hair was tousled as he had just got out of bed but despite all this he was an extremely good-looking boy, far better-looking than his father, but then Adrianne had been a very attractive woman and this was her son.

'Not going to school today then?' said Keith.

'Obviously not, otherwise I wouldn't be sitting here.'

'Fair enough,' said Keith. 'I wanted to talk to you about your mother. May I sit down?'

'Help yourself,' said the boy.

Keith drew out a chair and sat down. 'Look Adam, I know this is a terrible thing to have to ask you, but do you believe your mother could have committed suicide?'

Adam stopped eating, put his spoon down and regarded Keith in silence for a moment. 'It's not a terrible thing to ask,' he said.

'Why not?' Keith asked.

'Because you are the first person who has shown the slightest interest in my opinion. Everyone is either so-called "shielding" me or ignoring me, no one cares what I think about it. They don't seem to think my view is relevant. The other policemen hardly bothered to talk to me and if they tried to do so, my father stopped them.'

'So what do you think?' Keith asked.

'I don't think, I know there is no way Mum committed suicide. There is not even the slightest possibility that she ever thought about it, it is not how she was. Sometimes she and Dad would argue, sometimes she found work hard but …'

'What the hell is going on in here?' Jerry strode into the kitchen. 'Did I give you permission to talk to my son? I think not. Adam, go upstairs. You,' he pointed at Keith, 'come with me.'

'If this man is going to talk about Mum I'm going to stay and listen.' said Adam.

'You do as you're told, young man, ' said Jerry.

'Actually,' said Keith, 'I think it would be helpful if he joined us.'

'Don't you start telling me how to deal with my son.'

'I'm not,' said Keith standing up, 'but your son is also the son of our victim. By all accounts, he is a highly intelligent boy, I value his opinion as much as I value your own and I think it is important he knows what is going on.'

'And I think he needs protecting.'

'I will have to interview him,' said Keith. 'I can do it down at the station if you prefer.'

'Oh for Christ's sake,' Jerry glared at Keith, looking close to hitting him.

'I'm going to stay, Dad, whatever you say,' said Adam. 'I can't imagine you are going to beat me up in front of a policeman.'

'I've never laid a finger on him,' Jerry began.

'Look, look,' said Keith. 'Let's all calm down. I'm not accusing anybody of anything. I would just like to talk to you both in the hope that something you have to tell us may help us discover what exactly happened on that beach in Gunwalloe.' Keith walked past them and out into the hallway, heading back towards the sitting room; father and son followed.

When everyone was seated, David looking extremely anxious, Keith began addressing Jerry. 'I'm afraid I have nothing new to tell you, Mr Beckett.'

'No change there then,' Jerry said.

'We've seen the Cleavers and we've talked to your wife's colleagues and everyone seems to corroborate what you and your son believe, that your wife would not have taken her own life.'

'Then for Christ's sake find the bastard who did,' Jerry shouted.

'There is just one inconsistency,' said Keith, ignoring the outburst. 'It appears that your wife never worked on Thursday afternoons and by all accounts didn't come home. Do you know what she used to do on Thursday afternoons? Was it the gym or something similar?'

'I've no idea what my wife did when she wasn't at home or at work,' Jerry said. 'We were both very independent people who liked our own space, I wouldn't dream of checking up on her.'

'Only it seems to have been a very consistent arrangement,' said Keith. 'There was an occasion last year, I believe, when there was a major car crash on the A30 and nobody could get hold of her, not even you.'

'She had turned her phone off because she wanted some peace and quiet,' said Jerry.

'You're not telling the truth, Dad,' Adam said. Suddenly he had gone very pale and was clearly nervous about contradicting his father.

'What do you mean?' Keith asked.

'I mean Dad knows exactly where my mother used to go on Thursday afternoons, he is lying to you.'

'How dare you!' Jerry half rose from his chair and then thought better of it and sat down again. 'How dare you,' he said again, feebly.

'Mr Beckett,' said Keith, 'if you are not telling the truth, then you do realise that you could be facing a very serious charge of perverting the course of justice. If you do know where your wife went on Thursday afternoons then it is your duty to tell us.'

'If he won't, I will,' said Adam. Jerry remained silent. 'She went every Thursday afternoon to a flat in a terraced house just up from Truro station on the left hand side, I don't know the number.'

Keith glanced at Jerry who was staring down at the carpet.

'And do you know why she went there?'

'I can guess,' said Adam.

'And what would that guess be?' Keith asked.

'She used to meet Roger Cleaver there. They were having an affair, have done for some years I think.'

'And you knew about this, Mr Beckett?' Keith asked.

Jerry remained mute, still staring down at his feet.

'Well, if I worked it out,' said Adam, 'I can't

imagine my father hasn't.'

'That was a bit of a surprise,' said David as he and Keith climbed back into the car and Keith began the torturous business of reversing out of the Beckett's driveway.

'Hadn't it occurred to you that this secrecy about Thursday afternoons could mean an affair?'

'Blame it on the innocence of my youth,' said David with a smile. 'I just assumed, like you said, that she was going to the gym or a Pilates class or some such thing.'

'If I was a woman married to Jerry Beckett, I reckon I'd have an affair too,' said Keith, grumpily.

'Yes, but think about it,' said David, 'fancy for falling for somebody like Roger Cleaver – talk about out of the frying pan into the fire.'

'That is certainly true,' Keith said.

When Keith reached home that night he hoped against hope that he would find Felicity there but the house was in darkness. He and Harvey trudged up the stairs and having fed the dog and poured himself a glass of wine, Keith slumped down at the kitchen table contemplating yet another evening alone. There was no sign that she had been in the house during the day. Her mobile phone was still where she had left it, but as he rose to top up his glass, his phone rang. He grabbed it eagerly but the number displayed was unrecognisable. For a moment, such was his mood, he thought he would block the call and then realised the stupidity of doing such a thing – the call could be about the case, about Felicity.

'Hello,' he said, cautiously, 'Keith Penrose here.'

'Keith, it's Otto Juniper.' On the phone his voice sounded thin, reedy; the voice of a very old man.

'Otto, how nice of you to ring,' said Keith. 'How are you?'

'Struggling on day to day,' said Otto, 'trying to make some sense of it all, of life I mean, without Sophia. And you, how are you doing, how did Felicity react, you have told her that you saw me?'

'Yes,' said Keith, 'yes, I told her and I'm afraid it didn't go very well, in fact it went very badly. She was so angry I didn't get a chance to explain anything really, she stormed out of the house and I haven't been able to find her since.'

'That's dreadful,' said Otto. 'Did you expect her to react so violently?'

'I thought she would be very angry,' said Keith, 'because she had expressly told me not to make contact with you but I didn't think she would walk out of my life like this. It's awful.'

'It must be,' said Otto. 'Mind you, mother and daughter, my Sophia was very volatile, too, as I think I told you.'

'Yes indeed,' said Keith.

'I would so love her to come to the funeral,' said Otto. 'There will be so many people there from the music world and the press of course, but I have no family. Sophia had no family except for yours. I know this sounds feeble but I really need you there.'

'I can understand that,' said Keith, deeply touched. 'We still have five days to find her. Believe me, Otto, I will do everything in my power to try and get her and her family to join you.'

'Thank you,' said Otto. 'You're a good man. I'll wait to hear from you then.' The phone went dead.

Am I a good man? Keith thought. From where I am standing, it doesn't feel like it. With a sigh he drew his notebook out of his coat pocket and stared sightlessly at the notes he had made after the meeting with Jerry Beckett. Adam's dramatic exposure of how his mother spent Thursday afternoons had not been denied by Jerry. He had just gritted his teeth and said he hoped they had got what they came for and would they now get out. He hoped Jerry would not be too hard on the boy. He was, after all, doing what every right-minded citizen should do, answering truthfully to a police enquiry.

The revelation opened up several possibilities – one that Roger Cleaver had murdered Adrianne because she had threatened to tell his wife of their affair – maybe she was jealous of the new baby. Alternatively, maybe she had decided to end the relationship and that had angered Roger. There were several reasons why he might have killed her and equally the same applied to Jerry. Having discovered his wife was having an affair, maybe he had decided to kill her – the fact that he had attempted to hide his knowledge of the affair from the police in itself did suggest an element of guilt. Then there was Adam, was he so disgusted with his mother and her goings on that he murdered her?

Somehow Keith couldn't see a sixteen-year-old meticulously sewing up two coat pockets. Besides it was clear he was deeply fond of his mother and not over-enamoured with his father. So, which of the men might have done such a thing? Roger Cleaver was a surgeon, so he would know how to sew presumably. That made him the most obvious suspect. The next thing was to find out if he was left-handed. Clearly he and David would have to go to see Roger Cleaver again in the morning and at some point that poor girl with her tiny baby was going to find out that her husband was having an affair with her best friend. Awful the tangled webs we weave, he thought, which of course brought him full circle back to Felicity and where she could have gone. Somehow he had to get her to her mother's funeral.

Suddenly he had an idea; suddenly he knew where she would be.

13

Driving to work the following morning, Keith's thoughts were interrupted by a text. At the first available parking place, he pulled off the A30. In his mind, he was quite certain that the text would be from Felicity. It was not. Worse than that it was from Neil Mavers asking him to come and see him in his office before he did anything more with regard to the Beckett case. Already bad-tempered from lack of sleep, stress and concern for Felicity, this was all Keith needed. He swore under his breath as he started the car again. When he arrived at the station ahead, he was early for his agreed rendezvous with David so he took the stairs two at a time and rapped none too gently on Neil Mavers' door.

'Come.'

Keith entered. Neil was sitting with his feet propped up on his desk. He made no attempt to move when Keith came in, which Keith found not only annoying but extremely ill-mannered.

'You wanted to see me?' he said through gritted teeth.

'Ah yes, Keith,' said Neil, at last taking his feet off the desk but making no attempt to stand up by way of greeting. 'We've had a complaint from Jerry Beckett. Apparently you have been hassling his son and from what he says it sounds as if you could have been a great deal more gentle with the boy, particularly as he had just lost his mother.'

'Have you talked to David Sterling about this?' Keith asked.

'No, not yet.'

'When you do, you will find that I was extremely gentle with the boy. He is a nice kid under a lot of stress and I was aware of that. The reason you've had a complaint from Jerry Beckett is absolutely nothing to do with my handling of his son.'

'That is not what he says,' said Neil.

'Jerry Beckett lied. He lied to a serious enough degree that if we wanted to be vicious we could pull him in for perverting the course of justice. Of course we're not likely to do that when he has been so recently widowed and is obviously in a complete state. The fact remains, he lied and his son told the truth and that is what he doesn't like.'

'It seems to me you trapped the boy, boxed him in,' said Neil, when Keith had explained about the

Thursday afternoons and how Jerry had first denied knowing about them until Adam had explained what his mother got up to on Thursday afternoons.

'What do you mean, boxed him in?' Keith said.

'Well, you said you wanted the boy present, then you asked his father what his mother did on Thursday afternoons. With the boy present, not unreasonably, Jerry did not want the boy to know what his mother was up to. What is the boy's name, incidentally?'

'Adam,' said Keith.

'It really isn't unreasonable for a father to protect a sixteen-year-old boy from the knowledge that his mother was having an affair, so he had no alternative but to lie in front of Adam. You placed him in a position where, if he told the truth, it could damage his son.'

'But his son already knew,' said Keith.

'Yes, but did Jerry know that? I think you were wrong to insist on interviewing them together.'

'Jerry Beckett lied to me when his son was not even present, when he had no one to protect but himself.'

'And his wife's reputation.'

'His wife is dead and we need to find out why,' Keith thundered.

'I'm aware of that,' said Mavers with a supercilious smile.

'The important thing,' said Keith, 'is the knowledge that Adrianne Beckett was having an affair with her best friend's husband which in turn gives us at least three suspects.'

'How do you see that?'

Keith sighed with frustration. 'Well, it's obvious isn't it, Roger Cleaver, Jane Cleaver, Jerry Beckett – they all had a reason for wanting Adrianne dead.'

'I think Jerry Beckett is genuinely upset about his wife's death, devastated I would say,' Mavers said piously.

'That doesn't preclude him from being a murderer,' said Keith. 'In my experience, murderers often feel remorse, particularly if they have killed someone close to them. It is easy for their behaviour to be misconstrued as nothing more than grief.'

'A crime of passion,' Neil said.

'Hardly,' said Keith, 'you don't gather stones and meticulously sew them into the pockets of your intended victim in a moment of passion. It was a calculated murder. Whoever wanted Adrianne dead, planned it.' Keith stood up and began pacing the room. 'Having said all that, I don't see Jerry Beckett as the killer, I think it is far more likely to be Roger Cleaver, assuming that he is left-handed.'

'Why left-handed?' Neil asked.

'Because Horace Greenaway reckons whoever

sewed the stones into those pockets was left-handed and there is also the fact that as Roger Cleaver is a surgeon there is a good chance that his stitching might be rather neat.'

'So have you established whether he is left-handed?'

'That is where I am off to this morning.'

'You are putting a lot of store by the path lab.'

'He is an old horror but he is top of his class is Horace when it comes to sniffing out a mystery.'

'Just don't go upsetting anyone else, Keith,' said Neil, standing up. 'I have to go now, I have back-to-back meetings all morning.'

Pompous idiot, thought Keith as he strode back down the corridor.

David was waiting for him at the door to the canteen. 'Want a cup of coffee before we go?'

'No thanks,' said Keith. 'Let's go up to the hospital and see if we can make Roger Cleaver squirm a little.'

'I gather you are not flavour of the month over your handling of Jerry Beckett yesterday?'

'And I gather you will be called upon to defend my honour,' said Keith.

'Don't worry, I'll do that.'

'Only if you think it's right.'

'I do. I didn't when we started but if Adam hadn't been present when we interviewed his father, we would never have known about Adrianne's affair.'

'Exactly,' said Keith.

There was no waiting for the great man today; Roger Cleaver had come in on his day off to catch up on some urgent paperwork and was in his office.

'Oh, not you two again,' he said. But at least, unlike Neil Mavers, he had the manners to stand up and shake both their hands.

'This won't take long,' Keith said, 'I gather you were having an affair with Adrianne Beckett, something you neglected to tell us yesterday?'

'I didn't neglect to tell you,' said Roger Cleaver with a slight smile, 'you neglected to ask me.'

'We'll let that one pass, sir,' said Keith, 'but I would have thought that as we were discussing a possible murder victim, it's information you should not have withheld from us.'

'How did you find out?' Roger Cleaver asked.

'Adam Beckett knows.'

Roger let out a low whistle. 'Did he now and how long had he known?'

'I've absolutely no idea,' said Keith, 'how long has your affair been ongoing?'

'About six years,' said Roger.

'So maybe,' said Keith, 'it was getting a little stale, maybe you'd had enough, particularly with your wife at home with a new baby. Maybe you felt it was time to make more of an effort where your marriage was concerned, in which case Adrianne Beckett was in the way. Did she perhaps threaten to tell Jane, after all she was supposed to be her best friend?'

'I can see where you are going with this,' said Roger, 'but I can assure you I did not murder Adrianne, I both liked her and admired her and yes, we did meet once a week, so obviously I found her physically attractive as well but we were both happy with the arrangement, neither of us wanted to break up our marriages. I am good friends with Jerry and, as you say, Adrianne was best friends with Jane.'

'Wasn't it awkward when the four of you met?' David burst out.'

'You are a very young man,' said Roger, 'when you are young, passions run high, jealousies are all-consuming, insecurities often lead to self-destruction. Adrianne and I were relaxed and secure in our relationship – we enjoyed our Thursday afternoons but that's where it stopped, in its own self-contained bubble. When we met at other times in the week it was absolutely no problem for either of us. I suppose you could say we had a sophisticated attitude to our relationship.'

'Some might use different words to describe

cheating on your respective spouses, I would have thought,' said Keith. 'And your wife had absolutely no idea?'

'Absolutely none. She is a dear girl, without a mean bone in her body. It would never have occurred to her that Adrianne and I were anything other than good friends and in most respects that is how it was.'

'And if she had found out, Jane, I mean, could this have resulted in her reacting violently, women's' hormones can be all over the place after childbirth?'

'She would have been devastated, yes,' said Roger, 'but violent, no. You've met Jane, you must see that.'

Keith nodded in silent agreement, and stood up. 'Well, thank you very much for your time. Oh, just one thing, the stones in the pockets of Adrianne's coat had been sewn into place with very neat cross stitch. I imagine as a surgeon, sewing must be something you are pretty good at?'

'I am a consultant surgeon,' said Roger, 'it is years since I sewed up anyone.'

'Are you left or right-handed?' Keith asked.

'Right-handed,' said Roger, in an instant blowing apart his theory.

'Damn it,' said Keith, once they were outside the hospital, 'I had him all fitted up for it.'

'Me too,' said David. 'Although I have to admit partly because I cannot stand the man, he is such a slimy toad.'

'Say what you mean, won't you, David! Come on, let's go and see Horace again, he will be very pleased to meet you. He is a huge fan.'

Horace kept them waiting a few minutes and then appeared looking particularly rotund in his theatre gown and wellington boots.

'Oh my God,' he said, 'it's David Sterling. I am extremely honoured to shake you by the hand, young man, and who on earth is this you have dragged along with you?'

'Only the boss,' said David, smiling.

'Boss, he's not even a real policeman any more! All righ, Penrose?'

'All right until I walked in here,' grumbled Keith.

'I'm in the middle of chopping up a body so can you make this quick?'

'Are you absolutely sure,' said Keith, 'that the stitching on those coat pockets of Adrianne Beckett's was done by a left-handed person?'

'I can't be absolutely sure,' said Horace. 'After all some people are ambidextrous and some people do one thing with their right hand and another with their left. For example a lot of left-handed people eat right-handed.'

'I understand that,' said Keith, impatiently.

'Good,' said Horace, mildly. 'I do believe that the person who sewed up those pockets did so using their left hand and holding the coat with their right hand, that is all I am saying. Got it?'

'Yes,' said Keith, tersely.

'I'd have thought you would have got your man by now, Penrose. Losing your touch?'

'And good morning to you too, Horace,' said Keith, as he stomped out of the lab.

'Are you two always like that?' David asked as they climbed back into Keith's car.

'Yes,' said Keith. 'We were at primary school together; we've been friends ever since.'

'Ah,' said David, 'forgive me, that's friendship?'

'Certainly,' said Keith, 'and what I have to say about old Horace, is that he is rarely wrong. The other thing he mentioned was insulin as being a means of stunning a non-diabetic person so they could not prevent themselves from drowning but non-detectable at autopsy. Could you have a go on your computer again this afternoon and see if any member of the Beckett or Nicholls family are diabetic?'

'Getting access to medical records is not easy, as you know, sir,' said David.

'You'll think of something,' said Keith.

'What will you be doing this afternoon?'

'Thinking,' said Keith.

Having dropped off David, Keith made for Malpas, his favourite thinking venue and a good place also to walk Harvey. He walked along the side of the estuary for a while with Harvey, then gave him a bowl of water and a Bonio and sat down on a bench, Harvey beside him. He reached into his pocket and pulled out his mobile, searching through his contacts until he found the name Josh Buchanan. He had realised the previous evening that whenever Felicity was in trouble or sad, like a homing pigeon she always returned to Oxford. She maintained, and he believed her, that she had settled into life in St Ives and had no desire to leave Cornwall again, but none the less, when things went wrong she made for Oxford. Normally, in the past, she would have gone straight to her best friend Gilla but Gilla was dead and without doubt, Josh was the next best thing. He was Gilla's former lover and father to Felicity's god-daughter, Ellie. Keith wasn't particularly fond of Josh. He had only met him a few times – Josh was good-looking, clever and amusing, but he also knew it and Keith could never abide people who were pleased with themselves – still needs must.

Keith did not really expect him to answer the

phone, assuming he was at work. Josh had been a partner in the law practice of which Charlie Paradise had been the senior partner, but much to his surprise Josh answered on the first ring.

'I've been waiting for your call, Keith,' he said without preamble.

'What do you mean?' said Keith. 'How did you know I was going to ring you?'

'I've been sworn to secrecy, so I couldn't ring you because I promised Fizzy I wouldn't, but I knew it was only a matter of time before you worked out where she would be.'

'So she is with you! Is she all right? Is she safe?' Keith asked anxiously.

'She was with me,' said Josh. 'She left this morning.'

'Damn,' said Keith, 'where has she gone now?'

'Well, she came here by train. I think she was sufficiently in a state that she didn't want to drive, so she left her car in Truro I think, or maybe , I'm not sure. In any event, she has gone off by train again, and is planning to stop off at Exeter.'

'Exeter!' Keith's heart did a double beat. 'Did she say why?'

'No, in fact she has been most un-Fizzy like. She has said absolutely nothing at all about anything. I have just assumed that you two have had a row. Am I right?'

'Yes,' said Keith.

'And I suppose you are not going to tell me what it is about either?'

'No, I'm not,' said Keith, 'but not because I am trying to withhold anything from you, Josh. I'm very grateful she has been with you, it's just that I am sworn to secrecy as well. I've promised to tell no one what is wrong.'

'She's not ill, is she?' said Josh.

'No, no,' said Keith. 'It's nothing like that. Did you get the impression she was going to stay in Exeter overnight?'

'Yes,' said Josh, 'I think so, well I presume so really, she didn't leave here until an hour, hour and a half ago. It would be a bit late to go on down to Cornwall tonight.'

'And she gave you absolutely no hint as to why she was going there or where she was going to stay?'

'Absolutely nothing, old boy, sorry.'

'Right,' said Keith. 'I'd better get in the car, drive to Exeter and try and find her.'

'Bit of a needle in a haystack, won't it be? There are hundreds of hotels in Exeter.'

'Well, I'll just have to try,' said Keith. 'Thanks Josh.'

'If she does get in touch with me again, shall I tell her that you are on your way to find her?'

'Probably not,' said Keith, after a moment's

pause. 'Just say I've been in touch with you and I send my love – keep it simple.'

'OK,' said Josh, 'but when this is all over I expect a full explanation from you both. Keeping me in the dark like this is a true test of friendship.'

'Promise,' said Keith and rang off.

In the days when he was a full-time policema, he always kept a clean shirt, razor and toothbrush in his office so that he could travel at the drop of a hat, but not any more. He drove round to Tesco, bought a few toiletries and a clean shirt for himself and some dog food for Harvey, then he headed out of Truro towards the A30.

It was nearly half-past-six when he reached Exeter. On the way up A30, he decided that it would be best to check one or two of the hotels immediately around the station. It seemed to him improbable that if Felicity was to stay the night she would go very far from the station.

It was a beautiful spring evening. He parked his car in the station car park and clipping a lead on Harvey, thought he might as well start with the hotel at which he had stayed what now seemed a lifetime ago. As he crossed the road he saw a signpost for the cathedral and suddenly without a shadow of doubt he abandoned all thoughts of hotels and started out towards the cathedral. That is where he would find her, he was certain. Felicity adored evensong; she was not particularly religious but she loved the sound of choristers and if ever they were in Truro or Oxford in the late afternoon she would look longingly in the direction of the cathedral – she found evensong the perfect way to end the day.

Harvey was rather nonplussed by the bustle of the city but once they got out on to the cathedral green, he visibly relaxed. One of the doors was open and the beautiful sound of the choristers' voices rose into the evening air. All around the green were restaurants and bars, the sky was still a bright blue but mellowed slightly by streaks of orange, it was beautiful. He realised that with Harvey in tow, he could not go into the cathedral so he would have to wait for the service to finish. The question was which door to stand by? He was so convinced that Felicity was there, it never occurred to him that he might be waiting in vain; it was just a question of making sure he didn't miss her. He did a complete circuit of the cathedral and decided there was only one likely exit from which people would leave and he stationed himself close by and sat on a wall to wait.

As he waited he tried to work out what he would say to her when he saw her. So much depended on why she was here. Had she simply come to the cathedral to pay her respects to her mother in her own way? It was still four days before the funeral but this is where her mother would come and maybe this was where Felicity wanted to say goodbye. The other alternative was that she was going to see Otto Juniper, that she had decided she wanted to know more about her mother or even that she wanted to go to the funeral. Somehow Keith doubted this, but maybe their days apart had made her think. A woman hurried by, someone he recognised but for a moment couldn't place. Then he remembered it was the woman from the newsagents; obviously she was coming to collect her son, the chorister. It must mean the service was nearly over. He stood up and sure enough a trickle of worshippers began to walk out of the exit he had favoured. There was a surprising crowd of people.Keith peered anxiously, terrified of missing her. Suddenly beside him, Harvey stiffened, ears pricked and there she was strolling across the grass, head down, lost in thought, oblivious of their presence. Keith unclipped Harvey's lead and the dog bounded across the grass towards his mistress, yelping with excitement.

'Harvey!' she cried and knelt down to scoop him into her arms, then she looked up and saw Keith walking towards her. Her eyes were filled with tears and she smiled at him a little uncertainly.

'How on earth did you know I would be here?' she asked.

'Don't be daft,' he replied, 'I'm a policeman.'

14

They didn't touch but stood awkwardly like a couple of teenagers staring at one another, trying to read how each was feeling.

'Are you staying overnight here?' Keith asked. Felicity nodded.

'Where?'

'There is a hotel opposite the station.'

'That's where I thought you might stay,' said Keith, 'it's where I stayed. Are you hungry?'

Felicity shook her head.

'When did you last eat?'

'I'm not sure, yesterday I think.'

'Right,' said Keith. 'Here's what we'll do. Let's go back to the hotel. I'll feed Harvey and put him in my car and then we'll go out to dinner. You see that little Thai restaurant over there,' he pointed to the far side of the cathedral green, 'that looks a nice place. I'll nip over there now, if you hold Harvey, and book a table.'

They didn't talk much on the short walk back

to the hotel. They parted outside. 'I'll meet you in the foyer in, what, fifteen minutes,' said Keith, very anxious not to crowd her.

'OK,' said Felicity. She looked forlorn as if their lack of intimacy upset her, but instinctively he knew he had to be very careful not to frighten her off. He fed Harvey in the back of his car then settled him on a blanket on the back seat, an arrangement of which the dog clearly did not approve.

'I'll be back very soon,' Keith lied.

In the foyer Keith sat in a leather armchair pretending to read the paper. What if she did a bunk again? But why would she, surely there was no point? Then suddenly there she was, wearing the mad purple coat he loved and a bright red scarf.

'I've suddenly realised I might be hungry,' she admitted.

With the food ordered and a bottle of wine between them, Keith took a deep breath and started. 'So, why did you go to Oxford?' he asked.

'I always run away to Oxford, don't I?' she said. Keith nodded. 'I went and looked at my old home, not the home I shared with Charlie, the house where I grew up in Staverton Road. There was a teddy bear sitting in the window of the room that used to be my bedroom. It was rather comforting to know another child lives there now. It is a lovely old house. Being there made me appreciate that throughout my childhood, I had every possible comfort: a private education, a car on my seventeenth birthday, skiing holidays with the school – my father did his very best and I wanted for nothing. Compared with most children, I was hugely privileged and, yes, I lost my mother but some children lose both their parents or are abused by them and end up being pushed from one foster family to the next. I was so lucky and it made me realise I've been making a huge fuss. It made me feel ashamed in ever thinking myself to be some sort of victim.'

Keith thought it wisest not to comment. 'So why are you here in Exeter?' he asked.

'I wasn't intending to come but when I realised the train was going to travel through Exeter, I remembered you said my mother's funeral would be here next Wednesday so I thought I would stop off and…'

'And what?' said Keith.

'I'm not sure, really,' said Felicity. 'I went to evensong as clearly you knew I would. I hadn't really thought beyond that.'

Keith topped up their glasses. 'Can I stay the night?' he asked.

'It is a double room,' Felicity said, 'but what do we do about Harvey?'

'There is a side entrance to the hotel and back stairs which take you up to all the floors, we can smuggle him in.'

'Is that the way you smuggled in your woman the other night when you stayed over?'

'Yes,' said Keith, 'I brought them both in that way!'

They chatted throughout supper about Josh and Oxford, how Ellie was doing, about Keith's case – anything but the purpose for which they were both in Exeter. Felicity went up to the hotel room while Keith collected Harvey and crept up the back stairs. Harvey was overjoyed to see his mistress again. They took turns in the bathroom, they were oddly shy together. Keith was in bed first, followed by Harvey who jumped up and settled himself on the end of the bed.

'That's not allowed,' said Felicity, frowning as she came out of the bathroom.

'Just this once,' said Keith. 'He's had a tiring day, he's missed you and he's not the only one.' He held out his arms. For a moment she hesitated and then flew into them.

It was only just after three but Felicity knew she was not going to sleep again that night. Keith was flat out beside her and the light from the street outside highlighted the dark circles under his eyes, which she had first noticed at dinner. The poor man was clearly exhausted and that was hardly surprising. She knew she had not been fair – how could she expect him to understand how she was feeling when she barely understood herself? Why was she here in Exeter? Why the mad dash to Oxford? Being without her mobile phone had been a blessed relief for her but not for those who cared about her. They must have been worried sick. She wondered if he had told Martin and Mel, or indeed anyone else, about her mother – could she blame him if he had? Slipping out of bed, she tiptoed to the bathroom, shut the door and sat on the bath looking into the mirror over the basin. Staring at her reflection she saw that she had changed. She was no longer frantic, no longer running. She loved Keith. She was with him again and for the first time since she had picked up the newspaper at Paddington Station, she felt safe. She must have gone temporarily mad, she thought, to put the man she loved so much through this ordeal when he had just started working again. It was so selfish. She stood up, suddenly needing to be close to him again and when she opened the bathroom door, she saw him struggling into a sitting position in bed.

'There you are,' he said. 'I was worried where you had gone.'

She climbed in beside him and he slipped an arm around her. 'I won't be running away any more,

Keith,' she said, 'provided that is you still want me to stick around?'

'I'll have to think about that one,' said Keith, but she could feel him smiling. 'So what do you want to do tomorrow, I mean today?'

'Go home,' said Felicity.

'And not see Otto Juniper?' Keith asked.

Felicity turned in his arms.

'Are you serious? You still want me to do that?'

'Yes,' said Keith, 'yes, I really do.'

'But why, Keith? Why, when you know how much I hate the man, how I don't ever want to go anywhere near him?'

'That is exactly why I want you to meet him,' said Keith.

'But if I am comfortable putting the whole thing behind me, why can't you be?'

'Because I want to spend the rest of my life with you,' said Keith, 'and I want to spend the rest of my life with someone who is at peace with themselves. I don't care what you say, this opportunity will pass and it will never come back – and there is something else, you didn't give me a chance to tell you the other day.'

'What?' Felicity asked.

'It wasn't his fault that you didn't see your mother again. It wasn't his fault and it wasn't hers, either.'

'How is that possible?'

'I'm not prepared to tell you,' said Keith. 'The only person who can tell you properly is Otto.'

15

Keith and Felicity presented themselves at Otto's imposing front door at ten-thirty the following morning. The same dragon of a woman answered the door and appeared only slightly less frosty until she saw Felicity. She stared at her very hard and then managed a small smile.

'If you would like to come with me,' she said, 'and wait in the hall, I will tell Otto that you have arrived.'

'Who is she?' Felicity whispered when she disappeared through a doorway.

'The housekeeper,' said Keith. 'She is absolutely terrifying. I had an awful job getting past her the first time but she certainly knows who you are, doesn't she?'

'She stared at me long enough, that's for sure.' Felicity shivered, it was obvious she was very nervous.

'And smiled,' said Keith, squeezing her hand. 'I didn't believe she could smile, amazing!'

Otto was standing by the fireplace when they entered the drawing room. He, too, was clearly very agitated. Keith had rung ahead to say that Felicity had agreed to see him and he had dressed for the occasion. He wore a soft grey suit with a purple waistcoat and purple matching tie. With his white hair and extraordinarily distinguished features, he was quite a sight to behold. When he saw Felicity he gasped and put a hand to his mouth.

'Oh, my God,' he said, 'you are so like your mother.'

Felicity stood rooted to the spot. She had gone very pale and didn't seem able to speak. They stared at one another for a long moment and then Otto's impeccable manners surfaced.

'I am so sorry. Coffee Keith, Felicity?'

'Not for me,' said Keith. 'I am going to leave you two together. I will be back in say, what, half an hour?' Both Otto and Felicity looked at him beseechingly.

'Do you need to go?' Felicity managed.

'Honestly, it is best if you get to know one another without me cluttering up the place.' He smiled at her; it was like leaving a small child on her first day at school. 'I'll be back,' he said and hurriedly left the room to avoid further argument.

Outside the dragon housekeeper eyed him with something approaching approval. 'Would you like to wait in the study?'

'No, thanks,' said Keith. 'My car is just outside. There is a dog who needs walking and I have some phone calls to make.'

'She is so like Sophia,' the dragon said.

'Is she?' said Keith.

'Oh yes! It is marvellous that you brought her here. It will make all the difference to Otto.'

'I hope so,' said Keith. He glanced towards the closed door. 'We'll just have to hope for the best, she was very reluctant to come.'

'Otto will make her feel pleased she did, everyone is always pleased to be in his company. It is one of his many gifts.'

Keith smiled. 'I can imagine that, I will be back about eleven.'

Back in his car Keith called David Sterling.

'Where are you?' David asked.

'Exeter,' said Keith.

'What still?'

'Yes.'

'You haven't been to see …'

'No, I haven't been to see the Nicholls. I know the rules. I can't even blow my nose without permission. What's happening?'

'Nothing,' said David. 'I've checked everyone and none of them are diabetic and please don't ask me how I found out.'

'I won't,' said Keith, 'other than to ask you if you are absolutely sure.'

'I'm absolutely sure.'

'Well,' said Keith, 'so much for Horace's theory that we were looking for a left-handed diabetic. If he is right, that rules out the immediate family.'

'I don't know why we are assuming it might be someone close to Adrianne who killed her. For all we know, we should be searching for some random killer and the only common link between Morwenna and Adrianne is the fact that they were in the wrong place at the wrong time.'

'OK,' said Keith, 'but presumably the nationwide search threw up nothing?'

'What nationwide search?' David asked, puzzled.

'When you have two or more unexplained deaths with several common features, it goes without saying that you check the national database for any matches. Please tell me Mavers organised that?'

'No, definitely not.'

'What! I'm sorry David, but all leave is cancelled. Please get on with it right away. Good God, what was the man thinking of?'

'It's going to take a while, sir.'

'Not really,' said Keith, 'if you look for unexplained deaths or presumed suicides involving young to middle-aged women in the last, sa,y ten years. If we are looking for a random killer then he – presumably it is a he – will have killed more than these two. I just assumed the search had been done before I became involved. It is unbelievable, it's standard procedure.'

'OK,' said David, 'I'm on to it. When will you be back?'

'I'm not sure,' said Keith. 'I think you'd better write me off for today.'

'You are OK, aren't you? In view of this, it would be good to have you here. There's nothing wrong, I hope?'

'No, I'm fine,' said Keith. 'It's just a personal thing that needs sorting out. I'll be at the station at nine o'clock tomorrow morning but don't hesitate to call me if anything breaks.'

After giving Harvey a short walk and feeling full of trepidation, Keith rang the doorbell of Otto's house once more. The dragon answered almost immediately.

'It is going well, very well,' she said. Her face was transformed, she looked almost friendly.

'Are you sure?' said Keith.

'Yes, absolutely sure. Shall I bring you some coffee? Go right in.'

Keith opened the door to the drawing room to see Felicity and Otto sitting close together on the sofa with what was clearly a photograph album open on their knees. They were talking so intently that they didn't hear him come in. Then Otto glanced up and saw him.

'Keith,' he said, 'I'm showing Felicity pictures of her mother when she was about the same age as Felicity is now – they are so alike.'

Felicity looked up at Keith. 'He is an old flatterer,' she said. 'My mother was much better-looking than me.'

'Should I be the judge of that?' said Keith. They handed the photograph album to him. There were several pictures but the one that grabbed his attention was of Otto and Sophia sitting on a swinging seat together, obviously on a terrace somewhere hot. Otto was looking straight at the camera and Sophia at Otto with such love in her eyes. It was an expression that Keith knew and recognised because he had been the recipient of such a look and he knew suddenly in one heart-stopping moment how lucky he was. 'Otto is right,' he said, smiling at them both. 'Two peas in a pod! Tell me Otto, did Sophia ever take any notice of anything you said?'

'Never,' said Otto.

'And she was a woman of great mood-swings and passion?'

'Absolutely,' said Otto.

'There you go,' said Keith, 'carbon copy.'

The coffee arrived.

'Come and sit with us, Margot,' Otto said to the dragon. 'So what do you make of Sophia's daughter?'

'Lovely,' said Margot. 'A great comfort to know Madam lives on in someone. Do you have children, Felicity?'

'Yes,' said Felicity, 'I have two and four grandchildren.'

'I hardly know how to ask,' Otto began, suddenly looking very vulnerable.

Felicity touched his arm. 'It's OK, you don't have to ask. I will bring them all on Wednesday if that is what you would like.'

'What I would like! It would make everything possible. It would make sense of her death to know that she continues to live through you and your children and if you all come, I will play, once more – just once more.'

'You'll play?' said Keith, increduously.

Otto looked across at Margot. 'Margot has been trying to persuade me to play for one last time. I said no, I will never play the violin in public again, not without Sophia. But as Margot said, I would not be without Sophia. She will be there too as always, and if her family are there, I can do it,' he hesitated. 'Please tell no one, the press will go mad and the public will turn Sophia's funeral into a concert.'

'Of course not,' Felicity and Keith said in unison.

'I think that is a wonderful way to end a truly marvellous career,' said Keith, visibly moved.

'Exactly,' said Margot. 'Exactly, this is how to end it.'

An hour later Keith edged the car off the slip road onto the A30. Felicity had been quiet since leaving Otto Juniper's house. She had been leafing through the photographs he had given her, but now she placed them back in the large envelope and put them in her bag.

'You were right, of course,' she said.

Keith smiled at her as she put her hand on his knee. 'It's the "of course" that really blows me away,' he said.

'Don't let it go to your head,' said Felicity, 'but I am so grateful, Keith. I shall always be grateful that you made me see him and hear their story.'

'I'm just hoping it doesn't make you feel angry with your father. I was worried it would affect your view of him. I presume Otto told you all about the court cases?'

'Yes,' said Felicity, 'and strangely, no, it doesn't change anything much. You see, it was impossible to get to know Father well. He was such a buttoned-up person, and in an odd way it came as no surprise that not only had he fought to keep me, but that he hadn't told me anything about it, not even when I was grown up.'

'Was he ashamed, do you think?'

'No, I don't think so. I just think he was a terribly poor communicator. He simply didn't know how to tell me. In a strange way it is almost comforting.'

'Really?' said Keith. 'I thought you'd be angry and sad at the missed opportunities.'

'I'm sad that I never saw my mother again. I'm sad too never to have met Otto because, had I done so, I would have understood how she felt about him.'

'Really?' said Keith again.

'Absolutely,' said Felicity. 'He is marvellous, isn't he?'

'Yes,' said Keith, 'yes he is, marvellous in every way.'

'And to think she saved his life. If it was not for my mother, he would have died.'

'How exactly did they meet?' Keith asked.

'You're aware he is Jewish?'

'Yes,' said Keith.

'His parents were taken away one day from his house. His mother put him in a cupboard to hide him. After the soldiers were gone, he went out into the street looking for his parents – it got dark and he was lost. My mother was returning from the British Embassy. Her father had arranged for her to be brought home because of what was happening in Berlin. Otto was sitting on the pavement trying to keep out of the wind, there is no way he would have lasted the night, the temperature was sub zero. She took him home, fed him and made him warm and the following day organised for him to go onto Kindertransport. They had to wait for two days and the Embassy told them not to leave the house so they spent the two days together. She was nineteen, he was four and that is when they bonded, for life as it turned out. I suppose when you are in danger it heightens everything. If my mother had been discovered harbouring a Jewish child, she would have suffered God knows what fate and as for Otto, undoubtedly he would have ended up in a gas chamber.'

'It is an extraordinary story,' said Keith. 'I know what it cost you but you must be inordinately proud of your mother, she was so young to do such a brave thing.'

'I am proud of her now,' said Felicity. 'I wasn't. I've spent all my life thinking she was a hard-hearted bitch. That sounds terrible, doesn't it? A terrible way to speak about your mother, but that is what I told myself. Now I know she wanted to see me and now I know what she did for Otto, I feel quite differently about her.'

'And do you regret not seeing her when you grew up?'

'Yes I do,' said Felicity.

'That was the other thing that was worrying me,' said Keith. 'I don't want you feeling guilty about not seeing her.'

'I was starting to,' said Felicity, 'and then Otto made me look at it in a different way. He said that Sophia never really expected me to get in touch because she knew how hurt I must have felt. She also suffered huge guilt about choosing Otto over me, she felt it was terribly wrong but equally she didn't feel she had any control over her feelings. Once she found him she had to be with him. He felt the same, and of course, when she made the decision to leave she thought I would come too.'

'Their relationship is the stuff of legend in the music world,' said Keith. 'A grand passion, I'm not sure they exist anymore.'

'Oh, I see,' said Felicity, 'so you have no feelings of grand passion so far as I'm concerned.'

'We are the exception,' said Keith smiling, 'there will be plenty of grand passion when I get you home, you'll see.'

'Promises, promises,' said Felicity.

16

James Paradise replaced the receiver. He had been sitting in the den watching the ten o'clock news when he received the call from his mother. it was a long call and once finished he went he got up abruptly and walked into the kitchen where Trish, his wife, had covered the kitchen table in invoices.

'That was mother.'

'Oh, how is she?' Trish asked. 'I've been meaning to get in touch with her, Jamie. I was going to suggest that she and Keith came up and spent the weekend with us.' When he didn't reply she looked up and saw an odd expression on his face that she couldn't place. 'What's up? She's all right, isn't she?'

'Well yes, sort of, I think, but I have to say she never fails to amaze me.'

Trish gave up all attempts at trying to sort out invoices and started to close down her laptop. 'Come on then, spill the beans.'

'Well it appears until recently I had a

grandmother.'

'What on earth do you mean?' said Trish.

'My mother's mother died a week ago.'

'That's impossible, she died when Fizzy was very small, five or six, something like that.'

'Apparently not. That was a cover story she and her father told the world. In fact her mother ran off, would you believe it, with the violinist Otto Juniper.'

'That woman! I've heard of her,' said Trish. 'She's a legend, she was his muse.'

'Not any more, she has just died and apparently she was my grandmother.'

'Oh Jamie,' said Trish. 'You look shattered.' She got to her feet and put her arms around him.

'Well there is no reason for me to be is there, except I would have loved to have known her.'

'And I would have loved to have met Otto Juniper,' said Trish.

'Well that is easily arranged, we are going to the funeral this Wednesday in Exeter.'

'Are we? We will have to take the boys out of school.'

'We will, it's their great-grandmother's funeral, they have to be there. Mother is insisting for Otto's sake apparently.'

'I am not beginning to understand any of this,' said Trish.

'Believe me,' James replied, 'it is a long story.'

'OK,' said Trish. 'Wine, beer, coffee, tea?'

'Brandy, I think,' said James, 'a large one and then I will tell you the most extraordinary story.'

Keith was just emerging from the shower when Felicity came into their bedroom.

'How was Jamie?'

'Well fine,' said Felicity, 'but he would be wouldn't he, bless him? He takes everything in his stride. He was just concerned that I was all right and said, of course, he would be there. We have agreed to meet at Exeter. Jamie doesn't want to take the boys out of school for too long. I said I would book them into a hotel.'

'I bet he had a lot of questions,' said Keith, towelling his hair.

'Yes, he did.'

'I bet Trish will be surprised and more than a little miffed,' said Keith, smiling, 'you know Radio Three is her constant companion. She will be livid to have missed out on all these years of knowing Otto Juniper.'

'It's not too late to put that right,' Felicity reminded him.

'No, so you haven't tackled Mel yet?'

Felicity shook her head. 'I told Jamie not to ring her until tomorrow, I can only cope with one of them at a time. I thought I would ask them all over to lunch tomorrow to break the news.'

'Good idea,' said Keith.

'Mel is going to throw a wobbly, isn't she?' Felicity said, sitting down on the bed.

'Probably,' said Keith. 'You know I am devoted to your daughter but somehow she will turn this story round so it is all about her missing out on a grandmother.'

'Jamie just remembers Charlie's mother but Mel never met her. They both knew my father, of course, but he was hardly a cosy grandpa and when he went into a care home they were very bad about visiting him.'

'However, history has not repeated itself – Jamie and Mel's children have a perfectly splendid grandmother,' Keith said, kissing her soundly.

'Mel and Martin would prefer to come to lunch on Sunday rather than today,' Felicity shouted down the stairs to Keith.

'That's fine,' said Keith, 'except I may not be here tomorrow.'

'Why not?'

'I really need to do some work. I'm hoping to catch up with David tomorrow because we should have the results back from the nationwide search for crimes of a similar type. Of course, there may be no matches in which case that is that, but if there is anything that looks hopeful we need to get our ducks in a row ready for Monday.'

'Couldn't you do it today?' Felicity asked.

'No, today is Saturday,' said Keith coming up the stairs.

'So?' Felicity said.

'On Saturday, David plays rugby. Not only would he never forgive me if he had to miss a game, but as far as I can understand it neither would the rest of Cornwall.'

'Ah, I see' said Felicity. 'Well as this is so important, they will jolly well have to come for lunch today, I'll mention roast lamb that should do it.'

Trying to persuade a three- and a five-year-old to sit at the table and eat a meal was a full-time occupation for the four adults and it wasn't until Charlie had been taken downstairs for a nap and Minty was settled in the sitting room with a Brio trainset, that Felicity could explain the reason for the lunch. She told the story as briefly as she could. She attempted to explain why she had told no one about her mother, and then paused, looking hopefully from Martin to Mel, seeking their understanding.

'Well,' said Martin, 'I am very sad for you of

course, but I am also in a weird way strangely relieved.'

'Why?' Keith asked.

'I just couldn't work out how it could be that you two had fallen out in what appeared to be such a serious way.'

'Hang on a moment,' said Mel, pouring herself another glass of wine. Keith and Felicity groaned inwardly. 'You're telling me that I've had a grandmother all these years and I never had the opportunity to meet her because you were bearing a grudge. That is bad enough but fancy not telling me, fancy not letting me make my own decision as to whether I wanted to meet her or not.'

'I told no one,' said Felicity, 'not even your father. The only person who ever knew about her, until I told Keith, was Gilla and she only knew because she was there when it happened.'

'I don't think you had the right to keep this to yourself,' Mel said. 'I think it is disgraceful. My children had a great-grandmother and they never got the chance to meet her, I don't know what you were thinking about Mum, it is awful to keep a secret like that, it is so selfish.'

'I wonder if you would say the same thing if I had abandoned you when you were six years old,' said Felicity.

Keith could tell immediately that Felicity was

close to tears so he waded in hurriedly to support her. 'Minty will be six next year, Mel. Can you imagine what it would be like for her if you suddenly disappeared out of her life? Then, as she grew older, it became increasingly clear that you had disappeared not because you had died or been separated as people are by war or circumstances. How would she feel if she knew you had gone simply because you wanted to live with another man other than your father, that you had chosen him instead of her. Can't you see how it would affect the whole of her life?'

'I would like to think that Minty would have the good sense to share the experience with her children.'

'I couldn't,' said Felicity. 'The only way I have dealt with this is to bury it. I never thought about it, I never ever thought about my mother – it was the way I coped. My father and I dreamed up the cover story of her dying and that was so much easier and after a bit it seemed real…' she hesitated. 'I have to admit that she did try to contact me both when I married and when Jamie was born.'

'Oh, so she didn't bother to contact you when I was born?'

'I think she had given up by then, Mel.'

'It is just so selfish of you.'

'I think that is enough now, Mel,' said Keith. 'I

think you should do some hard thinking before you say any more.'

'And who are you to tell me what I should do?' Mel said.

'Keith is right,' said Martin. 'Just shut up for a minute Mel, could you. Felicity, you want us at the funeral, I imagine?'

'Yes, I want you all at the funeral including Charlie. Otto does too, very much.'

'It's a bit late now, isn't it? Mel said.

'This is not about you, Mel, I am asking you to do it for me,' said Felicity quietly.

'We'll be there,' said Martin.

'Jamie and Trish and the boys are coming,' Felicity added, her voice trembling.

'And I suppose golden boy Jamie was all sweetness and light, telling you what a wonderful mummy you were for not telling us we had a grandmother.'

'He didn't say that,' said Felicity, 'but he did seem to understand.'

'I'm not at all sure I will be going to the funeral,' said Mel, standing up, 'and I think we should go home now.'

Martin also rose from the table. 'Well, I will be there, Fizzy,' he said, 'and I will be bringing Sophia's great-grandchildren with me.'

'You're just so disloyal,' said Mel and

thundered off down the stairs. 'I'll collect Charlie, you bring Minty,' and with that she was gone.

Keith and Felicity sat in silence after the door had slammed shut behind them. They looked at one another.

'Families!' said Keith.

'I knew she was going to react like that, but it still hurts.'

'Don't let it, you are doing what Otto asked, what you know is right. Your children including Mel will be there and so will your grandchildren and that is how it should be.'

'I hope Mel doesn't make another scene.'

'She won't,' said Keith, 'Martin can handle her and anyway she will be overcome by the occasion. There is bound to be a mass of celebrities there and the press. The cathedral is going to look amazing and then, as you and I know, Otto is going to play for us – no, not for us of course, for your mother. It is going to be spectacular. Mel will be literally out of her depth. Trust me darling, it is all going to be absolutely fine.'

17

David was already at his computer when Keith arrived at the station on Sunday morning.

'We've had a hit,' he said, 'in fact two.'

Keith drew up a chair beside him. 'What do you mean?' he asked.

'Two bodies, both on the North Norfolk coast, same scenario, stones sewed into the pockets of their jackets, ten years ago.'

'North Norfolk?' said Keith. 'That's about as far as you can get from Cornwall, extreme west to extreme east.'

'Nonetheless,' said David, 'it all fits in. The first body was found just inland from Blakeney Point, about four years before Morwenna died. Apparently the water channels in very quickly over a bar between Blakeney Point and the mainland and any number of people have drowned there over the years as the tide comes in. So, it was just another body as far as the police were concerned.'

'But the stones must have suggested it was suicide?'

'Yes,' said David, 'and if you are going to commit suicide in that part of the world, it is a pretty sensible place to do it.'

'And the second body?' Keith asked.

'A few miles along the coast on the beach at Sheringham. Here again, it is a bit of a black spot. The beach is all pebbles, big ones, no sand at all and the waves can be very ferocious there with a big undercurrent. Again there have been deaths.'

'And was it a woman and were there stones sewn into her jacket?'

'Affirmative in both cases,' said David. 'I've arranged for both the coats to be sent straight to Horace and we are just waiting for files on both the dead women to be released to us, but there doesn't seem to be any problem and they should be e-mailed over by tomorrow morning.'

'So it looks like we could be dealing with a serial killer then?' said Keith.

'Yes,' said David. 'I haven't widened the net any further. We searched for women between sixteen and fifty. We could extend that if you wish.'

'I think what we've got is good enough for the time being,' said Keith. 'When was the Sheringham death?'

'Nine months after the Blakeney one.'

'So first there was the Blakeney death, then nine months later, Sheringham. Then a gap of two and a half years before Morwenna and then strangely a gap of six years before Adrianne. There could be more, I suppose. What have you been searching for – suicides or suspicious deaths?'

'Suicides and deaths with open verdicts – any deaths really that the coroner couldn't decide upon but which fell into the criteria of what we were looking for.'

'So maybe it would be a good idea to run unresolved murders as well?'

'Could do,' said David. 'Shall I go ahead?'

'I think so,' Keith suddenly frowned and stared hard at David. 'You look awful.' He had a deep gash over his left eye and his left cheekbone had completely disappeared under a swelling which half closed the eye. He also looked exhausted. 'I assume the injuries are from your game yesterday and not a Saturday night brawl?'

'Yes,' said David, grinning. 'We won and I hope you're impressed, sir. Rather than going out on the lash with the boys after the match, I came here. I've been up all night.'

'I am impressed,' said Keith, 'but if you are going to be any use to me at all tomorrow, I think you'd better shoot off home and get some sleep.'

'So do you think this means that we've been

chasing shadows?' David asked.

'You mean Morwenna's affair with Roger Cleaver and a possible spin-off from that?'

David nodded. 'I can't see that an orthopaedic surgeon or a solicitor working in Cornwall would have the time or the inclination to go and murder two unknown women in Norfolk.'

'If they were unknown women,' Keith said. 'Widening the net like this might provide us with the common denominator we've been searching for.'

'Or it may just be some random crazy in which case we are going to have an awful job tracking him down.'

'Yes,' said Keith. 'It's the water that's the problem. By the time we get our hands on the bodies, any sort of evidence has been washed away, that and the fact that no one has seen anything suspicious. I can understand that at Gunwalloe, the season hasn't started yet and it can be a pretty isolated place. It is quite likely that there was nobody else on the beach when Adrianne went into the water but I am still struggling with how Morwenna managed to drown, at Porthminster beach of all places, without anybody noticing.'

'Very late at night?' David said.

'Well, yes, that's the only possible explanation, but even so.'

'Maybe they didn't go into the water at either beach,' said David. 'Maybe they were thrown into the water from a boat and the bodies simply came ashore.'

'I've thought about that,' said Keith. 'The harbour master in St Ives has often told me that in order for a body to end up anywhere but on one of the St Ives beaches, you have got to go out pretty far to sea, well beyond Seal Island – then the body will end up at Padstow and Newquay. But with the tide and the wind in the right direction, Morwenna could have gone off the pier or out of a boat in the harbour or just beyond.'

'And at Gunwalloe?' David asked.

'I don't know,' said Keith, 'but that's something I could find out.'

It was just after midday as he drove into the village of Gunwalloe. It was a dank, miserable and overcast day, chilly, too, for March. He parked outside the pub, the Halzephron Inn. The wind was coming across the fields from the sea, it was bitter. He climbed out of the car, the car door almost whipping from his hand, and hurried into the pub. They were obviously expecting a brisk Sunday lunch trade and were busily preparing for it, but at the moment the pub was relatively empty, with three or four people propped up at the bar and a couple already seated at one of the tables. Keith approached the barman. Without his warrant card he felt positively underdressed, it made everything so difficult. Fleetingly, he thought of the woman in the newsagents in Exeter who said he looked like a policeman; he hoped that was true.

'I am investigating the recent drowning down on Church Cove,' he said. 'Is there anybody here who could tell me about the tides and currents down there?'

The barman nodded to a man sitting on a barstool. 'Dan will help you, he used to be a coastguard.'

A tall but stooped old man sat on the edge of the barstool nursing the remains of a pint, he peered at Keith from under shaggy eyebrows looking none-too-friendly. Keith nodded at his glass.

'Can I buy you the other half?' Immediately he brightened and there was even the trace of a smile. 'Same again then please and a glass of red wine for me.'

'You certainly know the way to Dan's heart,' the barman said.

Keith wasted no time. 'You know there was that drowning here a couple of weeks back?' The old man nodded. 'I am investigating the case. A body was found on Church Cove. Does that mean the victim was likely to have gone into the sea there?' Dan reached for his new drink and took a long draught followed by an equally long silence to the point where Keith was beginning to wonder whether he should ask his question again.

'The body could have gone in anywhere,' he said, at last, 'off the cliff path or even at Dollar Cove.'

'Dollar?' Keith queried.

'It's the first cove you come to when you go down to the beach. There is a rip current there. They say if you get caught up in the rip at Dollar Cove and you don't fight it, you will be landed in Church Cove.'

'When you say "they say",' said Keith, 'do you mean that is a fact?'

The old man took another swig of his beer. 'I reckon,' he said. The two men sat in silence for a moment, Keith wondering on earth to say next. 'I reckon she went in at Dollar,' Dan said, at last.

'What makes you say that?' Keith asked.

'I arrived before the police,' Dan said. 'I was down there walking my dog. A visitor spotted the body, a young woman she was and she couldn't stop screaming. I went to see what I could do to quieten her down, stayed with her until the police arrived so I got a good look at the body.'

'And?' said Keith.

'And the poor soul had been pretty badly bashed up by the rocks, covered in bruises and cuts. Now if she had walked into the sea at Church Cove, she'd have simply been washed back on to the beach. In that case, she probably would have had a few grazes but there are no rocks at Church Cove – she would not have been nearly so severely injured. But, if she went in at Dollar and the rip took her round the church to Church Cove, then the chances are she would have ended up looking like she did, God rest her.'

'Was there anything else you noticed specifically about the body?' Keith asked.

'No,' said Dan and that was clearly the end of the conversation.

Keith finished his wine, thanked the old man and left the pub. He drove up the road which then dropped down towards the beaches. He parked in the National Trust car park and walked along to the church. He saw immediately what the old man had meant. First he came to a rocky, wild-looking beach, Dollar presumably. He walked over the shingle, the tide was out, on the road to his left a couple were walking their dog, otherwise it was deserted. Whether Adrianne had committed suicide or been murdered, this was an ideal spot. He then walked on towards the church, skirting around it and onto the second beach, Church Cove and again he could see immediately what Dan meant. If Adrianne had walked into the sea at Church Cove, drowned and then been washed back up onto the beach, she would have sustained very little damage. He walked back to his car slowly, feeling uncharacteristically melancholy and more than a little defeated. Briefly, when he had discovered Adrianne's affair with Roger Cleaver, he had thought they were getting somewhere. Now with these two new murders in Norfolk, if the details of the cases matched – and it looked as if they would – it changed everything. It was a question of going back to the drawing-board and starting again. He needed a much bigger team and an office to himself, in order to progress this case. He would have to talk to George Staple in the morning.

While Keith was marching around Gunwalloe, Felicity was ironing his suit for the funeral and a dress and coat for herself. She felt slightly disorientated by the events of the last few days. The secret that had been hers for so long was now public knowledge. She had been around to Annie to ask her to look after Harvey while they were away at the funeral and told her the whole story. As well as Mel and James, she had also felt obliged to ring Josh and explain to him what had really been going on during her brief visit. There was no point in keeping it a secret any more. In one way it was a relief, she acknowledged that, but the reality was also disturbing. She had coped with her mother's abandonment by choosing to believe the cover story her father had concocted, that her mother was dead. Of course she knew it wasn't true but if you say something often enough, it takes on its own sort of reality. Knowing now that a week ago her mother had been alive made her feel extraordinarily sad and rather vulnerable.

Of course, in many respects, it was good to hear from Otto that he and her mother had tried hard to make her part of their lives. However, her absolute rejection of her mother, when Sophia had tried to contact her as an adult, made her feel churlish, downright unkind and unreasonably unforgiving. Otto had tried to reassure her that she should feel no guilt, that her mother had understood completely why she had not wanted to make contact – but it still felt wrong. Was she glad that Keith had taken matters into his own hands and exposed the truth of her mother's life and death? Yes, she supposed she was. It just seemed incredibly sad that she should be ironing a dress to attend her mother's funeral when in all the preceding years, they had never met.

It was interesting that Otto and Keith clearly liked each other so much; strange that the love of her mother's life should be instantly drawn to the love of her own, when the two men, apart from this one common thread, had really nothing in common, either in background or lifestyle. Felicity tried to imagine her mother as the nineteen-year-old, alone in Berlin, trying to take care of a little Jewish boy. It had been an extraordinarily brave thing to do, but then again at nineteen, one knows oneself to be indestructible. It was amazing that the child and the teenager should have formed such a bond in those few terrifying days, a bond that the years could not shift. Yet was it? – Otto Juniper was an extraordinary man, he had probably been an extraordinary little boy.

How strange life was. If her mother had taken a different route home, Otto would have died. If her father had not taken her mother to the concert at the Sheldonian Theatre, would she ever have found Otto again? He was adamant that without the support of her mother, he would never have reached the dizzy heights of performance that had turned him into an international star. Was that the case? Without her mother, would he have simply been a good and reliable musician? She would have grown up with a mother and father, all of them together, or would she? Would her mother have stayed with her father even without finding Otto again? It was hard to tell, impossible to know but in the last few days, she had come to acknowledge that her parents were hugely wrong for each other. Her mother – excitable, volatile, amusing, a great talker; and her father – silent, conventional, dedicated to his work. It was extraordinary that they had ever got together. Maybe her mother had married him because losing Otto and not being able find him again had affected her life, her whole life. Yet he had only been a little boy, surely not important to Sophia as a young woman. She would never know now and that too made her sad.

When Keith walked into the house half an hour later Felicity stepped straight into his arms. 'I'm sad,' she said.

'Me too,' Keith said, holding her close to him.

'Thank God we have each other,' Felicity murmured against his chest.

'Amen to that,' Keith replied.

18

A text had arrived for Keith during Sunday evening telling him to be at the station in Truro at eight o'clock the following morning for a meeting with DI Neil Mavers.

Apart from his many other unattractive attributes, Mavers was not subtle. 'Ah, there you are, Penrose! You're off the case!'

'What!' said Keith. 'Why?'

'We're dealing with a serial killer now,' said Neil. 'This is no job for a part-time retired policeman. We have to throw considerable resources behind it.'

'I was going to suggest the same thing myself,' said Keith, 'but I rather thought I could be involved.'

'No,' said Mavers. 'It's out of the question. By all means, I am happy to authorise you to have continued access to the Nicholls file since that was your original case. Certainly, as the situation develops, we may need to refer to you again, but essentially your services are no longer required.'

'What about David? What's happening to him?'

'He will be working directly for me now.'

'You can't just drop me like this, surely?' Keith said.

'Of course I can,' Mavers replied. 'As I have just explained, when we took you on – which frankly was against my better judgement – it was because we had a cold case of which you had specialist knowledge and which we believed was linked to a current crime. That is not the case anymore.'

'How do you know?' Keith said. 'How can you possibly know that there isn't still a link? Have the files arrived from Norfolk?'

'They've arrived, yes.'

'And they match up with the cases down here, same modus operandi?'

'As I have said, Keith, you are no longer on the case. Now, I really must get on.'

'You hadn't even bothered to look outside Cornwall – I cannot imagine what makes you think you are fit to run this investigation!' With that as a parting shot, Keith left the office.

He was still seething with rage when he reached his car. He immediately dialled George Staple's number.

'I've been taken off the case,' he said without preamble.

'I know,' said George. 'I'm sorry Keith, but there really is no alternative.'

'Why?' Keith asked.

'As I am sure Neil Mavers will have explained to you, as if you need to have it explained, we can't have the hunt for a serial killer headed up by someone who is no longer even in the police force. Apart from the fact it is inappropriate, imagine if the press got hold of it, they would have a field day. While we had two fairly low-key investigations which were suspicious but probably just suicide, it was a whole different ball game.'

'How can you ever have believed they were suicides when neither woman had a motive and their coat pockets were sewn up in identical ways?'

'It could have been a copy cat,' George said, defensively.

'So Adrianne Beckett remembers the details of a woman who died in St Ives six years ago and thinks one day, "I know, I'll do the same thing"? I don't think so,' said Keith, fighting to keep control of his anger.

'Look, Keith, there is no point in us arguing over this. I am extremely grateful to you because, but for you, the search would never have been widened beyond Cornwall but the fact is, as a result of your good work, we are now in a completely different league.'

'Headed up by a man who didn't have the foresight to look beyond Cornwall in the first place,' Keith said.

'Keith,' said George. 'Enough – in all honesty, there is absolutely nothing I can do about this. I am sorry.'

'This is not a vendetta on my part,' Keith said, 'but if you want this case solved you are going to have to look above and beyond Neil Mavers.'

He turned off his phone without saying goodbye, hurled it onto the passenger seat and sat brooding. Eighteen months ago the case would have been his. He would have been heading up the whole operation, overseeing developments both in Cornwall and in Norfolk – he knew exactly how he would handle it, what he would do, who he would recruit. He would insist on getting back his old sergeant, Jack Curnow. Jack had often understood him better than he understood himself. What a challenge to get to this guy, whoever he was, before someone else died. He could feel the adrenaline pumping around his system, his head swimming with ideas and all for nothing. He was no longer a policeman – that was the bottom line.

While Keith was driving glumly home, Felicity was

sitting in Annie's cosy kitchen drinking tea and eating one of Annie's famous drop scones.

'I should not be doing this,' she said, 'I only have one decent dress to wear at the funeral and it barely fits me. After a couple of these, it is going to be hopeless.'

'Rubbish!' said Annie. 'You're as thin as a wand.'

'I am so not,' said Felicity. 'Ever since Keith and I got together I've been steadily putting on weight, it's cooking for him and, well …'

'Being happy?' Annie suggested.

'That too,' Felicity admitted.

Annie cocked her head on one side, looking at Felicity shrewdly. 'So, tell me, how are you feeling about the funeral tomorrow?' Felicity took a sip of tea and considered it. 'I don't really know,' she said. 'I'm not dreading it exactly. I don't know what to expect. I just don't know how I am going to feel.'

'It must be very strange,' Annie said. 'I expect because you've always told everyone that your mother was dead, that holds more reality for you than the truth – the fact that she was alive until a few days ago.'

Felicity nodded. 'Yes,' she said. 'I did my mourning, my grieving for her, many years ago when I was a little girl. You can't feel sad about losing somebody you've already lost, somebody you don't even know …' The sentence hung in mid-air.

Annie studied her in silence and then, leaning forward, she placed her little bird-like claw on one of Felicity's hands.

'I think, my girl, you should expect to feel a great deal more deeply than you are anticipating at the moment. I think you may suddenly realise whose funeral it is and it will come as a great shock to you.'

Felicity shook her head, vehemently. 'No, it won't, Annie. I didn't even know that she was alive. She could have been dead for years for all I knew. The fact that she would live to be so old had never occurred to me. I didn't believe she was still alive.'

'Nonetheless,' said Annie, 'my advice, for what it is worth, is to expect to feel some pretty strong emotions on Wednesday. Thank heavens for that policeman of yours, he'll look after you.'

'A policeman no longer,' said Felicity.

'I thought he was back on a case?'

'Yes, he is but it is a cold case and he has to work with someone who is still in the force. He has no powers of arrest or the ability to interview anybody without someone in the force being present.'

'That must be very hard for him,' Annie said.

'To go from being a Chief Inspector to someone who has to drag an inexperienced junior officer around with him, some boy who has got more power than he has. It must be really hard. Is he enjoying it?'

'I think so,' said Felicity. 'He is certainly fired up about it all. It may be a big adjustment, but he really had nothing to do all day, Annie. He was making jobs for himself but he really had no sense of direction. This case has definitely given him a new lease of life, something to think about and, of course, he is very good at his job.'

'If we are talking about criminals, it was a criminal act to retire him when they did with all his experience and expertise,' Annie said.

'He was tired though,' said Felicity, 'particularly after that last case.'

'We're all tired,' said Annie, 'but all the better for working. You know the old saying – if you want something done, ask a busy person.'

Felicity smiled at her fondly. 'I'd better be going,' she said.

'Well take care of yourself, my girl, and remember what I say about Wednesday – it will be harder than you expect but I will be thinking of you, all day.'

'That means a great deal to me,' said Felicity, giving Annie a hug. How lucky she was to have such a friend, an unlikely friend but a true one.

Annie's thoughts on the difficulties of Keith's job had inadvertently prepared Felicity for the sight of Keith climbing the stairs, dejected, brow furrowed.

'Keith, what on earth is the matter?' she said, taking his coat, holding his hand and looking up into his face.

'Oh, nothing really, it doesn't matter,' said Keith.

'What doesn't matter? Whatever it is, it is serious.'

'I'm off the case, that's all.'

Felicity stared at him, stupefied. 'Off the case? Why?'

'They think there is a serial killer on the loose. David did some work and unearthed two more victims, exactly the same modus operandi, sewn-up pockets and all that, on the North Norfolk coast. There is no question that the deaths are linked.'

'So surely that means that they need you more than ever?' said Felicity.

Keith shook his head, miserably. 'Because I am not a policeman, now that the case has become such a big one, they have got to bring in somebody who is actually on the force – that is Neil Mavers of course – to head the thing. To quote from him, they can't have a part-time retired policeman in charge of such a big case and unfortunately George Staple is backing him up. They are worried about the press apart from anything else.'

'But that is ridiculous! You're clearly the man for the job.'

'Not any more,' said Keith. 'I do understand, I do see that as I am no longer a policeman, I shouldn't be heading up such a big case, but it is so frustrating, I'm ...' He hesitated.

'You're gagging to have a go at it,' Felicity said, smiling at him.

'Yes, yes I am.'

'And you know just what to do. You've got it all sorted in your mind, haven't you?'

Keith nodded again. 'Of course.'

'And you think Neil Mavers is going to make a complete bodge-up of it?'

'There is absolutely no doubt about that,' said Keith, smiling properly at last.

'So you're having nothing more to do with the case?' Felicity said. 'I'd better fetch you a glass of wine, I think.'

'They've left me the cold case, the Nichollses. It's a bit like throwing a bone to a hungry dog, a bone with very little meat on it,' he added, bitterly, 'but I suppose it is better than nothing. The problem is I have a feeling it is going to be difficult to persuade them to release anyone to come with me if I want to conduct any more interviews. Everyone is very stretched at the moment.'

'So will you pursue it?'

'Yes,' said Keith, 'but not until after Wednesday. The good thing that has come out of all this is that I can now concentrate one hundred percent on you and the funeral.' He put his arms around her and held her close. 'How are you feeling about it all?'

'Annie asked me that just now. I popped in to see her to make arrangements to drop Harvey around to her tomorrow morning and she said she thought I would feel more than I expect when it actually comes to the funeral.'

'Knowing Annie,' said Keith, 'she is almost certainly right and it makes sense. It probably will hit you quite hard when it actually comes to seeing the coffin.'

'I don't know,' Felicity said, a little uncertainly. 'I just don't know what I'll feel.'

'Well, whatever you feel, my love, I will be there, right beside you.'

'That's also what Annie said,' said Felicity.

They were up and about early the next morning. Felicity was conscious that Keith had not slept well but decided it was better not to raise the whole spectre of the case again. They dropped Harvey round to Annie's and were off up the A30 by nine o'clock. Martin, Mel, Minty and Charlie were coming up after lunch, and James and his family would be arriving in the early evening. They had all agreed to meet for dinner at the hotel into which they were all booked and which was close to the cathedral, within walking distance.

Felicity had a long conversation with Margot and while Otto was very keen to meet Sophia's family, they had all agreed and Otto had not argued, that it would be too much for him to do so the day before the funeral. He needed to conserve his strength and being expected to meet new people and four boisterous children was asking too much. It had been arranged that Felicity and Keith should go round for an early evening drink with Otto on their own, before meeting Mel, James and family back at the hotel.

They arrived in Exeter in time for lunch and having checked into their hotel went to a pub for a snack before wandering around the city. Inevitably, they ended up at the cathedral.

'Would you like to go inside?' Keith asked. Felicity nodded. Inside preparations were obviously being made for the funeral the following day. Several women were arranging flowers. There seemed to be a purple and white theme in the bouquets and there were going to be a lot of them, already the cathedral smelt of their scent. Up by the altar the full choir was rehearsing. 'Would you like to stay and listen for a while?' Keith said. Felicity nodded. They sat down in a pew near the front of the cathedral and held hands in silence.

'It is odd to think,' said Felicity, 'that all this preparation, all this fuss, is for my mother.' Keith nodded in agreement. The reality is starting to get to her, he thought, I wonder how on earth she is going to feel tomorrow. The choir reached a crescendo; Keith wished he was not such a philistine when it came to music – whatever it was, it was beautiful. The choirmaster then dismissed the choir and they all began hurrying off. A group of boys laughing and jostling one another, obviously a reaction to the discipline of the choir, hurried down the aisle past where Felicity and Keith were sitting. Keith suddenly recognised the bright red hair of one of the boys.

'Excuse me a moment,' he said to Felicity, hardly knowing what he was doing, but following some sort of instinct. 'Graham,' he called out. The boy stopped and turned around. 'You won't remember me,' he said.

'Yeah, I do,' Graham said. 'You came to call on my dad the other day. He told me who you are, you're a policeman, you tried to find out what happened to Mum.'

'That's right,' said Keith. 'Is your dad working anywhere close this week, close to Exeter, I mean?'

'He's not working at all,' said Graham. 'He did his back in last week and the doc has given him a week off, so he is at home resting, well, shouting at the television mostly,' he grinned.

He was a nice lad, Keith thought. 'I was wondering if I might call in to see him on Thursday morning,' said Keith. The boy looked suddenly wary. 'Don't worry if it is not convenient – I haven't got any news of any particular sort, I just wanted his advice, to be honest.'

'OK,' said Graham. 'I'll tell him, what time will you come?'

'About nine?' Keith asked.

'OK, what's your name?'

'Keith, Keith Penrose.'

'See you then,' said Graham and he turned and hurried off after his friends.

'Who was that?' Felicity asked, after he rejoined her.

'That was Graham Nicholls. He is the younger of the two boys who were left motherless when Morwenna Nicholls walked into the sea at Porthminster.'

'I thought you were off the case, Keith?'

'I am, well I'm off the main case but remember, I still have the Nicholls. I've just arranged to go and see Colin Nicholls on Thursday morning. I've made an appointment for nine o'clock. I hope that is OK, but it seemed silly not to while I'm here in Exeter?'

'Hang on a minute,' said Felicity, 'I thought you weren't supposed to interview anybody without having someone with you?'

'I'm not interviewing him,' said Keith, 'I'm asking his advice.'

'Keith, hold on, you could get into trouble,' Felicity said.

'Could I?' said Keith. 'Could I really? So what are they going to do? They can't make me redundant, they've already done that.'

'You're sounding very bitter, that's not like you at all.'

He smiled at her and took her hand, giving it a squeeze. 'I'm sorry, today and tomorrow are all about you and here I am wittering on. I just thought I would tell Colin Nicholls about the Norfolk women and see if he has got any ideas, any links.'

'Surely the police will be doing that anyway?'

'You would think so,' said Keith, 'but heaven knows what sort of dog's dinner Neil Mavers will make of everything. I don't like Jerry Beckett or Roger Cleaver, come to that, I don't particularly trust either of them, nasty types, the pair of them. You can see why they are friends. By contrast, Colin Nicholls is a decent bloke who a terrible thing happened to. I trust him and I just want to pick his brains.'

'Well, on your head be it,' said Felicity. 'The "Super" is going to go ballistic if he finds out.'

'I think I can live with that,' said Keith. 'Now, enough of me and this case, let's concentrate on you and tomorrow. The kids will all be arriving soon and ...' Keith glanced at his watch, 'we are off to Otto's in an hour, so let's go back to the hotel, freshen up and prepare ourselves.'

'You're making it sound like an ordeal,' said Felicity, in a small voice.

'I think it is going to be an ordeal,' Keith said, looking around the cathedral. 'Tomorrow this place is going to be crammed to bursting point and you and Otto are the chief mourners. You are Sophia's next of kin, you are bound to feel overwhelmed by it, I imagine.'

'Between you and Annie, you are making me thoroughly nervous.'

'That's not the intention. It is just because we both love you and are anxious that tomorrow goes as well as it possibly can and that you don't find it too overwhelming.'

Felicity gave him a small, frightened smile, 'I hope so too,' she said.

19

Neil Mavers and David Sterling were standing in George Staple's office. It was evident they were not there for a cosy chat which normally took place in the far end of his office with coffee and comfortable armchairs. Instead, they were standing in front of his desk like a couple of naughty schoolboys.

'So whose idea was it to spread the search nationwide?' George Staple thundered.

'Not mine,' said Neil Mavers, smugly. 'I reckoned we had enough to do here in Cornwall. I see this case very much as a Cornish problem that needed clearing up – we just need to satisfy ourselves that the Beckett suicide was just that, suicide. I didn't see the need to look any further, certainly not.'

'So whose idea was it then,' George said, 'if not yours?' Neil did not answer immediately, but his expression was full of self-satisfaction.

'Chief Inspector Penrose, sir,' said David.

George ignored the use of the inappropriate

title. 'So this retired nobody, as you would have me believe Keith Penrose to be,' he said, addressing Neil, 'this waste of space who should be put in a retirement home, was the only person to think outside the box? It's a bloody scandal! Surely the most obvious thing was to check that a similar incident had not occurred anywhere else in the country? Surely, Mavers, even you can see that the identical nature of these two women's alleged suicides in Cornwall has to mean that there is more to it than meets the eye, which is why I brought in Penrose.' The smug expression had left Neil Mavers' face. He had obviously thought that it was Keith Penrose who had got it wrong. It had never occurred to him that it could be him. 'So,' George shouted, slamming his first on the table, 'what is happening now?'

'We are looking through the files from Norfolk,' said Neil, 'and waiting for the path lab to confirm that the coats all have the same stitching.'

'Looking, waiting – what is this?' George shouted. 'Chase, search, dig, think. While you're sitting around scratching your asses, someone else could be dying. There has to be a link, find it and fast.'

The cathedral looked magnificent and as Keith had predicted, it was full to bursting. Otto, Felicity and

Keith sat in the front pew on the right hand side, James, Mel, spouses and children sat on the left. The number of people and the magnificence of the building even seemed to make an impression on Charlie who, at three and normally hyperactive, was surprisingly quiet. Felicity looked at Otto and on impulse put out her hand, took his and gripped it. He turned to her, surprised, and smiled. He looked very pale but composed.

'Thank you for being here,' he said. 'I don't know what I would have done without you and your family.'

It was true, Felicity thought, Otto, having never married and had children of his own, his adoptive parents and older siblings long dead and all his German family having perished in Dachau, there was no one for him but her and her family. She turned to Keith, he was staring solemnly ahead at the altar and her heart went out to him. What a good man he was and how right he had been to get her to this point. The thought of this poor old man who had loved her mother all his life, sitting here alone, didn't bear thinking about. She felt tears well into her eyes, not for her mother but for Otto, Otto who, for all of her life until a few days ago, she had loathed and despised – what a change.

The drink with Otto the previous evening had been just right. He had looked very frail and with such a big day ahead of him, Felicity was glad she'd had the good sense not to bring any of her family with her. Otto had insisted on a bottle of champagne as a celebration of Sophia's life and as they sat drinking it with Margot around the fire, he had suddenly turned to Keith and asked him if he would do a reading at the funeral, at the end during the Committal.

'Me,' said Keith, 'why me? Of course I would be delighted, honoured, but …'

'Because you brought me Felicity,' said Otto, 'and because I admire you very much.'

'That is quite a compliment, coming from you,' said Keith, clearly embarrassed.

'I have the reading here, it is the Irish Blessing, Sophia always loved it, it is so full of hope. Are you happy to do that? There will be a big crowd but it is a very short piece, and I imagine as a Chief Inspector you've done your fair share of public speaking.'

'As I say,' said Keith, 'I shall be very honoured to do this for you and for Sophia.'

It had been a touching gesture and Keith had been practising the brief reading until he knew it by heart. He was a good public speaker, as Otto had anticipated, and he loved the idea that Otto had thought to involve him in the service, it was just right.

Interrupting her thoughts, the organ suddenly burst into life filling the cathedral with sound. Everybody stood and, turning, Felicity saw the coffin being borne down the aisle. It was carried, Otto had told her, by some of the younger members from various orchestras with which he had played over the years, many of whom had become friends as well as colleagues.

Keith gripped her hand. 'All right?' he asked. She nodded.

Otto, closest to the aisle, had his back turned towards her, facing the coffin as it made its slow progress towards them. She was glad in a way that she could not see the expression on his face, but looking across the aisle she saw, to her surprise, Mel looking at him and biting her bottom lip, clearly close to tears.

The service was wonderful. The music was magnificent and an old friend of Otto and Sophia's gave a short and touching eulogy. He was a grand old man of music, a former music director at Covent Garden. Although in his eighties, his voice echoed around the cathedral. He spoke movingly of the little boy freezing to death on a December night in Berlin so many years ago and of the love that began that day and lasted, undiminished, until Sophia's death. Then, right at the end, he added that 'the truly miraculous thing about today is that

Otto is blessed with having Sophia's daughter and family with him – I know just how much it means to Otto and I know just how much it would have meant to Sophia.'

Up to that point Felicity was doing very well. Keith was about to slip an arm around her shoulders but instead Otto, leaning in close and taking her hand, whispered 'We're doing great, we can get through this together.'

Her self-control, however, vanished, when at the climax of the service, Otto rose to his feet, took up his violin and played Vivaldi's violin concerto, the Autumn movement from the *Four Seasons*. Not only did Felicity openly weep, there was hardly a dry eye in the whole cathedral, for not only was the playing superb, so full of feeling, but many knew that this would be the very last time Otto Juniper would ever perform in public.

And then it was Keith's turn. He climbed the steps to the pulpit and read the Blessing in this strong, comforting voice, with its soft Cornish lilt. Only at the last sentence when he met Otto's gaze, did his voice falter. 'And until we meet again, may God hold you in the palm of his hand.'

Two hours later they were back at Otto's house. Only the family had been invited and after the grizzly business of the crematorium, and the added pressure of fighting off the press, Otto looked completely wiped out. Margot fussed around him, sat him in a chair by a blazing log fire and handed him a brandy, ordering him to drink it immediately. Then, one by one, the children and grandchildren were presented to him, beginning with James. Otto visibly brightened as one by one the young people shook his hand and Felicity explained who was who. Mel, she noticed, was still red-eyed. When it was her turn to introduce her family, Otto seemed instinctively to recognise that Mel was the tricky one. He spoke to her gently, telling her how much it meant to him that she had come and brought her children and strangely Mel seemed almost starstruck and for once had little to say.

'You know Melanie, you and I have something very unique in common.'

'Do we?' Mel said.

'Yes, but for your grandmother, Sophia, neither of us would be alive,' he smiled at her. 'Now let me meet your children.'

This was the moment that Felicity, on the one hand, had dreaded and on the other hand, felt might bring Otto some comfort. Mel introduced Martin and he then stood aside and Minty stepped forward. Of course, from an early age, Felicity had recognised her mother in Minty but now at five, with the baby fat gone, this beautiful little girl was the spitting image of her great-grandmother. She watched, waited, as Otto first gasped and then tears started in his eyes. He looked at Minty and then up at Felicity.

'Should I have warned you?' she asked.

'What is it, Mum?' Mel said. Otto and Felicity ignored her.

'No, no, you did the right thing,' he said. 'It was best as a surprise, a wonderful surprise.' He turned to Mel. 'Your daughter, Melanie, has skipped a couple of generations. She is,' he shrugged, 'Sophia reborn.'

'Mum, you must have known,' Mel said, Felicity nodded, trying not to cry herself, 'every time you looked at her?' Felicity nodded again. Minty was obviously slightly bemused, looking from her mother to her grandmother.

'Ah, Minty,' said Otto. 'I am very pleased to meet you. Now, is this little chap your brother and what is his name?' The moment of high emotion passed, drinks were poured, canapés consumed.

When everyone's glass was full, Keith called for hush. 'Legally,' he said, 'I am not really a member of this family, but you've welcomed me into it. I am proud and privileged to feel a part of it and I would like to feel that you can extend the same welcome to Otto.' There were murmurs of approval all around. 'You and Sophia, Otto, have opened up a whole new dimension for this family, enriched it beyond measure and I believe brought great comfort to Felicity after all these years. So ladies and gentlemen, I'd like you to raise your glasses to Sophia.'

'Sophia,' they all said.

They left shortly afterwards, aware of Otto's exhaustion, Felicity and Keith promising to come back and see him in a week or two. Back in the hotel the children were fed, bathed and put to bed and finally the six adults regrouped in the hotel dining room for dinner. Felicity was expecting an interrogation from Mel as to how she had managed to keep her mother secret when Minty looked so like her, but whether her own sensibilities had kicked in or whether Martin had warned her off, Mel was surprisingly restrained.

'I think you are right,' James said to Keith, 'I think it is important we give Otto some support from now on, that's if you agree, Mum?'

'Yes, I do,' said Felicity, 'I don't mind admitting I have spent most of my life hating him, not the man of course, but the name and the idea of what he did. But, of course, he is wonderful, I can quite see why my mother loved him – I think I am a little in love with him myself.'

'Oi,' said Keith, 'enough of that!' There was a general relaxing of tension and smiles all around.

'Without his music,' said Keith, 'and without Sophia, I know he has the dragon Margot for company, but I suspect he is going to be quite lonely. He told me last night that he is probably going to sell his London house so he will be based in Exeter, which is easy anyway for Fizzy and I and for you too,' he said, looking at Martin.

'Absolutely,' said Martin, 'and even if we can't always get up here, we can at least call him, send him the odd postcard and keep in touch generally.'

'It will be nice for the children,' said Mel, suddenly. 'They have no grandfather other than our adopted grandfather, Keith, of course,' she said, smiling at Keith.

'I should be very pleased to share the honour of grandfatherhood with Otto,' said Keith.

They took coffee and brandy in the hotel drawing room and after a while Mel and Trish disappeared off to check on their respective children.

'There is a question I would like to ask you, Mum,' said James, 'but please don't answer it unless you want to.'

'Jamie, I know what the question is,' said Felicity, 'and I am happy to answer it.'

'Do you?' he asked.

'Yes, you're wondering whether I regret having not seen my mother during all these years and having kept her existence a secret from you and Mel?'

'That's the general gist of the question,' James admitted.

'Yes,' said Felicity, 'yes, of course I do, in some respects. Now I know that Otto is not an ogre, now I know they tried really hard when I was growing up to see me. I understand why she made the decisions she did now and so I can take the hurt less personally. However …' She paused and took a sip of coffee. 'However, I do not think I could have coped with losing my mother when I did if I had tried to keep her memory alive. The only way I survived was to blot her out.'

'But you didn't do that when Dad died?' James said.

'No,' said Felicity, 'but that wasn't a rejection, was it, Jamie? Your father died in a horrible hit and run, somebody killed him, he didn't want to die, he didn't want to leave me, or you, or Mel. He should have had years of life ahead of him. In my mind, at the time, my mother rejected me, she left me for Otto. There will always be part of me that wonders how she was able to do that, I could never have left you and Mel for any man.' She smiled across at Keith. 'Not even that one. Then, of course, I think about what Otto's music has brought to the world, the pleasure it has given and I think of their life together and how worthwhile it has been. Now, at last, happy with my children, grandchildren and Keith, I do feel I will be able to forgive and forget.'

'Tell me to shut up because I am afraid I am twisting a knife in the wound,' said James, 'but I want to understand – don't you wish you had seen her before she died?'

Felicity shook her head. 'Not really, she would have been a stranger to me and I a stranger to her. We spent six years together. She was a wonderful mother from what I can remember and from what I've been told. She chose her life and I chose how to cope with her decision. From everything Otto has told me about her, I am absolutely certain she understood the decision that I made.'

20

At nine o'clock the following morning Keith presented himself at the Nicholls house. Colin answered the door; he was still in pyjamas and a dressing gown.

'Sorry about this, Inspector, only my back is giving me so much trouble, it is just easier to stay in pyjamas all day. Come in.'

'Did you have a fall?' Keith asked, as Colin led the way down the passageway towards the kitchen.

'No. I just overdid it. It goes with being self-employed.'

The house looked tidier and cleaner than it had last time Keith had been there, possibly because he was expected or possibly because Colin had the time to clean up as he was not working.

'Tea? Coffee?'

'A cup of coffee would be great,' said Keith. 'Look Colin, before I say anything, there is something you need to know.'

'There's been a development?'

'No, sorry, not that sort of thing,' said Keith, 'I do apologise, I expressed myself badly. What I am trying to tell you is that I am not supposed to be here without a member of the police force accompanying me. I am retired now, as you know, and I am not allowed to interview people because I am just a citizen and I have no rights to talk to you. So given all that, if you want to give me my marching orders, please feel free. I will completely understand.'

'Why would I do that?' Colin said, filling the kettle. 'You were good to me and my family. You did your best. As far as I am concerned you will always be a policeman.'

'I'm afraid that's how I feel,' said Keith. 'It's a difficult thing to shake off.'

'I can imagine,' said Colin. 'So what can I do for you? It makes no difference to me what you are, I know who you are and that is what is important.'

'Have they told you yet that there have been two more suspicious deaths – in Norfolk this time?'

'No, nobody has been in touch at all,' said Colin.

'That's ludicrous,' said Keith under his breath. 'We did a sweep of the country to see if we could find any more similar "suicides" and two turned up, one in Blakeney on the North Norfolk coast and one a few miles along the coast at Sheringham.'

'Same thing, stones in the pockets?'

'Yes,' said Keith, 'because I am not on the investigation team for those particular incidents I don't yet know how similar they are to Morwenna's death. I know the coats have been sent to our path lab but I haven't seen a report on them so I can't say whether they are identical or not.'

'If there are two more bodies in Norfolk,' said Colin, suddenly looking animated, 'then what that means is that Morwenna didn't commit suicide, it was a crime and somebody killed her.'

'I have to say, I agree with you,' said Keith. 'It was a pretty long stretch of the imagination to think that two women could have killed themselves in identical ways six years apart in the same county, but four women on opposite sides of the country: no.'

'You said there had been no developments,' said Colin, 'as far as I am concerned this is a massive development.'

'I suppose it is,' said Keith, with a sigh, 'but the thing is, Colin, after all these years, the only kind of development that I feel is appropriate where you are concerned is me arriving on your doorstep and saying I've found who murdered your wife and I have him in custody. That, to me, is the only result which is acceptable.'

'And that is why you will always be welcome

here,' said Colin, 'because I know that's how you feel.'

'Morwenna had no connections with Norfolk?' Keith asked, as he sipped a rather insipid cup of instant coffee.

Colin shook his head. 'No, none at all. We were both Cornish, Morwenna and I, as you know. I only brought the boys up here because there is more work. There is so much new development going on in Exeter and I felt we all needed a change. I don't think any of us have ever been to Norfolk. I am certain me and the boys haven't and, as far as Morwenna is concerned, she certainly did very little travelling outside Cornwall.'

'So no relatives, no friends, nothing connected to Norfolk?' Colin shook his head. The two men sipped their coffee in silence, Keith feeling increasingly frustrated with his lack of achievement. 'Colin,' he said, 'is there anything, anything about Morwenna which was out of the ordinary, anything to do with how she grew up, where she went to school about her siblings, her parents, anything at all?'

Colin looked at him. 'She was in care.'

'Was she?' said Keith. 'Did we discuss that at the time?'

'I don't think it came up,' said Colin.

'How come she ended up in care?'

'Her father died of cancer when she was twelve. Her mother had five children to raise on her own. Morwenna was the eldest and her mother just couldn't cope, not financially, not in any way and the three eldest children were taken into care.'

'And they lived in a children's home?' Keith asked.

'No, the two younger girls were fostered with a family together and Morwenna was fostered on her own some miles away – ghastly system but I can see how it happened.'

'You mean there should have been a few foster parents who would be prepared to take three girls?'

'Exactly, apparently the younger two were very close in age but Morwenna was quite bitter about it, felt Social Services could have tried harder to keep the family together.'

'So when did she go into care?' Keith asked.

'Oh, at about thirteen I think.'

'And did she ever go back to live with her mother?'

'No, no she got on very well with her foster parents, in fact she kept in touch with them after she left. She was fonder of them, I think, than she was of her own mother. She was supposed to leave when she turned sixteen but they kept her on until she was eighteen so she could go to college. I met them a few times, nice people.'

'I suppose you don't remember their names, do you, or where they lived?'

'Well, I know where they lived,' said Colin. 'St Austell; as for their names … it was something to do with Black … Blackburn, Blackmore, something like that. I know the mother was called Hayley.'

'And do you think they are still alive?' Keith asked.

'I would think they could be. I felt bad actually because when Morwenna died, I should have got in touch with them and told them.'

'I'd have thought they would have read about it in the papers, there was enough coverage.'

'Maybe they did, maybe they didn't or maybe they have moved away, I don't know,' said Colin, 'but they certainly made no attempt to get in touch at the time and, of course, I was so devastated, as you know, I made no effort to contact them. They must have thought it strange that Morwenna hasn't been in touch with them, she was so fond of them.'

'Did they foster other children?' Keith asked.

'Oh yes, I think so. I think there was a steady stream. They had a child of their own, one or two children, I think. I can't remember now, but they certainly had a birth child so the fostering they did out of the goodness of their hearts, it wasn't because they couldn't have children. Morwenna reckoned she was quite a handful by the time she ended up with them, but they really sorted her out.'

'Good people, then.'

'Definitely.'

'Thank you,' said Keith, 'that could be very helpful. Now I'll leave you in peace, and I hope your back is better soon.'

'Would you mind if I didn't get up to see you out, only I've just managed to get myself comfortable for the first time in days.'

'You stay right there,' said Keith.

Back in his car he took a deep breath and dialled Jerry Beckett's number. There was no reply. Searching through his phone, he found a telephone number for Jane Cleaver. He wondered whether she knew of her husband's affair with Adrianne Beckett. Still that was hardly relevant at the moment. He dialled her number. She answered sounding flustered, the baby was crying in the background. He introduced himself.

'I'm sorry, I thought we'd talked already,' she said, sounding extremely stressed.

'Yes, we have,' said Keith, 'and I am really sorry to trouble you. There's just one question I want to ask you.'

'The baby needs feeding.'

'It's a very quick one,' said Keith.

'Go on then,' said Jane.

'Was Adrianne ever in foster care?'

There was a moment's pause. 'Yes,' she said, 'briefly.'

'Why was that?'

'Her mum had a nervous breakdown. She was an only child and her father couldn't cope and hold down his job. I don't think she was in care for much more than five or six months.'

'And do you happen to know where she was in care?'

'Oh yes, yes I do. She was placed with a family in St Austell, a lovely couple apparently.'

'And did she keep in touch with them over the years?'

'Yes, yes, she did.'

'Do you happen to know their names?' Keith asked.

'No, not a clue, I never met them but she always spoke very fondly of them.'

'Thanks so much for your help,' said Keith. He laid his mobile phone reverently on the passenger seat and let out a deep sigh. At last, at last, he was getting somewhere.

Felicity was sitting in Mel and Martin's kitchen with Charlie on her lap. Minty was doing some colouring at the kitchen table and Martin was making tea for everyone – a cup of tea for him and

Felicity and shepherds' pie for the children.

'I'm speaking slightly in code,' said Martin, 'because of flappy ears there,' nodding towards Minty's bowed head, apparently intent on her colouring book. 'Your daughter is very embarrassed about her outburst. We've talked everything through and she gets it now and, of course, it is wonderful having a celebrity such as Otto in the family. We're all totally starstruck. He's a marvellous man, isn't he?'

'Yes he is,' said Felicity. 'I adored him even from the first moment I met him and I arrived on his doorstep expecting to hate him.' She glanced at Minty, but she had clearly blanked out the boring adult conversation.

'Anyway,' said Martin, 'Mel is never going to be able to say sorry, that's not her thing, is it?'

Felicity shook her head, smiling. 'You know your wife very well, Martin.'

'She has many sterling qualities and I love her to pieces, as you know, but admitting she's wrong is one of the things she can't do. So can I say on behalf of us both I am really sorry about her outburst and I do hope that everything worked out for you, the funeral and everything, that you were glad you went.'

'Completely glad,' said Felicity, 'but I would never have done it but for Keith. It's odd, he and

Otto absolutely adore one another, instant soulmates.'

'I'm not surprised,' said Martin. 'They're both special people. How is he doing in his case, Keith, I mean?'

Felicity explained how Keith had been taken off the case and, if anything, Martin was more outraged than she herself had been. 'A year ago,' Martin spluttered, 'he would have been in charge of the whole damn shooting match, including what was going on up in Norfolk. He'd have been gyrating around the country like he normally does and getting results.'

'I know, I know,' said Felicity, 'but he's got something up his sleeve, something is going on.'

'How do you mean?' Martin asked.

'Well, he visited the first victim's family again on the day after the funeral and since then he's been walking around with a special sort of face.'

Martin laughed. 'What do you mean, a special sort of face?'

'Slightly knowing, not exactly pleased with himself but he is definitely a great deal more chirpy than he should be in the circumstances.' Charlie who had fallen asleep, exhausted from his day at nursery, let out a sigh and snuggled closer to his grandmother. 'Isn't this precious,' she said, 'aren't I lucky?'

'So is he,' said Martin, 'to have such a lovely, cuddly granny.'

'Anyway,' said Felicity, 'I've had an idea, it's why I am here really. I was wondering whether you would have Harvey for a few days.'

'Yes, of course, why?'

'I'm going to try to persuade Keith to take me to Norfolk because that's where the other victims were found.'

'But if he's off the case!'

'I know,' said Felicity, 'but if we got up there and rooted around a bit, I'm sure we could find out something useful.'

'Something that would increase the look on his knowing face?' said Martin, spooning shepherds' pie into two bowls. 'I think you'll have to feed Charlie as if he was a baby, he's so tired, poor chap.'

They removed Minty's colouring book which resulted in much protesting and then woke up Charlie who wailed a great deal. Eventually, though, peace was restored and once both children were fed, they perked up and disappeared into their playroom from where shrieks of laughter could be heard.

'I think it's a great idea for no other reason than it would do you both good to have a few days away together, after the emotional turmoil of the last week or so.'

'Yes,' said Felicity, 'and if we could beat bloody Neil Mavers in solving this case, that would be an added bonus.'

'Disgraceful, Fizzy!' said Martin. 'You're supposed to be putting the pursuit of justice way ahead of petty vendettas.'

'Absolutely,' said Felicity, grinning, 'but it would be good though, one in the eye for Neil Mavers, pompous idiot. How dare he sack Keith!'

Keith was not at home when Felicity and Harvey returned an hour or so later. He had been a little mysterious when he left in the morning as to his whereabouts and Felicity knew better than to probe too deeply. Instead she prepared some supper, cleaned the house a little in a rather perfunctory way and then took a glass of wine and some olives out onto the terrace. Although it was still early in the year, the sun set in such a way that it lit up her little terrace in the evenings and with a jumper on she felt quite warm. Harvey, sitting by her feet, heard Keith first and ran back into the house and started yelping joyfully as he came up the stairs.

'Oh, I see, lounging about in the sunshine drinking wine, all right for some.'

'Your supper is in the oven and the housework is done, at any rate partially.'

'Excellent, any more in that bottle? I'll come

and join you.' He was totally back to his old self. He looked tired but the knowing face was still in place. He kissed her, grinning happily and sat down on the chair next to her.

'Good day?' she asked, raising an eyebrow.

'Yes, very good.'

'Now I'm hoping that you are going to tell me all about it, but before you do, I have an idea.'

'Right,' said Keith, cautiously.

'Let's go to Norfolk for the weekend, well a bit longer than a weekend, if necessary. Go tomorrow and come back when we feel like it.'

'Norfolk?' said Keith, looking at her sceptically.

'If we rooted around a bit up there, we might find something that Neil Mavers hasn't discovered, though obviously my main reason for suggesting we go is to have a little holiday.'

'Of course,' said Keith, playing along.

'Only I can tell that you are getting somewhere with this case,' Felicity persisted, 'and if we actually go to Norfolk, which I bet it is more than Mavers would ever do, we might just crack it.'

'I wonder if David would help?' Keith said.

'In what way?' Felicity asked.

Keith ignored her question, staring thoughtfully out across the harbour. 'I'll ask. That's a really good idea, the best. Any ideas where we should stay?'

'The Blakeney Hotel,' said Felicity, 'I was just waiting for you to come back and agree. We can book three nights starting tomorrow night. I've checked availability, they have a nice room looking out over the quay.'

'You book that and I'll just make a call to David.'

'And then,' said Felicity, 'I want to know what it is you've discovered.'

Keith made his phone call in the sitting room. 'David, it's Keith Penrose,' he said. 'How's it going?'

'Not getting very far, I'm afraid,' said David. 'We have the files now on the Norfolk victims and Horace has confirmed that the stitching on the coats looks very similar, although again it's with different thread, older and more damaged. Clearly, there has to be a link, doesn't there?'

'Yes,' said Keith.

'I wish you were here,' David said, 'we could really do with some input from you and the "Super" is going mental.'

'I've got a favour to ask you,' said Keith.

'Oh Lord,' said David, 'is this going to get me in trouble?'

'Very probably,' said Keith, 'unless we're both sworn to secrecy, swearing on our respective grannies' graves or whatever we feel is appropriate.'

'What is it you're asking for?' said David.

'The names of the two Norfolk victims.'

'I can't give you that,' said David, 'you're off the case.'

'I agree,' said Keith. 'You couldn't give them to me if I was a member of the press or some random member of the public but I'm not going to rush in with two left feet and cause trouble. I thought you would have released the names by now anyway, surely they should be in the public domain?'

'I agree, but if I tell you the names then it is going to be obvious who leaked them to you. The "Super" wants to keep the Norfolk connection quiet for another day or so for some reason.'

'No one need know,' said Keith. 'I have a plan. I'm going up to Norfolk tomorrow and staying in Blakeney. I could easily ask around and find out the names of the victims for myself.'

'Why don't you do that then?' said David, not unreasonably.

'Because time is not on our side. While no progress is being made there is someone, somewhere who might die like these other women.'

'That's exactly what George Staple said,' David admitted.

'Well, there you go then,' said Keith. 'Why waste my time up in Norfolk trying to find the names of the victims when you could tell me right now?'

'You can't interview them,' said David, weakening by the moment.

'I agree, but I can be an interested tourist. I can say the same thing has just happened in Cornwall where I come from. It's not as if these deaths have just occurred; the families though they might still be grieving will be out and about back in the community, it shouldn't be difficult to track them down.'

'So what happens if I lose my job?' said David.

'It's obvious – you'll play rugby for England,' said Keith.

So David gave him the names.

21

The following morning they started early and reached Exeter Services by six-thirty. While Keith drove, Felicity was busy Googling both the Blakeney and Sheringham families to check for any information about them which might help. There were plenty of newspaper reports to read but nothing she read seemed to provide anything new. The previous evening had been hectic. Having eaten supper, they delivered Harvey to Mel and Martin, packed, shut the house down and then Felicity listened to Keith's findings. They were both exhausted by the time they finally went to bed. Keith had told Felicity of the link of a shared foster mother between Morwenna and Adrianne.

'You'd have thought that the fostering link was something Neil Mavers and crew would have found out by now,' Felicity said, as they drove. 'You are clever.'

'Not really,' said Keith, 'it was just a matter of asking the right question. Was there anything in

Morwenna's past that made her slightly different from everyone else? And that is when Colin came up with the news of foster care. I rang Jane Cleaver never really expecting to find that Adrianne had been in foster care, only to learn she had those few brief months in care while her mother had a breakdown. Then I was able to establish that the foster carers were the same one.'

'And now you're going to tell me you've found the foster mother.'

'I've found the family,' said Keith. 'That's where I've been today. Their name is Blackburn. The father, Sam, has been dead for some years and the mother, Hayley, the foster mother, is in a care home in St Austell. She has Alzheimer's, quite severe I understand. As well as all the foster children, they also had a son by birth. His name is Hugh, he is in his late forties, he is unmarried and still lives in the family home.'

'So he could be our killer?' Felicity asked.

'Maybe,' said Keith, 'but he doesn't sound the type, apparently he is very a unassuming, gentle soul. The woman I saw at Social Services sang the praises of the family to the rafters. Apparently, Hayley Blackburn was a wonderful foster mother, she didn't mind how difficult the case, how long or short a time the children stayed, she loved them all and did her very best for them. She had dozens of children over the years.'

'Maybe her own son felt pushed out?' Felicity suggested.

'Maybe, the important thing is he is still alive and he can tell us about Morwenna and Adrianne.'

'Well, you say that,' said Felicity, 'but if Social Services are right and there were literally were dozens of children who went through that house, he may not remember them.'

'Judging by the likely dates the girls were in care, I reckon the chances are the boy Hugh was still living at home when they were fostered, because he would be only a few years older than them. If nothing else, he will at least be able to tell us something about how life was. It could be that the killer was one of the other foster children who had some kind of grudge.'

'If that's true,' said Felicity, 'then we are really looking for a needle in a haystack. Isn't it about time you told your findings to Neil Mavers?'

'Yes,' said Keith, 'definitely.'

'So have you done so?'

'No.'

'Are you going to?'

'Not yet,' said Keith. 'I just want to be a bit further down the road. I need to establish whether the Norfolk women were in care too. It seems rather a long shot to assume that they were fostered by a woman in St Austell. It doesn't make any sense.'

'So that's what we are going to find out?' said Felicity, 'but, seriously Keith, aren't you perverting the course of justice or something by not putting Mavers in the picture?'

'I thought about that,' said Keith, 'but I don't think so. If it was a week ago and I was still working for the force with instructions to report anything I found to Neil Mavers, well then I would be quite in the wrong for not involving him. However, they took me off the case so what I do now is entirely up to me, surely? In any event I don't want to take this information to anyone until I've checked out the Norfolk end. The fact that the two victims down here shared a foster mother, however briefly in Adrianne's case, may have nothing to do with anything but if the common denominator also applies to the Norfolk victims, then we really do have something to tell George Staple.'

They returned to this theme when, many hours later, they saw a sign for Blakeney. During the journey Felicity had read up on the family who had suffered the tragedy in Blakeney. The victim had been named Eleanor Long and she left behind Terry, her husband, and Bea, her daughter, who was now twenty-two.

'Another devastated family,' Felicity said.

Keith nodded and they were silent for a few minutes.

'It sounds as if this one, Eleanor, may have been a little older than Adrianne and Morwenna, having a daughter, aged twenty-two at the time?' said Keith.

'Possibly, or maybe Eleanor was just a very early starter. There's not much to do up here in Norfolk, is there?'

'The same could be said of Cornwall,' Keith said.

'True. Keith, how are you going to approach this Terry?'

'I've been wondering about that,' said Keith. 'It's all so difficult. Just a year or so ago I would have presented myself at the local station and somebody would have driven me around to his house. I just have to hope he is a pub man.'

'It's Saturday night,' said Felicity, 'if he is a pub man, tonight's the night.'

Keith glanced at his watch as they began the slow descent into the village. 'Well, it's only five o'clock, once we've checked in if we collapse for an hour we can then take ourselves off to the most likely hostelry and track him down.'

'But what are you going to say to him?' Felicity said. 'How can you possibly ask him any questions without raising suspicions?'

'Do I look a suspicious character, then?' Keith asked, smiling.

'No, not if you're short-sighted and the light's poor.'

'Look,' said Keith, ignoring her, 'there is only one question I need to ask him – was your wife ever in foster care and if so where and with whom? If he answers no, then I'll simply tell bloody Mavers of the link between the two Cornish victims and leave him to figure it out from there. I promise I'll drop it.'

'And if Eleanor Long was in foster care?'

'Then we have to go to Sheringham and check out the other one. She was the first victim. What did you say her name was?'

'Daisy,' said Felicity, 'Daisy Daniels. She never married. She just had a brother as her next of kin, called Peter. I suppose we could go to Social Services up here, Keith, and ask some questions.'

Keith shook his head. 'I got away with it in St Austell because everyone knew who I was. Some random bloke turning up at Norwich Social Services, or wherever their headquarters are, and saying I used to be a policeman in Cornwall, is not going to cut much ice, is it?'

'No,' Felicity agreed.

'OK, well let's just see how we get on.'

After a quick sleep and a shower they were

restored and ravenously hungry. It was just after six-thirty in the evening when Keith and Felicity presented themselves to the receptionist at the hotel.

'We're looking up a friend of a friend,' Keith said. 'He's a local man, Terry Long, do you know him?'

'Everyone knows Terry around here,' the receptionist said.

'I was wondering if we might catch him in the pub as it's Saturday night. Where does he drink, do you know?'

'He's not much of a drinker, despite ...' she stopped in mid sentence. 'You're not journalists, are you?' she asked, suspiciously.

'No,' Felicity said, hurriedly. 'We just promised to try to catch up with him while we're in Blakeney, on behalf of a friend.' The woman, who was fairly elderly, squinted myopically through her glasses at them for some time.

'You don't look like journalists,' she said at last. Then she frowned at Keith, 'you look like a policeman.'

'So I'm told,' said Keith, 'I used to be one but I'm not anymore.'

'I don't want that poor man hassled, he's been through enough, they never leave him alone.'

'We're not here to hassle, I promise,' said Felicity, 'honestly.'

'He drinks at the King's Head, just along the quay on the Morston road, you can't miss it.'

'That's really helpful, thank you,' Keith said. They made their exit hurriedly, aware that the receptionist's eyes were boring into their backs.

'She doesn't believe us,' said Felicity.

'Can you blame her?' said Keith, taking her hand.

It was a breathtakingly beautiful evening, the tide was full, the water like glass. The sky was very different from Cornwall, an oily green grey reflecting the marshes below, but nonetheless very beautiful in its own way.

'This is actually fun,' said Felicity, 'if it wasn't for the sad reason we're here. We ought to have weekends away more often, if we can afford them.'

'Your wish is my command,' said Keith. 'That is what we'll do in future – maybe two or three times a year. It's a good idea.'

The King's Head was busy with what looked and sounded like mostly locals, with a few yachting types thrown in.

'They're the same on every coast, aren't they?' said Keith, nodding towards a group who were braying very loudly, all dressed in yellow wellies and guernseys.

'Now, now,' said Felicity, 'we're not here to criticise.'

283

Keith ordered drinks and waited until he was paying the young man behind the bar, before he asked if Terry Long was in the pub. The young bar man looked down at his watch.

'Terry isn't usually in here until about eight.'

'OK,' said Keith. 'That's fine, I just wanted to catch up with him. Could we order some food, we'll sit at that table over by the fire. Will you let us know when he comes in?'

'You want to catch up with him but you don't know what he looks like?' The barman said, suspiciously.

'We've been put in touch with him by a mutual friend,' said Keith, firmly.

'He doesn't come in every Saturday, mind,' the barman said.

'Well, let's hope he does this Saturday,' said Keith.

They ordered a crab salad with local crusty bread and when they had finished that and their glass of wine, they moved onto coffee.

By quarter-past-eight Keith was getting restless. 'It doesn't look like this is one of Terry Long's pub nights,' he said. 'Maybe he's been warned off.'

'What from meeting us?' said Felicity. 'Surely not.'

'The locals seem pretty protective of him,

don't they, and who can blame them.'

At that moment a tall, lean, grey-haired man came up to the bar. He had a strong, weather-beaten face and wore sea boots and an old tatty waterproof jacket. The barman pulled a pint for him without asking what he wanted and then nodded in the direction of Felicity and Keith.

'There's our man,' said Keith. He stood up and met Terry half way between the bar and the table. 'Terry Long?'

'Yeah, who wants to know?'

'My name is Keith Penrose and this is my partner, Felicity Paradise.'

The man's craggy, rather formidable impression softened as he broke into a semi-toothless smile. 'Felicity Paradise, what sort of name is that?'

'I know,' said Felicity, 'awful isn't it? But I'm stuck with it and I'm sort of used to it now.'

'Takes some getting used to, I shouldn't wonder,' said Terry.

'Can you spare us a minute?' Keith asked.

'S'pose,' he said.

'I've been thinking,' said Keith, 'while I've been waiting for you to arrive, of all the different reasons I could give for wanting to talk to you and I've decided that the very best one is to tell you the truth.'

'I should hope so,' said Terry, taking a long slurp of his beer. 'What is all this about anyway, you're not a journalist, are you?'

'I promise I'm not, I'm a retired policeman.'

'OK,' said Terry, warily.

'I was a Chief Inspector based in Cornwall. The thing is, Terry, we've had two deaths down there very similar to your wife, Eleanor's.'

'I don't want to talk about it,' Terry said, half rising out of his chair.

'Please,' Felicity said, putting a restraining hand on his arm. 'Please, we're trying to stop this happening to another family, please just hear what he has to say.'

The man sank back into his chair and stared aggressively at Keith. 'You've got two minutes.'

'OK,' said Keith, 'I was the investigating officer on the first apparent suicide in Cornwall.'

'My Eleanor did not commit suicide.'

'I know,' said Keith, 'that is what I am trying to prove. Hear me out, please.'

'OK.'

'I was the investigating officer on the first case,' he repeated, 'and there's been another one just recently, in the last couple of weeks. Then we discovered that there were two more victims, your wife here in Blakeney and the other poor lady in Sheringham. All the circumstances surrounding

286

their deaths are the same, in particular the stones sewn into the jacket pockets. Apart from that, we've had nothing to go on until at last, I found another connection between the two victims in Cornwall and I just wanted to see if that same connection applies to your wife.'

'What connection would that be?'

'What sort of childhood did Eleanor have?' Keith asked.

'What do you mean by that?' Terry was aggressive again; for a moment it looked as if he was going to leave them once again, but he was clearly intrigued. He wanted to know more.

'Well, was there anything unusual about her childhood, about her upbringing?'

There was a long pause. Keith and Felicity could barely breathe. Felicity found her heart was thumping in her chest. 'Well, it wasn't easy,' he said. 'North Norfolk wasn't much of a tourist destination in them days, when we were growing up. Then we had the terrible floods in 1954 and that did no end of damage to the land as well as put off the tourists.' Felicity could hardly bear it. 'Anyway her dad lost his job and took to the bottle and she and her brother, Chris, were put into care.'

Keith let out an enormous sigh.

'What, what it is?' Terry asked, alarmed. 'What have I said?'

'Where was she in care?'

'Where? In Norwich.'

'Norwich?' said Keith, crestfallen.

'Yes, that's where they lived, well on the outskirts, a village just outside Norwich, I think. Can't remember the name.'

'Was she in care for long?'

'Two or three years,' he said, 'then she got a job. She went into service at Holkham Hall. We met on the beach one day, we married when she was only nineteen.'

'Do you know the name of her foster carers?'

'No, she never kept in touch with them.'

'Why was that?' Keith asked.

'I don't know. I don't think she was especially close to them, but I believe they were kind, she always had a nice word to say about them.'

'How old was your wife when she died?' Keith asked.

'Only fifty-one, waste of a life, our daughter can't get over it, neither can I, come to that.'

You've been incredibly helpful, Mr Long,' said Keith. 'Can I get you another pint?'

'Well yes, I suppose you can. I don't like talking about it, you see.'

'I understand,' said Keith. 'Stay here and I'll fetch one.'

'Why is he asking all these questions if he is

not a policeman anymore?' Terry Long said to Felicity as soon as Keith had left the table.

'Because he has always believed that the first victim in Cornwall did not commit suicide. He got close to the family. The woman who died left two little boys; one was only five. You, more than anyone, can imagine the impact it had on the family, you of all people should know what it felt like.'

Terry nodded and downed the rest of his pint. 'So what is he trying to do then?'

'He is trying to prove that the two victims in Cornwall and the two here in Norfolk, which includes your wife, did not commit suicide but were murdered.'

'We all know that,' said Terry quietly, 'but I'd give my right arm to have your man prove it.'

Sunday morning found them in Sheringham. The church bells were ringing and the sun was shining but they found it a bleak little town compared with Blakeney. The North Sea stretched out before them, crashing onto a pebbly beach. It was a grey, lifeless sea.

'We're spoilt,' said Felicity, her arm through Keith's. 'The quality of light in St Ives, the extraordinary colour of sand and sea and sky that has brought painters to the town through the decades, it spoils you for everywhere else, doesn't it?'

'I was thinking,' said Keith, 'standing here, that this is a pretty appropriate place to commit suicide.'

'That's an awful thing to say, Keith,' said Felicity.

'You know what I mean though, don't you? It's all so grey and bleak and so much concrete.'

Felicity nodded. 'It's certainly not what we're used to.'

'Right, so enough of this, let's try and find Peter Daniels.'

The pubs were all closed and were not opening until twelve o'clock. That was the first disappointment, so they made their way up the high street until they came to a village shop. The stout woman standing behind the counter was staring aggressively at them before they even opened their mouths. Felicity knew it was going to be hopeless.

'We're looking for Peter Daniels, I wondered if you could help us? We're friends of friends of his.'

'No you're not,' she said, 'you're snoopers, journalists I wouldn't be surprised.'

'We're not,' said Felicity. 'We promised we would look him up when we were in Sheringham.' This had worked very well in Blakeney but not so here.

'I'm not telling you where he is,' she said. 'I don't trust you. I don't like the look of you.'

'Right,' said Keith, 'well, we'll just have to find him without your help.'

'You'll have a job,' she shouted after them, as they left the shop.

'Oh, so friendly!' said Felicity. 'Now what?'

'I think we should go and sit on the seafront and wait for the pubs to open.'

'I'm not sure he is going to be a pubgoer, is he?' said Felicity as they walked back down towards the sea. 'Brother and sister both unmarried, I have visions of nice cups of tea in front of the television.'

'You're stereotyping,' said Keith, 'and if there is one thing I've learnt in my job, that is a very dangerous thing to do.'

A signpost pointed to the lifeboat. 'Why don't we promenade along the promenade,' said Keith 'and try and get a feel for the place.' It didn't help there was nothing but boarded-up beach huts, a discarded bandstand and very little else but the endless grey sea and pebbles.

'In fairness we are out of season,' Felicity said. 'Oh look, brilliant, a lifeboat, better than ours.'

'Bigger certainly,' said Keith, 'but then it would have to be to cope with the North Sea.' He glanced at his watch. 'Come on, ten minutes to opening time.'

'Anyone would think you were an alcoholic,' said Felicity.

'If I stay much longer in this place I will be,' said Keith, turning on his heel.

They tried five pubs: the Crown, the Two Lifeboats, the Lobster and the Dunstable Arms but it wasn't until they arrived at the Windham Arms that they struck gold. The landlady was friendly and while at the other pubs they had made enquiries without buying a drink, instinctively Keith thought this was the one at which to linger, and he was right.

'Yes, I know Peter,' she said. 'He lives a little further up the street.'

'That's marvellous,' said Keith. 'Thank you so much. Do you happen to know what number?'

'No, but it is the one with the blue door, about half-way up on the right. You can't miss it.'

'Do you think he is likely to be in?' Keith asked.

The landlady shook her head. 'Don't know. He is rather a law unto him self. He has not been right since his sister died. Mind you, I'm not sure he was right before then, poor chap.'

'Goodness, I wonder what we're in for?' said Felicity, as they hurried up the street towards Peter Daniels' door.

Peter Daniels was a slightly disturbing sight

when he cautiously opened his door to Keith and Felicity. He was about Keith's height, well built but pale with dark circles under his deep brown eyes, He looked like he never ventured outside. His eyes were curiously blank, he didn't seem to be focusing on either of them.

'Yes?' he said.

'I was wondering whether I could come and talk to you about your sister,' said Keith. There didn't seem much point in beating about the bush.

'Why?' Peter asked.

'Because I need your help,' said Keith. 'We have other cases similar to your sister's and we are trying to establish a link between them.'

'I don't talk about my sister.'

'I understand that,' said Keith, 'but this is really important. It could help enormously.'

'All right,' said Peter. 'You'd better come in.' They went into a darkened hall and then into a kitchen which was surprisingly cosy, with a Rayburn in one corner. It was also spotlessly clean. 'Do you want something to drink?' Peter asked.

'No thanks,' Keith and Felicity shook their heads.

'What is it you want to know?'

Peter Daniels was a man of so few words, Keith decided that although potentially he was leading the witness, he would do best to ask the direct question. 'Was your sister ever in foster care?' he said.

'Why?' Peter asked.

'Because it could be the link with the other cases.'

He was silent for a moment, apparently staring at some point over the top of Keith and Felicity's heads.

'We were both in foster care,' he said, 'me and my sister.'

'In Norwich?' Keith suggested.

'Yes.'

'Do you mind me asking why?'

'My mother died, our mother died and our father didn't want us. We went into foster care and then after a while my mother's sister took us in.'

'That must have been hard on you both,' Keith said. Peter merely nodded. 'Mr Daniels, do you remember the name of your foster carer in Norwich?'

'Hayley,' he said, immediately.

'Do you remember her second name?' He shook his head.

'But her husband was called Sam, we weren't allowed to call them Mum and Dad, we had to call them Hayley and Sam, I remember that.'

'And did you like being with Hayley and Sam?' Keith asked. He felt as if he was talking to a child.

'Yes,' said Peter.

'They were kind to you?'

'Yes.'

'Thank you Mr Daniels, I won't take up any more of your time. It was very good of you to see us.'

'That's all right,' said Peter.

Moments later they were back out on the pavement, the blue door shut firmly behind them.

'Wow, amazing! That was odd in lots of ways,' said Keith.

'He is certainly a strange man,' said Felicity.

'And he is the only relative who hasn't immediately protested that the victim was not suicidal. Everyone else is adamant that the death of their relative could not have been suicide. Peter didn't seem interested in proving that point which either means he knows it was suicide …'

'Or he knows it wasn't?' said Felicity.

'Exactly,' said Keith, 'but the really important thing is that clearly the Blackburns lived in Norwich before they moved down to St Austell. That is why these victims are older than the ones in Cornwall.'

'I don't get it?' said Felicity. 'I don't see how it fits.'

'The Blackburns clearly fostered the Norfolk children earlier than the Cornish ones. They must have lived here in Norfolk and fostered children here and then moved down to Cornwall and started fostering children down there.'

'But whoever has gone on this killing spree must have known them in both places,' said Felicity. 'I did find Peter creepy.'

'Yes,' said Keith. 'Let's get back to Blakeney and the hotel, I need to ring George.'

'There's another thing,' said Felicity, 'did you see his knitting?'

Keith shook his head. 'No, I missed that.'

'It was on a chair, well, on a footstool by the chair near the Rayburn. It looked like a Guernsey sweater he was knitting, and of course they are very intricate, different patterns around the neck mean different things.'

'So you're saying if he can knit, he can sew.' Felicity nodded. 'But, there again,' said Keith, 'what on earth could his motive be?'

They reached the car and climbed inside. 'His sister was the first victim, wasn't she?' said Felicity.

'Yes, then Eleanor Long, then Morwenna and now Adrianne. It seems unlikely that he would travel to Cornwall and anyway, why? So he kills his sister for whatever reason, then kills other girls who were fostered by the Blackburns?'

'But he wouldn't have known the ones in Cornwall, surely.'

'Unless he's not telling us the truth,' said Keith, 'unless he went down to Cornwall with the Blackburns.'

'My money is still on the Blackburns' son, Hugh,' said Felicity.

'We've done all we can now,' said Keith, 'I think we will have to turn it over to George Staple and hope he gets involved himself in unravelling this one.'

'Do you think he is going to be angry with you for interfering?'

'Very,' said Keith, 'but in a good way, I hope.'

22

Felicity sat in the hotel restaurant looking out over the wonderfully changing light across the mudflats. The tide was way out now. After a while she ordered a drink for herself and sandwiches for them both. It was a long telephone call and when Keith appeared, he went straight to the bar returning with a large glass of red wine.

'I'm definitely needing this,' he said.

'Was he angry?'

'To start with,' said Keith, 'until I explained everything. I told him exactly what we had done and why and he understood. As I was talking I suddenly realised that there is a third possible suspect.'

'Who's that?' Felicity asked.

'Eleanor's brother, Chris. Terry Long said that she and her brother went into foster care, maybe he had some sort of motive.'

'Maybe,' said Felicity, 'but again only if he stayed with the Blackburns when they moved to

Cornwall.'

'Anyway,' said Keith, 'we've done all we can now. Let's enjoy the rest of the day.'

'So you're not going to be clapped into irons?'

'No, but we are going to have to leave very early tomorrow morning. George wants to set up a debriefing meeting with Neil and some of the boys so they make sure I've missed nothing.'

'That's going to be fun,' said Felicity.

'I know, there are going to be some very snide comments flying around, no doubt. I said we could be in Truro by about four if they want to hold the meeting tomorrow afternoon or else I will come in first thing on Tuesday morning. I suspect though it will be tomorrow evening. Can you entertain yourself in Truro?'

'I'm sure I can,' said Felicity. 'It might involve shopping.'

'In that case,' said Keith, 'I might leave you in a layby on the A30.'

The incident room was crowded when Keith arrived tired and stiff from hours of driving just after four o'clock on Monday afternoon. There was a variety of greetings shouted across the room from 'All right, Keith,' to 'Good to see you again.' It felt good to be back. It felt like home until he saw, standing by the whiteboard, not only George Staple but also Neil Mavers, who looked uncomfortable and thoroughly disgruntled. George got straight to it. He began by unnecessarily introducing Keith to the assembled crowd and then explained that he had asked him to be involved, since he had headed up the original inquiry. There was no mention of Keith having been taken off the case.

In the Blakeney Hotel the previous evening – was it really only the previous evening? Keith had written up his notes on both interviews which he now referred to. He started in chronological order by explaining his conversation with Colin Nicholls which had revealed that his wife, Morwenna, had been in care and that a telephone call to Jane Cleaver had confirmed that briefly Adrianne also had been in care and that both girls had been looked after by the same family, the Blackburns. He then described his trip to Norfolk and discovery that both Terry Long's wife, Eleanor and Peter Daniels' sister, Daisy, had been in foster care, as had both their brothers, Christopher and Peter respectively. All of them had been in the care of the Blackburn family when they had lived in Norwich, prior to their moving down to St Austell.

'I don't know what year the Blackburns moved south,' he said, 'nor at the moment have I been able to synchronise the arrival and departure of the various children in their care to see whether they were all in the house at the same time or not; I suspect not – I suspect the Norfolk and Cornish children never met.'

'Surely that is the fairly fundamental piece of information we need,' said Neil Mavers suddenly.

'I absolutely agree with you,' said Keith, ignoring the criticism by implication. 'With all four victims having been, at one time or another, in the care of the same foster family, I think we can all agree that there is no doubt that their deaths are both linked and suspicious and the chances of suicide are now negligible.'

'Maybe they all belong to some religious cult,' said Neil, 'where suicide is considered fashionable.'

'I rather doubt it,' said Keith, trying to keep the sarcasm out of his voice. 'Something happened while they were in foster care or someone also in the household at the same time bore a grudge, which for some reason took many years to develop from a festering sore into a need to commit murder, not once but four times. As I see it there are three suspects. Peter Daniels who lives in Sheringham and whose sister, Daisy, was the first victim. He is odd, reclusive, avoids eye contact, altogether a strange man and possibly slightly autistic. He also knits for a hobby.'

'What has that got to do with anything?' said Neil.

'Because, man, if he can knit he can presumably sew,' said George irritably, before Keith could even open his mouth.

'Peter Daniels could have snapped for some reason, killed his sister and then gone on to kill the other women he knew from his childhood. The second possible suspect is Hugh Blackburn. He is the natural son, the son by birth of the Blackburn family – that is Hayley the mother and Sam the father. They just had the one boy who must be well into his forties by now. He has never married and still lives in the family home in St Austell, the address of which I will give you all in a moment. Maybe he was resentful, maybe Hugh felt his parents spent more time worrying about these endless foster children than him. Maybe over the years, this resentment built up to a point where he decided to plot his revenge. The third possible suspect is Eleanor's brother, Chris, about whom I know absolutely nothing other than the fact he exists. He went into care with Eleanor to the Blackburns. Eleanor,' he said to remind everyone, 'is the wife of Terry Long and was the second Norfolk victim. Why Chris would want to first kill Daisy Daniels and then go on to kill his sister, heaven knows.'

'They're a rum lot up in Norfolk,' said a joker from the front of the crowd.

'Some would say we are a pretty rum bunch down here too,' said Keith, with a smile. 'So in summary, we need to get hold of Social Services in Norwich and find out as much detail as we can about the Blackburns and who they fostered during the time they were there. We then need specific details from Social Services in St Austell as to their foster children once they moved down. Did they, for example, bring one of the Norfolk children down with them? Thirdly, we need to establish whether Hugh Blackburn was living in the family home when each of the four victims was there too, being fostered. Fourthly, Hayley Blackburn is still alive. Sam is dead, but Hayley is in a care home in St Austell but she has Alzheimer's. What I am not sure is how bad she is, whether it is even appropriate to question her but it is certainly worth taking advice from the care home, particularly given the gravity of our enquiry. Then I suggest that each of the three suspects are properly interviewed and alibis established – in any event for the time and date when Adrianne was killed. That should be easy enough to establish.'

'You didn't make any attempt to contact Social Services in Norwich while you were up there?' said Neil.

'Of course I didn't,' Keith said, his patience wearing very thin. 'I have no authority any more, now I've retired, to ask Social Services to release sensitive information about foster children. That's your job. Now,' he said, addressing George Staple, 'if you'll excuse me, it's been rather a long day.'

'Of course, of course, Keith, thank you for coming in,' said George.

Keith started across the room and then stopped. 'One final clue. The person you're looking for is likely to be a left-handed diabetic who can sew, that should narrow the field down a bit.'

A young officer who was standing close by the door said. 'That has a ring of Sherlock Holmes about it, sir, if I may say so. Are you going to tell us why?'

'Ask Horace Greenaway,' Keith said and left the room.

While he sat in Mannings Bar in Truro waiting for Felicity – they had agreed to meet at half-past-six – Keith felt miserable and frustrated. He knew Felicity would be happy to do the rest of the driving so he ordered a glass of wine and sat in the bay window watching the world go by. He hated being out of the loop, not part of the team. If he had been a working member in that incident room this evening, he knew exactly what he would do and in what order, who he would ask to do it and he knew he would have been lucky to have snatched more than a couple of hours' sleep all night – but the thrill of it! In the last few months he had started to come to terms with his retirement but this case had wound him up. What he really wanted to do was get back to work.

23

Tuesday passed for both of them in a haze of exhaustion.

'It's so annoying,' Keith grumbled to Felicity. 'I could have driven to Norfolk and back without a moment's thought a few years ago, now I feel absolutely knackered.'

'I don't think anybody of any age could drive from Cornwall to the North Norfolk coast and back within forty-eight hours without feeling pretty tired,' Felicity said. 'Just come and relax, I know you're fretting about the case but just try to put it out of your mind.'

Of course it was hopeless. Felicity collected Harvey from Mel and Martin, bought some groceries and then attempted to start planning her book illustrations, but it was impossible because Keith kept marching round the house and wouldn't settle to anything. Eventually, in desperation, Felicity shooed him and Harvey out for a walk on the beach but she, too, was preoccupied –

something felt wrong, there seemed to be something missing. It wasn't as simple as Keith not being at the centre of the case: she couldn't put her finger on it but it felt as though they had missed something vital. Over supper that evening they talked it all through again but got no further forward. Wednesday passed in much the same fashion and by Thursday Keith was positively frantic with frustration.

'Do you think I can ring in?' he asked Felicity more than once. She shook her head. Then on Thursday evening just as they were starting to prepare supper, they had two significant calls.

The first was from George Staple. 'Keith, I think it's only fair to keep you in the loop as to what is going on.'

'I have to admit, sir, I have been a little anxious,' said Keith.

'It's not good news, I'm afraid. We've pretty much ruled out the three suspects you highlighted. Terry Long's brother-in-law, Chris is the easiest to eliminate. He is living in Australia now and hasn't been home for twelve years. Everyone agrees with you, Peter Daniels is certainly an oddball but he has been nowhere near Cornwall in his entire life, never mind in the last few weeks. I don't know if you've noticed but he has a slight limp, apparently he had polio as a boy. His mother taught him to knit to give him something to do while he was convalescing. He lives a simple, lonely life but the general feeling is he hasn't got the gumption to kill anybody.'

'And Hugh Blackburn?' Keith said, with a sinking heart.

'Nice chap, by all accounts, has a live-in girlfriend and two children. They are not married but have been together for years. He is very outgoing, a lively, friendly sort of man.'

'What does he do?' Keith asked.

'He drives a courier van, long distance, not local.'

'A van is what would have been needed, at any rate for Adrianne.'

'I know, I know, ' said George, 'but during the period Adrianne disappeared he was up in Yorkshire. He has a cast-iron alibi. He is definitely not our man and as for hang-ups about all those foster children, he doesn't seem to have any. The officers who interviewed him said he is the type of bloke they would like to spend an evening in the pub with, he wouldn't drink too much but he would be a good raconteur, friendly and interested in everyone. It makes sense, you can see why his parents were so good at doing what they did.'

'And what about Hayley Blackburn?'

'We've missed the boat there, I'm afraid,' said

George. 'The care home said that even six months ago she had good days and bad days but now they are all bad. She has no idea what is going on, it would be entirely pointless trying to interview her and it might upset her.'

'That's a damn shame,' said Keith, 'because she could unlock this for us.'

'I know, I know.'

'Did Hugh remember the victims?'

'Not the Norfolk ones, he was only very little and there were so many, he doesn't even really remember living in Norfolk – just a slight vague memory but nothing tangible. However he does remember both Morwenna and Adrianne. Adrianne was very stuck-up, apparently and didn't fit in but she was only with them for a few weeks until her mother was better. He remembers her particularly because she was different.'

'So it's back to the drawing board,' said Keith.

'Well, not entirely Keith,' said George, 'thanks to you, we have established this common denominator, it just doesn't make any sense. Hugh Blackburn is going to have another think about them all and we are reinterviewing him again tomorrow, he couldn't be more cooperative. He is digging out some old photo albums to see if he can identify the girls and whether something or someone might jog his memory.'

'Of course,' said Keith, 'if he is a courier, it might be worth checking whether he was on the Norfolk run a few years back.'

'I thought of that,' said George.

'I wonder if Neil Mavers has?' Keith couldn't resist saying.

'Now, now,' said George, 'he's doing his best.'

'That is what worries me,' said Keith.

The second telephone call was from Margot, Otto Juniper's housekeeper. Felicity took the call.

'I didn't want to worry you but Otto has been in hospital for the last few days.'

'Oh no,' said Felicity, 'what's wrong?'

'At first I thought he'd had a heart attack or a stroke. He just collapsed on me. It was last weekend on Saturday, it was awful. However his doctor thinks he was just suffering from nervous exhaustion. The strain of the funeral and the last few weeks of your mother's life have taken an enormous toll on him.'

'And is he home now?' Felicity asked.

'Yes,' said Margot, 'that is why I'm ringing. I was wondering whether you and Keith, if he's free, felt like coming up to pay a little visit. I know it's a lot to ask but he keeps talking about you both.'

'Of course we'll come,' said Felicity, 'of course.'

'He's not terribly bright, I don't think he'll

want you to stay for more than half an hour or so, so I completely understand if you can't make it,' Margot continued. 'It's a long way to come.'

'We'll be there,' said Felicity. 'Let me just check with Keith.'

'Of course we'll go,' said Keith. 'I'll drive you up there tomorrow morning. Ask Margot what time of day is good for him?'

'Just before lunch,' Margot said. 'After lunch he tends to take a nap. If you came along about half past eleven, that would be ideal.'

'We'll be there,' Felicity promised.

'So are you driving me up to Exeter out of the goodness of your heart?' Felicity asked, smiling at Keith as she turned off her phone.

'Of course,' said Keith, 'and also I'd like to see the old boy.'

'Any other reason?' Felicity asked.

'I find it slightly disconcerting to be read like a book,' said Keith. 'We might just pop in on Colin Nicholls in the afternoon.'

'Thought so,' said Felicity, smugly, 'although he may be back at work, I suppose.'

'I doubt it,' said Keith, 'judging by how much pain he seemed to be in when I saw him last, poor chap. I'll give him a ring when we leave Otto's and if he's not around I promise I won't keep you hanging around in Exeter.'

'What do you want to see him about?' Felicity asked.

Keith smiled back at her. 'To be honest, I have absolutely no idea.'

24

Keith established on the journey up to Exeter the following morning that Colin Nicholls was at home during the morning but going to the doctor's in the afternoon.

'I'll drop you and Harvey off at Otto's, then go to see Colin and come back for you,' he said. 'It'll probably be nice for you two to have a bit of time alone anyway without me hanging about.'

'We don't know how he'll feel about Harvey yet, you may have to take him to the Nicholls.'

'I can easily take him but let's see what Margot the dragon says first.'

Margot the dragon was almost unrecognisable from the woman he had first encountered, Keith thought as he stood with Felicity and Harvey at the front door.

'Who's this?' Margot asked immediately, bending down to stroke Harvey.

'This is Harvey,' said Felicity. 'I don't have to

bring him in, he can easily …'

'Of course you must bring him in. This is the most extraordinary thing.'

'What is?' Felicity asked.

'Your mother, she had a long-haired Jack Russell. He died about two years ago, his name was Hector and he looked just like this. What a weird coincidence.'

Felicity looked slightly shocked. These kind of revelations about her mother she still found difficult. The person her mother had become was still unreal to her.

Come in, come in,' said Margot. 'Otto will be delighted to meet the dog.'

'I'm going to leave them here,' said Keith, 'I have an appointment. Would an hour be too long?'

'No,' said Margot, 'it'll be fine and if he does fall asleep Felicity and I can entertain ourselves.'

Otto was overwhelmed by the sight of Harvey.

'Just like Hector,' he said to Felicity, 'the spitting image. Your mother, she had three Jack Russells during the period we lived together. She made a terrible fuss of them all and spoiled them rotten. But Hector, the last, we loved the best, didn't we, Margot?'

Margot nodded. 'Coffee, tea?' she mouthed to Felicity.

'Coffee would be great, thank you.'

'Hector died about eighteen months, two years ago,' Otto said. 'Sophia was devastated not to have a dog in her life but didn't think it was fair to have another. She was turned ninety by then and knew that she would never live long enough to raise another dog.'

'Was she ill for a long time, then?' Felicity asked.

'No, no,' said Otto. 'Do you want me to tell you about it?'

'I think so,' said Felicity.

'It's a good story really,' said Otto. 'She was strong as an ox, never had a day's illness really. Then, shortly after her ninetieth birthday, which was a big celebration, she started having palpitations and was diagnosed with a weak heart.'

'I realised, of course, that she died of a heart attack,' said Felicity. 'I didn't realise she was ill before it.'

'She wasn't ill,' said Otto. 'She had pills. It wasn't painful, well not really, only occasionally a little uncomfortable. When you think what some people have to go through, it was nothing really and her heart attack was so quick, it was terrible.'

'Were you with her?' Felicity asked.

'Yes, we were here in Exeter as you know. She died in this room. She sat down on the sofa after lunch and just keeled over. We called a doctor but we knew it was pointless.'

'It must have been terrible for you,' said Felicity.

'It was,' said Otto. 'We had talked about it many times because of the age difference between us, but when it actually happened ...' His voice trailed away. 'What was marvellous was that she was so well mentally, no, better than well, she remained herself even into her nineties, sharp as a pin.'

'Did she ever talk about me in the last few years?' Harvey, sensing distress, jumped up onto Felicity's lap.

'Yes, always,' Otto said. 'You were a part of our life together, not physically of course, but in our thoughts always. We raised a glass to you at Christmas and on your birthday. We had no idea that your husband had died, that must have been awful for you.'

'Yes it was,' said Felicity, 'as I mentioned, it was a hit and run so it was totally unexpected.'

'You've got a good man now though, haven't you?'

'Yes.'

'For keeps, I imagine, you two?'

'I'd like to think so,' said Felicity. 'I do love him very much and I think it is reciprocated.'

'You're made for each other,' said Otto. 'Trust

me, as an old man I know these things and your children obviously like him and your grandchildren.'

'Yes, they do. They are probably relieved I've got someone else to look after me, so they don't have to.'

Otto laughed. 'Very probably.'

'I knew you'd see the likeness to Sophia straight away with our little Minty,' Felicity said, by way of changing the subject.

'Yes, yes, of course,' said Otto. 'It was quite a shock.'

'I'm sorry, maybe I should have prepared you.'

'No, no, a shock in a good way and at a time when I needed it. So you remember your mother enough to know how much alike she and Minty are.'

'I do remember her, yes,' said Felicity, 'and I have some old photograph albums with pictures of her as a child. I haven't looked at them for years, I sort of purposely didn't. However, as Minty started to grow I felt sure there was a serious likeness and when I checked the albums I couldn't believe it, a complete throwback.'

'I'd love to see some pictures of Sophia when she was small, I've never seen her as a child. All those sort of things she left behind in your family home.'

'Silly of me,' said Felicity. 'I should have brought them with me but I will next time I come.'

'I'd like that,' said Otto. 'Now tell me one thing, my dear, has the funeral, meeting me, talking about your mother, has it been a positive experience or a painful one?'

'You know the answer to that,' said Felicity, leaning forward and taking his hand in both of hers. 'All my life I've thought of you as some sort of ogre, the beastly man who took away my mother. Now I know the truth of what happened it's, well, restful. Does that make any sense?'

Otto nodded. 'I'm glad I'm no longer the ogre,' he said.

Felicity grinned at him. 'You'd make an absolutely hopeless ogre.'

Keith found Colin Nicholls in more pain than on his previous visit; the poor man was virtually crippled, bent, limping, wincing with pain.

'I tried to go back to work,' he said, 'but it only made it worse.'

'Well, I should think it would,' said Keith, 'you need a complete rest. Do you have to force yourself back before you're well?'

'It's not about money,' said Colin, 'although of course we never have enough, but it doesn't do me any good sitting around the house all day on my

318

own. It makes me think, makes me miserable. I can't help thinking about what life would have been like if Morwenna was still here. We'd be in Marazion for one thing, on the edge of the sea, instead of in this God-forsaken city.'

'It's a beautiful city,' said Keith.

'Yes, but I'm not a city man, I'm a Cornishman,' he looked at Keith, 'like you, we don't really fit anywhere else.'

'You're right about that,' said Keith, with a smile. 'OK, you make yourself comfortable and I'll make the tea, or would you prefer coffee?'

'Tea,' said Colin, 'thanks.' Keith busied himself with the kettle and mugs while Colin moaned on about his back. 'I'm going to see the physio this afternoon,' he said, 'not that he did any good last time. I've just done too much bending and lifting over the years.'

Keith put the mugs down on the table. 'In my view rest and painkillers are the only solution,' he said.

'You're right at that. I just can't stand it. Daytime television – now that is something I've never seen before, it's terrible.' He took a sip of tea and then looked at Keith. 'Sorry, sorry for the grumbling. Have you come to tell me anything useful?'

'In a way,' said Keith. 'You mentioning that

Morwenna was in foster care opened a can of worms. All the other victims, the two in Norfolk and the more recent one at Gunwalloe, they were all in care as well and all with the same family.'

'Wow,' said Colin, 'that's something, isn't it? You're not suggesting some sort of suicide pact are you, I hope?'

'No, no,' said Keith, 'I think it is absolute proof that the same perpetrator is responsible for each of the deaths.'

'Some sicko, you mean?' said Colin, vehemently. 'So he can't be too difficult to track down, can he, if they're all linked to this one family?'

'You'd have thought not,' said Keith, 'but there were three obvious potential suspects and each one has checked out clean as a whistle, so we're back to square one.'

'That's mad,' said Colin, suddenly angry. 'Surely all you have to do is check out every child who was ever fostered in the same home and one of them is going to be the culprit.'

'There were dozens over the years. Some stayed for a day or two and some for much longer. I understand an attempt is being made to trace them all but the three that stood out can't have been responsible, it's so frustrating.'

Colin was silent for a moment. Keith imagined

him trying to control his rage but, in fact, when he looked up from his tea, Colin's face was calm and thoughtful. 'Rather than trying to search for all the foster children, are you sure you've checked out everyone even vaguely connected with each death?'

'How do you mean?' Keith asked.

'Well, take me for example. I'm a potential suspect. You haven't asked me if I was ever in foster care with this family?'

'Were you in foster care?' Keith asked.

'No, I wasn't, but that's not the point, you didn't ask me. Have you checked out all the relatives and friends connected with each case and made sure none of them were fostered? It would be a much quicker exercise then trying to trace each child after all these years.'

'You mean someone who was also fostered with the Blackburns?'

'Yes, I imagine foster kids often stay friends after they have left the family they were boarded with.'

'But Morwenna was fostered with the same family as Adrianne. I don't know whether it was at the same time, but they certainly were fostered with the same family. When I asked you whether Adrianne meant anything to you, you said no.'

'And I meant no,' said Colin. 'I'd never heard of her until you told me of her death, but that doesn't mean to say that Morwenna didn't know her, the trouble is …' he hesitated, his face suddenly solemn and drawn, 'I can't ask her, can I? And neither can you.'

'But you surely knew each other's friends?'

'Yes, of course,' said Colin. 'We had a good marriage, you know that, but that doesn't mean to say that if she was sitting here now at the table with us and you asked her about Adrianne, she wouldn't say "oh, I remember that little girl" and I would know nothing about it. It's like old school friends, you lose touch but you remember them.'

'Yes, I take your point,' said Keith, 'sorry.'

'It's OK, all I am saying is, you have this very strong connection with all these kids fostered by the same family. Are you sure that they are the only people involved in the case who were fostered?'

'The quick answer to that is no,' said Keith.

'As I say, it would be a lot quicker to check that out than trying to track down all the foster children.'

'You're right,' said Keith. 'Pity you're not a bit younger, Colin. You've given me the only two decent leads I've had – a career in the police force would be ideal and possibly a little easier on the back.'

'Couldn't stand it,' said Colin, 'I don't know how you can.'

'Why is that?' Keith asked.

'Dealing with other people's pain,' Colin replied, quietly.

Keith relayed Colin's theory to Felicity on the way back to Truro.

'He could have a point,' she said.

'Yes, I agree,' said Keith, 'and they are making really heavy weather of trying to track down all the foster children the Blackburns looked after over the years. Of course they are long grown up, some of them in their late fifties, and the girls who've married, sometimes more than once, have changed their names. David says it is a nightmare.'

'You've spoken to him then?' said Felicity.

'Yes, I rang him just before I picked you up from Otto's. Basically, they are no further forward, so Colin's theory may not be a bad one.'

'So who are we looking at?'

'Well, excluding Colin, there is Adrianne's husband Jerry Beckett, then there are Roger and Jane Cleaver. It was Jane that told me that Adrianne had been briefly in foster care, for all we know Jane may have been there too which is how they met. As far as the Longs and Daniels are concerned, Eleanor's brother is out of it, he is in Australia but that does leave her husband Terry. Everyone has decided there is no case to answer for

Peter Daniels, Daisy's brother.' He let out a sigh. 'Without an incident room, I'm starting to get a bit tangled up now, it's a pity I haven't got an Agatha Christie solution to fall back on.'

'What's that?' Felicity asked, glancing at him as she drove.

'Well, as you know, the way she used to write her crime novels was to think up a hideous crime or series of crimes, then get all the likely candidates into the drawing room, conservatory or wherever and then Poirot or Miss Marple would explain who was guilty. The formula she used for choosing the guilty party was to pick the one least likely to have done it and then work it back, change the bus timetables, that sort of thing, until the person she had chosen was all fitted up for the crime.'

'Oh dear,' said Felicity, 'well, if you are going to adopt the Agatha Christie method, then I am afraid Colin is your man.'

25

Keith sat at the kitchen table sunk in gloom. At his request David had run through the names of Terry Long, Roger Cleaver and Jerry Beckett on the Social Services database and nothing had come up against any of their names. They had not been fostered, it would appear – so much for Colin's theory.

Felicity put a fresh pot of coffee on the table. 'Why don't you go for a walk with Harvey and clear your mind, it's a lovely day.'

'If I was in the thick of it,' said Keith, 'if I had the incident room and a team, then ...'

'But you don't and you haven't and you can't,' said Felicity, 'so there is no point in torturing yourself. You've made a huge contribution to this case; but for you, they would never have known of the foster parent angle.'

'Perhaps it's not relevant,' Keith said.

'Oh, don't be ridiculous,' said Felicity, 'of course it is relevant. How could it possibly not be?

Four random women, all fostered by the same family found dead in identical circumstances. Come on, Keith that has to be the main link and you found it.'

'And a lot of good it's doing anyone,' Keith grumbled.

'You know, I've had enough of this moaning,' said Felicity. 'You take the dog for a walk, we'll meet for a drink at the Sloop and, if you promise me that you will be smiling when we meet, I might even buy you lunch.'

'Smiling,' said Keith, 'that's rather a tall order!'

'Suit yourself, bread and cheese here or a nice lunch at the Sloop and all I am asking for is a smile.'

'I'll see what I can do,' said Keith, with scant enthusiasm.

'Well?' said Felicity, when they met at the Sloop an hour later. She was already waiting for him with a glass of red wine for him and a white for her, sitting outside in the sun.

'Well what?'

'Well, have you decided who is the guilty party?'

Keith sat down and took a sip of his wine. 'If you ask me for a gut instinct, I would say Roger Cleaver.'

'Because you don't like him?' Felicity said.

'I certainly don't like him, no, but also because he lied the first time David and I went to see him and the mere fact that he was having an affair with his wife's best friend, you can't be a very nice person to do that, can you?'

'Particularly when his poor wife has a new baby,' said Felicity.

'I didn't like Jerry much either, the husband, but you have to make allowances for him. He was in shock, angry at the suggestion that his wife had committed suicide and that he hadn't realised how miserable she was. Obviously, I didn't see him at his best.'

'But if Roger Cleaver had been in love with Adrianne, he would have been in much the same state, wouldn't he?'

'He certainly wasn't in a state,' said Keith, 'he was very cool, calm and collected whereas Jerry was all over the place.'

'But what is the Norfolk connection?'

Keith shook his head. 'I have absolutely no idea. I know the Cleavers moved to Cornwall a few years back when Roger got his job at Treliske Hospital but I don't know where they were before.'

'That should be easy enough to find out, shouldn't it?'

'Yes, but if he wasn't in foster care, then what

possible connection could he have with these four women?'

'Maybe he was a friend of the Blackburns,' Felicity suggested.

'I'll ask David to find out where the Cleavers lived before Truro.'

'Poor David,' said Felicity, 'is he finding it hard leading this double life?'

'I think he quite enjoys it,' said Keith. 'He can't stand Neil Mavers either who, from what I hear, has been sidelined. It looks like George Staple is running the show now.'

'That's rather unusual, isn't it?' said Felicity.

'I don't think these days they have anybody else of the calibre to deal with such a high profile case. Certainly George seems to be calling all the shots.'

David Sterling rang Keith back at ten o'clock that evening.

'Are you still at work?' Keith asked.

'Yes and I'm not through yet,' said David. 'There is a whole lot of work I'm supposed to be doing for the "Super" but, of course, that has been interrupted by unreasonable demands from a retired policeman.'

'I wonder who that might be?' Keith said.

'I forgive you because we have a breakthrough,' said David, his voice full of excitement. 'The

Cleavers lived in Norwich before they moved down to Cornwall. He, that is Roger, worked at the Norfolk and Norwich Hospital, that is where he specialised in orthopaedics.'

'This is just too much of a coincidence,' said Keith.

'I know,' said David. 'You couldn't make it up.'

'And you are absolutely sure that he had no connection with the Blackburns?'

'There is no record of it,' said David, 'none at all. I've double-checked in view of this Norfolk connection.'

'Can you give me the address and phone number of the Blackburns' son? Hugh, isn't it?'

'Yes,' said David, 'you're not going to interview him, are you?'

'I might,' said Keith.

'When, because I ought to come with you?'

'No, no, I'm not going to make it an official visit,' said Keith, 'I seem to be getting on quite well by telling people who I am and that they don't have to talk to me.'

'You're not supposed to do that.'

'I know, I know David, but this is all too important. Have you a phone number for him?'

'I have,' said David.

'Then please give it to me and I'll ring him now.'

'Now?' said David.

'Just remember what the "Super" said – if we don't find this bastard soon, some other poor woman is going to die.'

'OK, OK,' said David. 'Here it is.'

The phone was answered on the second ring.

'Hugh Blackburn?' Keith said.

'Yes.' The voice sounded slightly hesitant, presumably because of the lateness of the hour.

'My name is Keith Penrose.'

'Not Chief Inspector Keith Penrose?'

'I was,' said Keith, 'but not any more. I am actually retired, at least I am trying to retire but I have been dragged back to help out with a cold case.'

'This is about these poor women who my parents fostered?'

'That's right,' said Keith. 'I wondered whether it would be possible to come and talk to you about it. I need to make the point to you that I am not a police officer any longer and you are completely in your rights to tell me that you don't want to see me.'

'Stop right there,' said Hugh. 'I'm a huge fan of yours.'

'What on earth do you mean?' said Keith, genuinely surprised.

'Well,' said Hugh, 'you've been helping keep

Cornwall a decent place to live in for years. I've seen you on telly, I've seen you in the newspapers and I was very sad to hear of your retirement – before time I would have thought. Of course I will see you, when had you in mind?'

'I was wondering about tonight,' said Keith, 'it is rather urgent but it's a tall order.'

'No problem. Where are you?'

'St Ives,' said Keith.

'Lord,' said Hugh, 'that's a bit of a trek, we could meet in Truro I suppose but the problem is where at this time of night. I suppose the police station would do. Are you sure we can't do this over the phone?'

The thought of trying to interview someone at the station seemed a very bad idea. 'Now I know you don't mind me talking to you,' said Keith, hastily, 'yes, I am sure we can do it over the phone.'

'Fire away then,' said Hugh, 'what can I do for you?'

'Does the name Roger Cleaver mean anything to you?'

'It certainly does,' said Hugh.

'Really?' said Keith, unable to believe his luck; this was too easy.

'My parents fostered the bugger for years.'

'But he is not on the records?' said Keith.

'No, he wouldn't be,' said Hugh. 'It was a

private fostering arrangement, nothing to do with Social Services. Roger Cleaver's parents were tragically killed in a car accident, both of them. Roger was a right toffee-nosed little sod. He was at the private school, Greshams near Holt. The family came from South Africa and had only been in the country for a year or so when the accident happened so they had few friends and no relatives in England at all. I think there was talk of sending the boy back to an ancient grandmother in South Africa, but in the end as he was thirteen, fourteen maybe, it was decided he should stay on in the UK and finish his education iat Greshams. There was no shortage of money.'

'So your parents fostered him?'

'Yes. Initially he was at school as a day boy. My poor old dad used to have to drive him to Holt every day and fetch him in the evenings about nine o'clock, I was too young to remember, but it was quite a tie. Then, when we moved down to Cornwall, Roger became a boarder. He must have been about sixteen by then and he used to come to us for the holidays. He was an ungrateful sod, clever though. From Greshams, he got a place at Oxford to read medicine and we never heard from him again. Never said thank you, never sent a Christmas card after all my parents had done for him.'

'Would it surprise you to know that he is an orthopaedic surgeon at Treliske Hospital?'

'Wha, here in Cornwall? Bloody hell!' said Hugh. 'Well, if I ever bump into him in the street, I'll have to try and avoid knocking him to the ground.'

'So what have you got against him?' Keith asked.

'On the whole,' said Hugh, 'my parents tended to foster girls. They did that because they felt it was less competition for me. Of course there were exceptions, sometimes they used to take in sibling groups and that would involve boys, but where possible they stuck with girls. Undoubtedly, it was a tragedy for Roger when his parents died but he milked it. He was a lot older than me and he used to give me a very hard time, always behind my parents' backs of course and none of the girls liked him, he was creepy they said.'

'What sort of creepy?' Keith asked. 'Are we saying sexual harassment here?'

'If so, I don't know anything about it,' said Hugh, 'but do bear in mind I was little more than a toddler when Roger first came to stay with my parents and I was still in single figures by the time he went off to Oxford. I was a pretty dumb kid, I don't expect I would have noticed sexual harassment if it was staring me in the face.'

'Why didn't you tell anyone about Roger Cleaver before?' Keith asked.

'Because nobody asked me,' Hugh replied, not unreasonably. 'I have been interviewed several times about the girls and I have done what I could to remember each of them and when they were with us. I was pretty much useless where the Norfolk girls were concerned, but of course I could remember both Adrianne and Morwenna. I didn't know Roger Cleaver was involved in any way. Is he involved?'

'Yes,' said Keith grimly.

'Well, I tell you something for nothing,' said Hugh, 'if you can nail that bastard, it would be a great pleasure and honour to buy you a pint, Chief Inspector.'

Keith and Felicity sat up late into the night talking the whole thing through.

'He has to be the one, doesn't he?' said Felicity.

'I think so,' said Keith.

'So what are you going to do, ring George Staple in the morning?'

'There are a couple of things I'd like to clear up first,' said Keith.

26

'Oh God,' said Horace Greenaway. 'I had forgotten about these early morning visits. This is "me" time, Penrose. I like to prepare for the arduous day ahead in peace and quiet. The only relationship I will tolerate at this hour is with my coffee percolator.'

'Excellent,' said Keith, 'that means the coffee is on, shall I be mother?'

'Bugger off, Penrose.'

'I can't,' said Keith, 'it's too important.' He poured two cups of coffee from Horace's jug, adding milk to his and giving Horace his cup the way he liked it, black with one sugar.

'Why don't you make yourself at home?' said Horace, morosely.

Keith ignored him. 'I think I've found the man responsible for all these murders staged as suicides but I desperately need some DNA evidence. He is a really smooth operator, full of confidence, he is going to be a tough nut to crack. He is not going to confess easily.'

'But in the hands of such a talented policeman as Neil Mavers, he won't stand a chance, surely?' said Horace, giving Keith a sly grin.

'We can't let him anywhere near Neil Mavers,' said Keith. 'That man will make mincemeat of him.'

'So, what are you asking? I've been over everything with a fine toothcomb.'

'But I bet you haven't looked for DNA on the Norfolk jackets?'

Horace took a sip of coffee and studied Keith speculatively. 'It's true,' he said. 'I've compared the stitching which as far as I can tell is done by the same person, but I haven't looked for DNA on the Norfolk coats. I just assumed that had all been done and in any case we've nothing to match to anyone as until now there appeared to be no suspects.'

'Well, there is now,' said Keith, 'and I need something, anything. Please try.'

'The trouble is,' Horace mused, 'those coats were in salt water such a long time …' he hesitated. 'Maybe there might be something, some skin cells perhaps left around the stitching process.'

'If it's the man I think it is, he'll have worn surgical gloves,' said Keith.

'Let's just hope he pricked himself then or forgot to put them on. There is absolutely nothing on the Cornish jackets, I am certain of that.'

'Maybe the police up in Norfolk gathered some evidence on the jackets?' said Keith.

'I'd have thought they would have told me when they sent them down, but I will double-check and I'll have a good look. Blood isn't a feature in any of these cases, except after death when the bodies were smashed against a rock. I think the sewing of the pockets is our best bet. I'll start there anyway.'

'Thanks Horace,' said Keith, standing up. 'I appreciate it. He's just a slimy toad of the first order. It is bad enough killing four women but leaving their families with the shame and guilt of suicide as being the most likely cause of their death, is beyond cruel.'

'Slimy toad he might be but I bet this suspect of yours doesn't make unreasonable demands of his colleagues before eight o'clock in the morning.'

'I'm pleased you still think of me as a colleague,' said Keith.

Horace gave him a wintry smile, but a genuine one. 'Always that, old boy, always that.'

It was too much. He was in Treliske Hospital, he had to have another look at Roger Cleaver. He knew the dangers involved. He must not confront him, he could blow the whole case. He just wanted to have another look at him. He could pretend perhaps he was in the hospital for another reason and just popped in to see how he was doing. He could even say he was off the case. He just had to have a sighting of him. Why, he was not sure, but his instincts were undeniable. He took the stairs to Roger Cleaver's floor.

The nurse remembered him. 'Hello again,' she said, 'are you looking for Mr Cleaver?'

'I am,' said Keith.

'It's Thursday, it's his day off.'

'Of course it is,' Keith said. Idiot, he thought to himself, it was on Thursday afternoons that Adrianne used to meet him. 'Do you know where I might find him?'

The nurse shrugged. 'I don't know if he'll be there yet but on Thursday mornings he usually plays squash.'

'Where?' Keith asked.

'At the Truro Squash Club. Do you know where that is?'

'Under the viaduct?'

'Yes, that's it.'

'Thanks,' said Keith, 'I'll try and catch up with him there.'

'Can I …?' the nurse began.

'No, no, I'm fine thanks,' said Keith.

Felicity couldn't settle, she ranged about the house.

In a way she was glad that Keith was not there. The previous day she had accused him of being poor company. Today she knew her own mood was intolerable. The last time she had felt like this, she realised, was when her husband Charlie had died. She remembered coming down to St Ives and staying with Annie and how her moods had swung into black despair at the drop of a hat. It had been difficult some days to even get herself out of bed. She felt a little like this now. She was sitting at the kitchen table and seemed unable to do anything. Perhaps she should talk to Annie, she thought, but something in her shied away from the thought. She loved Annie and greatly respected her understanding of human nature, her common sense, her kindness but this somehow seemed to be a family problem.

She forced her tired brain to think, it was Thursday, Mel didn't usually work on Thursdays and Minty would be at school, Charlie at nursery school, maybe. She had never needed Mel; Mel had been the one who always needed her; the brilliant, talented child making huge demands, the dramatic teenager who had turned into an equally dramatic young woman; sure of herself on the one hand to the point of arrogance, insecure underneath and above all, a little girl who still missed her daddy. Maybe, just maybe, Mel would understand what she was going through. Over the years Felicity had learnt to tiptoe around Mel's moods and tantrums; that was how their relationship worked, but she was desperate. 'Stop thinking about it and just do it,' she said to herself and picking up her phone, she tapped in Mel's number.

Truro Squash Club was surprisingly busy for so early in the morning. Keith wandered through reception without being challenged and started checking the courts. At the fourth court, he found Roger Cleaver and mercifully his direction of play meant he was playing with his back largely towards Keith. He was an aggressive player and despite the fact that he had to be in his fifties, he was athletic and there was not a spare ounce of flesh on him, his movements fluid and confident. This was a man who was quite capable of heaving a woman's body in and out of a car and into the sea. This was a man who was quite capable of overcoming any woman. He was tall, strong and very sure of himself, his opponent was being soundly thrashed. Keith hovered for a moment or two and then thought it was time he went before he was spotted. Something, however, was niggling at the back of his mind. He started to leave and then turned back; it was the moment at which the ball was played near the front of the court. Roger Cleaver saw him and then missed the shot. Their eyes met and in that moment Keith realised what he had seen but initially had failed to register. Roger Cleaver was a left-handed squash player.

Mel opened the door and frowned at her mother. 'You sounded awful on the phone Mum, what's up?'

'I just needed to talk.'

'Come in,' said Mel. 'Sorry about the mess.' The kitchen table was littered with papers. 'It's this case I'm working on, it's driving me nuts.'

'I'm sorry,' said Felicity. 'I shouldn't have interrupted you, this is your work time, isn't it, when you have a chance to concentrate without the children?'

'It's OK,' said Mel. 'Coffee, tea?'

'I don't know,' said Felicity, 'nothing, I don't think.'

'So something is wrong and you've come to see me,' said Mel. 'I'm not trying to be controversial here, Mum, but when anything is wrong you usually go and talk to Jamie, not me.'

'This is a mother/daughter thing,' said Felicity.

'Are you still cross at me,' Mel said, 'for going off on one about you keeping your mother a secret?'

'Mel, this isn't about you,' Felicity wailed and burst into tears.

In the weeks and months following Charlie's

death, Felicity had always held it together, in public at any rate. Her mother sobbing uncontrollably was a completely new experience for Mel. She stood watching helplessly, then ever practical, went to the kitchen cupboard and found a box of tissues which she tentatively pushed in Felicity's direction.

'Thanks,' Felicity said. She blew her nose and wiped her eyes. 'Sorry,' she added.

'That's OK,' said Mel, clearly confused and upset herself. 'What's going on, Mum? It's not you and Keith again, is it?'

'No, no,' said Felicity, 'we're always fine.'

'You weren't a couple of weeks ago.'

Felicity ignored her. 'It's about my mother,' she said and the tears began to fall down her cheeks again. This time she didn't even attempt to wipe them away. 'I keep telling everybody that it's fine, I keep telling everybody the fact that we never saw each other again after she left did not matter, that she'd had a happy life and I'd had a happy life, that we were both fulfilled in our own ways and that made everything OK.'

'And that's true, isn't it?' said Mel, who was now sitting beside Felicity, watching her anxiously.

'Yes, of course it is. I've been so lucky. I loved your father very much. I have two wonderful children, four fabulous grandchildren and then Keith. Of course I'm lucky and my mother, well, she didn't really need anybody but Otto so she was fine too.'

'So ...' Mel said, frowning.

'Until Otto told me differently, I thought my mother had just walked out on me. I didn't know she had fought through the courts to try to get access to me. I don't believe it would ever have been practical for me to live with her and Otto because he travelled all over the world and it would have been hopeless educationally, apart from anything else. But ... but if I'd known they wanted me, it would have made all the difference, all the difference in the world. We could have met, had a relationship instead of all those lost years.' There was a fresh burst of sobbing.

'But you didn't know,' said Mel. 'If your father didn't tell you, how could you possibly have known what was going on?'

'And then,' said Felicity, as if she hadn't heard her, 'when I got engaged to your father and then had Jamie, she wrote to me congratulating me on the engagement and then the birth and asking if we could meet and I didn't reply to her letters.'

'Why was that?' Mel asked.

'I've been wondering,' said Felicity. 'I don't know whether it might have been revenge. She hurt me dreadfully so maybe I wanted to hurt her back – I'd like to think it wasn't that.'

'I don't think it was that,' said Mel. 'You're not that sort of person. You don't bear grudges, you never have. You always see the best in everyone.'

'Goodness, Mel,' said Felicity, looking up startled. 'I don't think you've ever paid me so many compliments, in fact I don't think you've ever paid me any compliments before. Thank you.'

'Maybe I'm growing up,' said Mel, with a small tight smile.

'If it wasn't revenge,' said Felicity, 'what was it?'

'Protection,' said Mel, 'the thing that got you through your childhood without a mother. Denial was so ingrained in you that as a young adult you couldn't simply shake it off. It was your armour, the thing that got you through.'

'I suppose so,' said Felicity, 'but what a missed opportunity, I wonder if she thought about me when she died.' She started to cry again.

'Of course she did,' said Mel. 'Ask any woman faced with death, all they can ever think about is their children and whether they will be all right – it's a survival of the species thing.'

'But if she did think about me, I wasn't there,' said Felicity.

'But Otto was.'

'Yes, yes, that's true,' said Felicity.

'Clearly Mum, theirs was the most

extraordinary love affair. You could turn this whole thing on its head and say that because of the stand you took, you actually set her free to be with Otto.'

'Maybe,' said Felicity. 'I would just so have liked to have known her.'

'But now there's Minty, the little lookalike, you're going to know her as she grows up.' Unexpectedly Mel took her mother's hand, glaring very hard at the table as she spoke. 'Thanks for sticking around while I was growing up, Mum, I couldn't have had a better mother.'

There was an awkward silence between them, then Felicity said, 'Do you know, I don't think anything that anybody has ever said to me has meant as much to me as what you have just said.'

'Oh, for heaven's sake, Mother, don't make a fuss,' said Mel, getting up abruptly. 'I don't think we should have tea or coffee, I think we should have a large gin and tonic. What do you say?'

Felicity smiled at her daughter through tear-filled eyes. 'Perfect,' she said.

27

It was after seven in the evening by the time Keith finally left George Staple's office, having debriefed him and a number of other officers involved in the case. Neil Mavers was conspicuous by his absence. By the time Keith left, Roger Cleaver was in custody 'helping the police with their enquiries'. George Staple himself was going to conduct the main interview. Jack Curnow, Keith's old sergeant, was doing a warm-up interview.

'So we know all the reasons for him being taken into custody,' said George, 'the enormous crossover of coincidences which put him right in the front line. What we still don't know is why?'

Leaving the other officers behind, George walked Keith to the door. 'How did you get on with Jane Cleaver?' he asked.

'Very well, I think,' said Keith. 'A nice woman, just married to the wrong man.'

'Maybe it would be a good idea if you popped round to see her, just to make sure she is managing.'

Keith looked hard at George. 'Is it all right for me to do that?'

'It's quite all right, Keith,' George said, 'I authorise it. Family liaison, that sort of thing, just to see she is coping with those children.'

'Got it,' said Keith. 'You're taking a DNA, I presume?'

'Done,' said George, 'we've rushed it over to Horace. Please God the instructions you gave him this morning will have borne fruit. Oh, and Keith, you might learn something from your visit, something helpful.'

Jane Cleaver answered the door almost immediately. 'Oh you,' she said. 'I'm sorry, I can't remember your name.' She had clearly been crying, her hair was all over the place, she looked absolutely exhausted.

'I just came around to see if you were all right?' said Keith.

'Come in, come in,' said Jane.

'Only if you're sure?

'Yes, I'd like to talk to you.' She led the way into the sitting room which was still carpeted with a range of toys. 'Sorry for the mess,' she said. 'I can't seem to settle to anything.'

'Are you coping all right with the children?'

She nodded. 'My mother lives in London. She's getting the sleeper down overnight, so she'll be with me tomorrow morning. She is great with the children.'

'Good,' said Keith.

'He won't be coming home again, will he?'

'I don't know,' said Keith, truthfully. 'It depends what he is prepared to tell us.'

'He won't tell you anything, you'll have to trick him,' Jane said.

'That sounds a bit harsh,' Keith suggested.

'He is an awful man,' said Jane, 'I realise that now, it's taken me years to work it out. I've never had much confidence, you see, and I thought it was me who was all wrong, but it wasn't, it was him.'

'You knew about his affair with Adrianne?' Keith said.

'Yes, of course, we discussed it.'

'You and Roger?'

'No, me and Adrianne. We never had secrets from one another, we knew each other so well.'

'Didn't that put a terrible strain on your friendship?'

'Not really,' said Jane. 'I fell out of love with my husband years ago. I wasn't worried who he had an affair with; there have been strings of them over the years. It was just that when he got involved with Adrianne, I was frightened for her.'

'Why?' Keith asked.

'He raped her when she was nine.'

'What?' said Keith.

'You heard,' said Jane.

'Was this at the Blackburns?' Jane nodded.

'So why, in God's name, did she want to have anything more to do with him after that?' Keith said.

'She didn't at first. When the four of us became friends, she was horrified when she realised who I had married. She didn't tell me, not for ages. I think he was concerned that she would tell me, tell the world come to that what he had done. He was a teenager, old enough to know better, in his late teens I think.'

'But ...' Keith began, still incredulous.

'I think he destroyed her sense of self-worth and when he suggested having an an adult relationship with her, she convinced herself that made the rape all right – that's all I can think, I'm no psychiatrist.'

'So Jane, please don't answer this question if you don't want to, remember I'm no longer a policeman, but do you think he murdered Adrianne?' Jane began to weep and mumbled something into her handkerchief. 'What did you say?' Keith persisted.

'Yes,' she said. 'Yes, I'm sure he did.'

'But you gave him an alibi for the night Adrianne disappeared.'

'I was scared, I thought he'd kill me too – the children, you understand?' said Jane. She hesitated. 'Will I be in trouble?'

'I doubt it,' said Keith, 'not in the circumstances.'

'And what about the other women, do you think he killed them too?' Keith asked.

Jane nodded. 'I think he must have been a paedophile, maybe he still is, but I suspect he's abused all the women he went on to kill and he killed them to silence them.'

'I wonder what triggered it?' Keith said, almost to himself.

'I don't know the answer to that, I am just so glad it's nearly over.'

It was like old times. Keith and Jack Curnow were sitting in easy chairs in George Staple's office. There was an air of quiet celebration. They knew they had to be cautious, there was still a long way to go, but there was a real feeling of achievement.

'The DPP seem happy with the way it's going,' George said, 'and we have young Jack here to thank for getting him to confess.'

'It wasn't me,' said Jack. 'It was Professor Greenaway's evidence.' A tiny fragment of skin cells was found on the jacket from the first death, just where a knot had been formed to start sewing up one side of the pockets. 'Thank you Eleanor,' Keith had thought at the time. Maybe she had moved or struggled: either way, she had made it possible for them to prosecute. He must tell Terry Long.

'Yes, old Horace was right in more ways than one, wasn't he?' said Keith. 'The fact that Roger Cleaver was ambidextrous certainly made it possible for him to have sewn up the jackets left-handed, just the way he sews up his patients when he has operated, or at least, how he used to before he became so grand. The insulin, that was a good guess too.'

'Yes, but not because he was a diabetic, simply because he had access to it,' Jack said. 'Nonetheless, I think Horace is probably the hero of the hour.'

'You've all done very well,' said George. 'I've afraid we've interrupted young Curnow just when he is trying to study for his Inspector's exams, but there is nothing like practical experience. You know, Jack, Keith was kind enough to say to me once when talking about our years of working together that he reckoned he had trained under a master. I think the same thing could be said of you.'

'You're certainly right about that, sir,' said Jack, giving Keith a fond smile.

Felicity was waiting in the car when Keith at last

came out of the station. He climbed into the passenger seat and gave a huge sigh. 'Thanks for waiting.'

'I couldn't have stayed at home, I had to know what happened. Have you got him?'

Keith nodded and smiled at her, taking her hand. 'Yes, yes, we've got him, the full works – DNA evidence, a confession. His wife will testify against him and two or three other women have already come forward to say they were abused or raped by him during the period they were in foster care.'

'I wonder why the Blackburns never found out?'

'Too many children, too much going on. They , they probably just trusted him.' Keith said.

'But you would think with all that knowledge of children ...'

'I know, I know but sometimes we don't see things going on right in front of our faces, do we? Hugh Blackburn hated him, but he didn't know why, he was only a child.'

'Poor little girls,' said Felicity. 'Why did he kill them when they were grown up? What was the motive?'

'Very simple,' said Keith. 'He admitted it all. Eleanor, his first victim, went to Norwich hospital, she had a very bad fracture, the bone had gone through the skin.'

'Ouch,' said Felicity.

'She was treated by Roger Cleaver and she recognised him immediately. She got hold of Daisy Daniels. That was a question I never asked when I was up in Norfolk, whether the two families knew each other – they did. The men weren't friendly, well, Peter Daniels would be a difficult chap to be friends with, I imagine, but the two women were friends because they had been in foster care together as children. She knew that Daisy had been abused by Cleaver. He didn't know exactly what they were planning but Eleanor told him that they were trying to get as many girls together as they could in order to expose him. She should never have told him that.'

'So he murdered them both making it look like suicides. He injected them with insulin which, if you are not a diabetic, can render you fairly helpless, certainly not active enough to be able to rescue yourself from the water. Then he sewed up their pockets to make it look like suicide.

'It was well known that both girls had endured a troubled childhood so it was thought not entirely surprising that they had killed themselves. As soon as he had done away with the two of them, he moved to Cornwall. He had formed a liking for the county while he was in foster care with the

Blackburns, but no sooner had he settled into Cornwall when Morwenna contacted him. Eleanor and Daisy had been making enquiries about the children the Blackburns fostered in Cornwall. When Morwenna learnt they were dead she had put two and two together and reckoned that he had killed them. She also confronted him, so he had to kill her too. Silly girl, why on earth she didn't go to the police, I don't know, or even just have told her husband.'

'It could be that Colin didn't know about her being abused as a child,' said Felicity. 'That's the trouble with child abuse, the poor little victims feel ashamed, feel as if it is their fault. It must be a very difficult thing to shake off.'

'Yes,' said Keith, 'that may well be it, but poor old Colin is going to have to know now.'

'I think you'll find that while it will come as an awful shock,' said Felicity, 'he will just be so relieved that the suicide tag has been lifted from her death.'

'Yes, you're probably right,' said Keith. 'I'll go and see him again early next week.'

'What about Adrianne?' asked Felicity. 'Was she threatening to expose Cleaver?'

'No, at least not until he wanted to end the affair. I think he was bored with her. He is a horrible man. He tried to end it and she said she would go to the authorities and tell them about her rape, so he killed her.'

'I hope they send him down for years,' said Felicity.

'I doubt he'll ever be released,' said Keith. 'I think he's demonstrated just how dangerous he is. I think life will mean life.' Keith smiled at her and then frowned. 'You're looking a bit frazzled. I've hardly seen you over the last few days, are you all right?'

Felicity nodded. 'I am now. I had a bit of a crisis about my mother.'

'Why didn't you tell me?'

'As you said,' she smiled at him, 'I've hardly seen you, but it's all right, I went and talked to Mel.'

'To Mel?' said Keith, unable to hide his surprise.

Felicity smiled. 'She was surprisingly helpful, in fact, very helpful.'

'I'm so glad,' said Keith, 'glad that she helped, glad that you felt able to talk to her. What would you like to do now?'

'Let's just go home,' she said.

EPILOGUE

Exeter, August 2011

The summons to lunch had been just that, a summons. It was a beautiful August day as Felicity and Keith stepped out of their car and knocked on Otto's imposing front door.

Margot answered, smiled warmly and embraced them both. 'Come along in, he is in the conservatory with a bottle of champagne.'

'Goodness,' said Felicity, 'how lovely, what is this all about?'

'You'll see,' she said. 'I'm just going to get on with lunch, he's got something to show you.'

Otto was clearly delighted to see them. He looked much better than he had a few months earlier but was still very frail and as he stood up, they both noticed he was using a stick.

'I don't use this in the house normally,' he said, defensively, waving the stick in the air, 'but I'm taking you into the garden, follow me.'

The garden was as beautiful as the house, full of nooks and crannies, twists and turns, little bowers and a rose walk. He took them to the end of the walk and pointed to a small plaque set into the ground. They both stepped forward to read it.

Sophia Charlesworth 1919–2011.
Lifetime love and companion to Otto Juniper,
mother to Felicity,
grandmother to James and Melanie,
and great-grandmother to Sam, Harry,
Araminta and Charlie.

That was all, very simple. Felicity turned to Otto and embraced him. 'That is perfect, Otto.'

'You don't mind being mentioned on her memorial plaque? I've put her ashes here. She loved this garden so it seemed the right place, but of course you must do with it as you think.'

'What do you mean?' Felicity asked.

He waved his stick expansively. 'I'm leaving this house to you, Felicity, and the bulk of my estate.' He glanced towards the house. 'Margot is well provided for with a little cottage and an annuity and I know you will keep an eye on her, but the rest comes to you.'

'But you can't,' said Felicity, 'you hardly know

me.'

'Don't be ridiculous,' said Otto, 'I know you through and through. I loved your mother all my life so how could I not know her daughter.'

'But …' Felicity began.

'Thanks to your mother I've had seventy-four years more of life than I would otherwise have done. Of course, everything must go to her only child.' Keith and Felicity stared at him, stunned.

'I can still remember it, all of it,' said Otto; his eyes left theirs and he stared out across the garden. 'The cold had stopped hurting which I think probably means I was in the first stages of hypothermia. I had given up, I was beyond hunger, beyond thirst, beyond any hope, but the darkest hour is just before dawn. She reached down and picked me up, my beautiful lady. I thought she was an angel. I still did, on the day she died.'